Look for these other Dog Lovers' Mysteries by Melissa Cleary!

MORE MYSTERIES FROM THE
BERKLEY PUBLISHING GROUP . . .

DOG LOVERS' MYSTERIES STARRING HOLLY WINTER: With her Alaskan malamute Rowdy, Holly dogs the trails of dangerous criminals. "A gifted and original writer." —Carolyn G. Hart

by Susan Conant

A NEW LEASH ON DEATH	A BITE OF DEATH
DEAD AND DOGGONE	PAWS BEFORE DYING

DOG LOVERS' MYSTERIES STARRING JACKIE WALSH: She's starting a new life with her son and an ex–police dog named Jake . . . teaching film classes and solving crimes!

by Melissa Cleary

A TAIL OF TWO MURDERS	FIRST PEDIGREE MURDER
DOG COLLAR CRIME	SKULL AND DOG BONES
HOUNDED TO DEATH	DEAD AND BURIED
THE MALTESE PUPPY	

CHARLOTTE GRAHAM MYSTERIES: She's an actress with a flair for dramatics— and an eye for detection. "You'll get hooked on Charlotte Graham!" —*Rave Reviews*

by Stefanie Matteson

MURDER AT THE SPA	MURDER ON THE SILK ROAD
MURDER AT TEATIME	MURDER AT THE FALLS
MURDER ON THE CLIFF	MURDER ON HIGH

DEWEY JAMES MYSTERIES: America's favorite small-town sleuth! "Highly entertaining!" —*Booklist*

by Kate Morgan

DAYS OF CRIME AND ROSES	WANTED: DUDE OR ALIVE

BILL HAWLEY UNDERTAKINGS: Meet funeral director Bill Hawley—dead bodies are his business, and sleuthing is his passion . . .

by Leo Axler

FINAL VIEWING	DOUBLE PLOT
GRAVE MATTERS	

PEACHES DANN MYSTERIES: Peaches has never had a very good memory. But she's learned to cope with it over the years . . . Fortunately, though, when it comes to murder, this absentminded amateur sleuth doesn't forgive and forget!

by Elizabeth Daniels Squire

WHO KILLED WHAT'S-HER-NAME?	REMEMBER THE ALIBI

HEMLOCK FALLS MYSTERIES: The Quilliam sisters combine their culinary and business skills to run an inn in upstate New York. But when it comes to murder, their talent for detection takes over . . .

by Claudia Bishop

A TASTE FOR MURDER	A DASH OF DEATH

THE MALTESE PUPPY

MELISSA CLEARY

BERKLEY PRIME CRIME, NEW YORK

THE MALTESE PUPPY

A Berkley Prime Crime Book / published by arrangement with
the author

PRINTING HISTORY
Berkley Prime Crime edition / May 1995

ISBN: 0-425-14721-5

Berkley Prime Crime Books are published
by The Berkley Publishing Group,
200 Madison Avenue, New York, NY 10016.
The name BERKLEY PRIME CRIME and the BERKLEY PRIME CRIME
design are trademarks belonging to Berkley Publishing Corporation.

PRINTED IN THE UNITED STATES OF AMERICA

10 9 8 7 6 5 4 3 2 1

For
D

Colorado is most beautiful in the fall. The intense heat gives way to cool air and the mud hardens into dirt or sand so that the sidewalks and roads actually become level for a few months. The brown Colorado rivers and streams turn clearer in the fall, when some of the first snows melt and the run-off dilutes the sediment in the polluted water. The leaves turn brown, orange, and yellow and the natives trade in their dirty summer T-shirts and cut-offs for colorful mountain clothing with neat Native American designs, purchased from companies back East that have their goods manufactured in sweatshops in the Golden Triangle.

Everyone is a little happier in the autumn in Colorado. Everyone, that is, except medical researchers who do not happen to be working to cure the dreadful scourge of modern times, AIDS.

For twenty-five years Dr. Linus Munch (pronounced "Moonk") worked at an institute named after himself.

There, he and his brother tried to discover antidotes for the deadly viruses that plagued mankind. They couldn't find a way to actually cure these viruses so early on they decided that the most effective way to handle diseases caused by viruses was to come up with vaccines.

Little by little, their long hours of painstaking research and experimentation paid off and vaccines were later developed that saved the lives of hundreds of thousands of people throughout the world. In the late 1960s Linus and Marvin Munch were honored with the Nobel Prize for medicine in recognition of their work.

In 1985 Marvin Munch, Linus's younger brother, retired from medical research. The reason was not widely known, but the fact was Marvin had become incapacitated by Alzheimer's.

Unfortunately, the race to cure Alzheimer's was not as glamorous as the race to cure AIDS. Linus tried, in vain, to tell people that far more people died every year from Alzheimer's than from AIDS, but no one listened. No one cared.

Indeed, Linus Munch soon found out that not twenty years after being honored from one end of the globe to the other as Nobel Prize laureates, the Munches had been written off as tired has-beens, irrelevant dinosaurs from another era.

It was bad enough that Linus Munch no longer basked in the bright light of publicity. He could do without irritating interviewers disturbing his research and his privacy morning, noon, and night. It was unfortunate too that Linus could no longer get the best researchers who followed the big money and publicity associated with AIDS. It was even worse that Dr. Linus had to give up his beautiful research facility in Green River to AIDS researchers and go back to the World War II-era facility in which he and his brother had started fifty years before. Munch didn't like all this, but he could live with it.

The problem was that Dr. Linus did not have access to the sort of money needed to support his research. His excuse was that he didn't have the time or the personality to keep making proposals to the federal government or charm philanthropists into spending their money on medical research instead of clothes, cars, and other frivolities.

In the depths of despair, about to close his research facility and announce his retirement, Linus was given a chance to go to Palmer, Ohio, a small rural town near the Kentucky border. A former student, John A. Brooks, who headed the Science Department of prestigious Rodgers University, offered Dr. Linus an opportunity to deliver a half-dozen lectures to the senior class for an honorarium, which, frankly, was quite generous compared to what the doctor had been offered in recent years.

It was an opportunity to redeem himself professionally. Dr. Linus accepted with alacrity. He also decided he would kill two birds with one stone in Palmer. While there, he would persuade the young female newscaster to whom he had spoken on the phone several times to interview him, and he would tell the world just what he thought of the narrow-minded bureaucrats who were now running things. He, one of a handful of living American Nobel Prize laureates, would tell the ignorant, illiterate beer swillers and hamburger eaters who controlled government funding that if they didn't wise up, the men (and women) who had been wrestling with all the other killer diseases of the world would be gone, and the bureaucrats would have only the theoreticians and New Age healers of the AIDS community to protect them.

Perhaps he would even open his vaults—taking out the viruses of long-since dispatched killers (among other things, Linus Munch had access to the only viable small-pox virus left in the world). Perhaps he would re-introduce these killers and slaughter a few innocent babies, a handful or two of indigents, maybe knock off a celebrity here and a sports star there—just to remind people what the world of their parents and grandparents had been like.

The serial killers of Linus Munch's generation were, after all, two microns long, and what people didn't under-stand was that he, who had always protected them before, did not have any obligation to protect them now.

They wanted him to give up his research and just be an academic. Very well, first he would teach them a very old lesson indeed—he who giveth can also taketh away.

CHAPTER 1

Jackie Walsh, film studies professor at Rodgers University, had attended many funerals. Like many professionals in the arts, she had seen a number of very talented, still relatively young artists waste away and die from the terrible Acquired Immunodeficiency Syndrome.

In addition, having been instrumental in solving several murders (Jackie was Palmer's amateur sleuth extraordinaire), the dark-haired young film instructor had also attended a number of funerals for those who had met a violent untimely end.

This funeral, for her mother's old friend Maggie Mulcahy (a sweet, shy, former telephone operator who had diminished day by day since her retirement to the point where she was carried away by a not-very-serious case of Shanghai flu), was one of the saddest goodbye ceremonies she had ever attended.

First of all, it was raining. Second, there were only a handful of attendees. Frances Cooley Costello, Jackie's mom, was bedridden with the same flu which had killed her oldest and dearest friend. So she wasn't there.

Maggie hadn't any family in the area and her friends from her phone company days had either retired to warmer climes or were unwilling, in these lay-off happy times, to risk a supervisor's wrath by asking for a day off to attend the funeral.

Even the regular members of the Thursday Night Gentle Ladies' Gambling Society (the weekly poker game held at Jackie's mother's house) couldn't make it.

Bara Day, another elderly cardsharp of Frances's and Maggie's generation, was home nursing a sick snake.

Milly Brooks, Jackie's friend and an English instructor at Rodgers University, had taken the day off to attend her adoption proceedings (Milly and her husband John were adopting two orphaned children who had once lived next door to Jackie).

Suki Tonawanda, another instructor in the Communications Studies Department, couldn't miss class since the teaching assistant they shared was already covering a film lab for Jackie.

Worst of all, as Jackie, Maggie's neighbor Marj Leaming (once in city government, now a semi-retired volunteer at the Palmer Museum), Jean Scott (the *Herald*'s ace book reviewer and another member of the Thursday night poker game), and Jason Huckle (Palmer's premier veterinarian) looked on, the pallbearers, who doubled as Calvary Cemetery's principal grave diggers, dropped the coffin when it was half in the grave.

"Boo!" was Marj Leaming's reaction. She was very critical.

"How about giving us a break here, lady?" Jesse "Slam" Sullivan, the bigger of the two gravediggers, requested.

"Yeah," Gene "Gopher" Bailey chimed in. "This ain't exactly a golf game here."

"I should hope not," the short, rather stubby museum volunteer barked. "Since, as I understand it, the object of golf is to get it in the hole."

Mumbling obscenities, the two gravediggers picked up the muddy white coffin and wrestled/slid it back into the lowering harness.

At the same time, Jackie noted, uncomfortably, that her puppy, a huge elephant mastiff mutt named Maury, was furiously digging nearby in the soft mud.

"Maury!" Jackie hissed. "Stop it."

Hearing his name, Maury turned and looked at Jackie. *Wasn't it great what he was doing? Wasn't it great?! Wasn't he just the best damn dog in the whole wide world?*

Jackie considered kicking the dog in the ribs. "Stop it, Maury! Do you understand me? Stop digging this minute!"

The gravediggers, now starting to fill in Maggie's grave, looked back over their shoulders.

"Not you," Jackie said impatiently. "Him." She pointed to the big dog.

"Hey," Slam Sullivan commented. "He wants to dig, we'll put him to work. We got two more graves to dig this afternoon."

"Yeah, and there's nothing worse than digging graves in the rain," Gopher Bailey added.

Jackie could think of something worse. Being stuck with this giant hellhound for the rest of her life. She grabbed the big dog's collar roughly and started pulling him toward the parking lot. "Maury. Come on!"

Maury agreeably turned toward his mistress, whom he loved with all his great doggie heart, but he didn't move.

While the big dog's front end stayed friendly and steady, his back paws, working furiously, tried to fill up the hole he had created.

"Maury!" Jackie tugged ineffectually on the dog's collar.

"Jackie!" Jason Huckle hissed. The thin, mustachioed veterinarian, who had the curly blond hair and rugged good looks of a young Art Garfunkel, moved to intercede. It was Huckle's impression that bribes, not discipline, was the way to control a beast. "I'm surprised at you."

"I'm trying hard to get him to stop," Jackie protested.

"No, Jackie," Huckle said, undoing the bottom button of his tan Burberry. "It's the way you're handling Maury."

"What's wrong?" Jackie asked, looking down as she did at his collar. "He snaps leashes as if they were rubberbands and they don't make harnesses big enough for a dog this size."

"I know," Huckle said. "But you don't need a leash if you treat your canine with URTL."

"URTL?" Jackie looked at the elegantly dressed vet as if he had turned stark raving mad.

Maury looked around with delight. *Where was this URTL? Where was it hiding? Could he eat it? Could he lick it? Could he roll it with his nose?*

Huckle's voice took on the tone and timbre of actor Levar Burton doing a PBS children's show. "URTL is 'understanding,' 'respect,' 'trust,' and good old-fashioned 'love.' Isn't that right, Maury? Isn't that all a good dog needs?"

Huckle then hunched down slightly, preparing to give Maury a hug. With a blood-curdling Apache cry of delight, Maury pulled away from Jackie and hit the veterinarian like a blitzing linebacker.

"Aaagh!" yelled Huckle, as he was licked, pawed, and rolled in the mud. "Get him off! Help me! Please! Get him off!"

Jackie took a step toward the muddy vet who had taken such good care of her pets over the years and asked, "Should I use 'understanding,' 'respect,' 'trust,' or good old-fashioned . . . ?"

"Use a baseball bat for all I care!" Huckle shrieked. "Just get him off me!"

"Really," Jean Scott said disapprovingly as she turned to Marj Leaming. "All this carrying on is terribly out of place at a funeral."

"I agree," the slightly overweight former councilmember sniffed.

Jackie reached into her black fanny pack and pulled out a plastic-wrapped doggie treat.

"Maury! Maury! Want a Spicy Bone?"

Maury turned around in a flurry of fur and skittery paws. There wasn't a moment of the morning, afternoon, or night that he was not in the mood for a Spicy Pete Doggie Treat.

Jackie watched her behemoth puppy chow down on the biscuit and then noticed Jason Huckle, holding onto Jean Scott's outstretched umbrella, pull himself to his feet.

"What do you think now?" Jackie asked.

"Put the dog on a chain," the grumpy vet snarled.

Trying not to say "I told you so," Jackie smiled and asked brightly, "Can I offer anyone a ride home?"

CHAPTER 2

As Linus Munch looked at his laboratory for the last time, he wondered if he should stop and say goodbye to his brother. No, he decided. The poor fellow was so out of it, he wouldn't remember him. Or if he did, ten minutes after Linus left, Marvin would have completely forgotten that his older brother had come to visit.

Such a bright young man, now a barren hulk waiting to die. The thought of his brother's condition hardened Linus Munch's resolve. What he was going to do was unpleasant, yes. Perhaps even horrible. But then it was a horrible world, wasn't it? And Linus was sure that if Marvin could be made to understand what his brother was going to do, somehow he would approve.

Jackie's red Jeep bounced through the streets. "What," Jason Huckle in the backseat yelled over the sound of the tape deck, "do you suppose happened to the money Old Man Goodwillie was supposed to give to the city?"

The vet referred to a settlement Stuart Goodwillie, Palmer's billionaire-pharmaceutical-maven turned bottled-water-baron, had promised the good citizens of Palmer after it was disclosed he had accidentally let a contaminant from his household cleaning-products factory taint the reservoir, giving the poor people of the town two years of mysterious illnesses and occasional bizarre behavior.

"What are you saying?" the slightly hard-of-hearing Jean Scott asked querulously. "You know, Jackie. It's bad enough we have to sit here crammed together like sardines . . ."

Jackie blushed beet red for it was true, Maury positively refused to ride in the back seat. He had to be the center of attention all the time, even when he didn't have anything to say.

"I'm sorry, Jean," Jackie shouted. "But Maury has to ride in the front seat and he has to listen to his tape. Loudly."

"It's cowboys, Jackie," Marj Leaming protested. "Why must this dog terrorize us into listening to themes from Dean Martin westerns, for God's sake?"

Maury turned around, a Mr. T glare on his face.

"I really wouldn't insult Maury, Marj," Jackie advised.

"Oh . . ." Marj scoffed.

Maury then made a sound like that of a blast furnace.

"Careful, Ms. Leaming," Huckle advised. "This dog is half elephant mastiff. Do you know why they call them that?"

"Because the English in India used them to herd those animals the way the Germans used Alsatian dogs to herd their sheep?" Jean Scott guessed knowledgeably.

"Partly," Huckle conceded. "And partly because they never forget."

The growl grew louder in the big dog's chest, giving the back seat passengers the impression that they were standing in an airport terminal as a jumbo jet landed.

"For God's sake! Apologize, Marj!" Jean Scott screeched. "He's half Baskerville hound and half Moby Dick."

"All right! All right!" Marj conceded. "I'm sorry."

Maury nodded reluctantly as if he were doing the museum volunteer a tremendous favor, then turned back around.

"What's this next song?" Huckle asked Jackie, as if trying to ingratiate himself with the big dog by showing an interest in his favorite tape.

" 'Bonanza,' " Jackie answered. "As sung by Lorne Greene."

"Kicky," Huckle commented.

"Well, it's not grand opera," Jackie said apologetically, knowing that to be the preference of the cultured vet.

"Hey, I'm no snob," Huckle lied. "I'd love to hear this."

Right on cue, Maury started howling, sputtering, whining, and groaning (his idea of singing along), completely drowning out the tape.

"Here's your stop, Marj," Jackie called out as she switched off the tape.

"Thank God!" Marj said. Unfortunately, the moment she reached for the door handle, Maury barked again.

"What now?" she asked.

"I don't think he's going to let you leave until you listen to 'The Alamo' again," Jackie responded.

Marj cried out in horror. "Again?"

"He's only a puppy," Jackie explained. "He keeps confusing being big with being right."

CHAPTER 3

As Linus Munch got off the plane, he was disappointed to be met, not by a cheerful throng of science groupies, but by a single gentleman of an ethnic background the good doctor would just as soon see kept out of the gene pool. The young man held up a sign with Munch's name on it. Misspelled.

"Dr. Munch!" the chauffeur called out.

"With one 'N,' " the good doctor snarled. "And it's pronounced 'Moonk.' "

The young part-time chauffeur (for two days a week he was a teaching assistant for a cinematography class at Rodgers University) grinned good-naturedly and grabbed the lighter of the doctor's two bags. "Sorry about that, Doc. I thought it was 'Munch'—like 'Munch, munch, munch a bunch of Fritos . . . ' "

"Yes," the doctor replied crabbily. "That is exactly what it is not. I take it, you, sir, are my driver?"

"Yeah," Ral Perrin replied. "You'll have to get another club to putt."

After finally discharging the last of her passengers, Jackie picked up her mobile Fona-Dict.

Maury immediately hushed, knowing that if he was quiet while his mistress talked into the funny mechanical square bone, he would get a tasty treat.

Jackie code-signaled the number of her friend Marcella Jacobs. When the secondary tone connect indicated that Marcella's answering line would pick up, Jackie pressed a button with a pre-recorded "leave" message and switched the communications device she had treated herself to (with some of the money she had made from a recent two-hour TV movie script) from "transmit" to "dictate."

"Third Year Film Studies," Jackie started. "Lecture number three. Access code format three. Good afternoon, filmmakers . . ."

Jackie launched into a lecture about film-enhancement techniques. Maury, bored silly by any talk that did not directly involve him, scratched his head on the passenger seat visor, eventually breaking it.

"Maury!" Jackie switched her Fona-Dict to "Pause" and fished out a couple of Spicy Pete Deluxe Doggie Gobbles. She tossed them into the floorwell and the Gobbles disappeared into Maury's mouth so fast it was as if the treats had been vacuumed up.

Jackie then switched her Fona-Dict back on.

After a few minutes, she was interrupted by a mechanical female voice. "Excuse me. You have a call waiting from . . ."

There was a pause and Jackie heard the voice of her friend . . .

"Marcella Jacobs."

"Oh good," Jackie said to herself. She switched from "Dicta" to "Fone" while taking a battered shoe out of a bag of mixed, used footwear that she had bought at the Palmer Stars and Stripes Thrift Shop and gave it to Maury to chew.

"Hello, Marcella?"

"Jackie!"

Swerving around a slow-moving Oldsmobile, Jackie asked, "Are we still meeting today?"

"Yes, but I'm on a story."

"Uh, oh."

"Give me a break, Jacqueline," Marcella requested. "Things are particularly cut-throat right now. Would you do me a favor?"

"Sure," Jackie said obligingly.

Jackie's sudden willingness to help her friend was not based solely on comradely feelings. Jackie had met Marcella the year before, when she had accidentally become involved in a murder investigation. Together they had unraveled a very tangled skein indeed, which had led to an almost complete housecleaning in City Hall and in the Palmer Police Department.

For the past few months the two women had been in frequent contact and Marcella had taken the first real step in earning Jackie's friendship by offering to borrow (and perhaps to keep) the massive Maury as a guard dog.

So anxious was Jackie to unload the unexpected off-spring of her own dog Jake, that she was willing to do just about anything to keep Marcella happy.

"Oh, thank you," the reporter gushed. "You're such a love. Listen. I'm supposed to interview Dr. Linus Munch today. You know, the guy who won the Nobel Prize a few years ago?"

"Lucky you."

"Well, maybe," Marcella allowed. "Word is, he's

become a bit of a crank who pretends to be hard of hearing unless you ask him a question he wants to answer."

"Oh. One of those."

"Yeah. After all these years I can handle those types, but not without a lot of preparation and a lot of drinks."

"You get them drunk?" Jackie supposed.

"I get us both drunk," Marcella laughingly admitted. "Then I flirt with him. I found guys' hearing and their aches and pains get a lot better when you lead them on a little."

"Isn't that dangerous?" Jackie inquired, steering around a raccoon who had wandered out into traffic and was actually moving faster than some of the cars.

"Hey, if he's still dangerous at seventy-three, God love him." Marcella paused to talk to someone, then came back on line. "Listen, Jackie. Sorry, but I gotta go. All you have to do is drive over and pick Dr. Munch up at the television station. Explain to him that I'm running late and that we can meet later for a get-acquainted dinner. He's in town for a week anyway. I'm sure he'll be fresher himself tomorrow.

"Drive him to the university, where you're going anyway, and take him to the science building. He's staying with the chairman, John Brooks. Do you know him?"

"Oh sure," Jackie answered quickly. "His wife Milly and I are old college roommates."

"Good. You're a doll."

"Wait a minute," Jackie protested. "I happen to know that Milly and John are going to an adoption hearing today. What if he's not back when I get there?"

"Then park the old gentleman with John's secretary and let him wander around the campus, or . . . I don't know. You'll think of something. If you have to, call me back, but I really have to go now. Give that big adorable dog a big sloppy kiss for me. Bye."

Jackie looked at the suddenly dead phone receiver in her hand, then turned to Maury as he spit the remains of an espadrille into the gear box.

"Thanks, pal!"

Basking in his mistress' obvious approval, Maury slobbered a "You're welcome."

CHAPTER 4

Station KCIN was located on the outskirts of Palmer. As Jackie drove toward it, she wondered what Dr. Munch was doing in Palmer.

Jackie knew he had something to do with Alzheimer's research and hoped he wouldn't run into her mother Frances and think something was wrong with her. Frances was eccentric, sure, but Jackie didn't think she had any disease.

Maury picked up on his mistress' uneasiness and growled uneasily. A quick sniff through the vent window confirmed his suspicion that this was rabbit land—where he had once sniffed out a miserable low-life wild Palmer hare (and incidentally flipped over his mistress' Jeep while trying to push it out of the mud).

Was his mistress afraid of rabbits? Never fear. He would protect her. Why he would take any miserable rabbit that might happen to leap for the throat of his wonderful, sweet-smelling, food-giving mistress, grab it by the neck, and shake it until he had pulverized every bone in its body. Why he would . . .

"Maury."

. . . He'd make short work of that rabbit, by gosh, and if an elephant were to come along, . . .

"Maury!"

The dog's short attention span swung to his owner who he decided needed a good old-fashioned kiss on the snoot.

Her day makeup entirely washed from her face, Jackie gasped for air and protested, "Would you stop?"

Maury lost his train of thought again and started looking around the car for a toy. *Whatever happened to that rubber mouse he used to have that made a noise when you smacked it?* he wondered.

"Maury! Listen to me!"

The big dog looked up, as always attentive to his mistress' every wish.

"I am going to have another passenger in a minute. Do you understand?"

Maury nodded agreeably. He didn't understand a word, *but why disappoint a good friend like what's-her-name?*

"I want you to ride in the back this time. I know it's uncomfortable, but I don't have any choice. Do you think you can sit there for ten or fifteen minutes without bothering the nice man who's going to be sitting in your seat?"

Maury nodded happily. He remembered what happened to that mouse. He ate it!

"Good dog," Jackie replied.

Maury nodded again (this phrase he understood). *And he was a good dog, wasn't he?*

"I'll be right back." Jackie opened her door and Maury immediately tried to follow. He loved stretching his four legs and wherever his mistress wanted to go, he'd be right by her side—defending her from . . .

Pushing with all her might, Jackie managed to close the door and lock it. "Now stay. Stay!"

Rubbing the spot on his head that had been banged by the door, Maury looked out the window and barked a "Hey, what gives?"

"Stay there!" Jackie repeated. "I'll be back in a few minutes. Be good!"

Maury got a little frantic. *What, was she going somewhere? When would she come back? Should he stay here or what?*

Scurrying away from her rocking Jeep and her squawking puppy, Jackie rushed by the brown sod lawn (no grass ever seemed to grow by the television studio—perhaps the broadcast waves hurt certain kinds of plants as well as people) and hurried up the front walk of the KCIN building.

Unlike the broadcast buildings in the big cities, this particular complex of one-story buildings sprawled over a good half-acre of prime industrial real estate.

As she nervously burst through the door of KCIN (whose motto used to be "We Tell the Citizens of Ohio Just What Their Neighbors Are Up To"), Jackie found herself totally disoriented.

The last time Jackie had come to KCIN was when the network was still located in the National Bank Tower downtown. But then, the conglomerate that owned the station (as well as the Palmer *Daily Chronicle*) decided to sell the old landmark building (which could not be significantly altered without a special commission's permission). By threatening to move their headquarters to nearby Wardville, the conglomerate had sold the unused sound studio for a song.

Jackie was looking around for a receptionist, when suddenly a nervous, thirty-three-year-old news producer with designer eyeglasses and slicked down raven-colored hair (with a little artificial gray streaked in to make him look older), burst out of the employees' day care facility, holding a baby who looked none too happy to be a part of the KCIN news team.

"Who are you?" the young producer bleated.

"Oh," Jackie smiled, her eyes dilating. "Is that your beautiful baby?"

"No way," the young man replied, wincing as the bambino snapped his suspenders. "And I asked you who *you* are."

"Ruben . . ." Jackie addressed the young man. "It's me, Jackie Walsh."

"Oh," Ruben Baskette answered. "So it is. Ow!" Ruben moved the baby to his other arm, not immediately noticing that she had unfastened his silver Rolex watch, causing it to fall into the paper recycle bin behind him. "You're Marcella's friend, aren't you?"

"I hope so," Jackie replied. "Are you doing a story on babies, or something?"

"No. Why?"

"Well, you are holding one."

"Ow." Ruben held the sore spot on his ribcage where the baby had kicked him and replied irritably, "It's my turn as monitor, isn't it?"

"I don't know," Jackie answered honestly. "Is it?"

"Of course it is," the young man snapped, as the baby pulled out his Mark Cross pen and let it drop into the coffeemaker.

"Oops, careful."

"Oh, that's okay," Ruben replied sarcastically. "It's only a pen. It's only a deathbed gift from my grandfather.

Perhaps one day we'll be able to revive the dead, and I can dig him up, bring him back, and get him to give me another one. Ow!"

The baby, startled by Ruben's loud voice, kicked out again, this time catching the news producer on the side of the jaw.

"Do you want me to take her?" Jackie asked.

"What do you take me for? She's my responsibility. I can't let her out of my sight. Imagine the lawsuit . . ."

"Sorry, I wasn't thinking," Jackie replied.

"Hah. The day of the Harvard Business School–trained producer like yours truly is gone, baby."

The child gurgled happily.

"I wasn't talking to you."

"No more, huh?" Jackie asked dutifully.

"You can kiss it goodbye," Ruben continued. The baby naturally made kissy noises.

"Isn't she cute?"

Ruben all but snarled and Jackie was reminded of W. C. Fields's comment on how he liked children (parboiled). "You know, when management rolled over and agreed to open these day care facilities for the employees, we assumed that there would be child care workers to actually do the work."

"What's the matter? Can't afford them?"

"Hell, we'd pay them anchorman money if we could find them, but they're scarce as hen's teeth."

The baby pressed her chubby cheeks with her little palms, making the drool on her lips form into one big bubble.

"But why am I talking to you?" Ruben said. "I have a news show to get on the air tonight and all of a sudden I'm *Home Alone* in the nursery. It isn't even really my turn. I just got snagged because my co-anchor went over to Marx-Wheeler hospital to cover the wildcat strike that's getting under way. I don't suppose you know if she's going to make it back here in time to film the 4:15 live promo?"

"No, I don't," Jackie replied. "Sorry. In fact I'm supposed to . . ."

Suddenly, the baby, clearly in a playful mood, started making "Come closer" motions. Ruben obliged, drawing her in until they were practically eye to eye. Then, giving Jackie a devilish wink, little Mary Mercedes started sucking on the young producer's nose.

"Help! Help!" Ruben called out. "Why is she doing this?"

"I think she thinks it's a nipple," Jackie replied.

"Stop it! Stop it!" the young producer howled. "Hold on. Hold on. I'll get you a bottle."

As Baskette rushed away, ace reporter Drew Feigl, a very tall, very thin, very inquisitive reporter with dark wavy hair and gigolo dark eyes, appeared out of his office, stage right.

"Oh, oh."

"What?" Jackie asked.

"I know who you are," Feigl said worriedly. "And whenever you're around, there's trouble."

Jackie gave the television snoop a narrow look. First, she wasn't that fond of men who wore black clothing exclusively, unless they were mimes or sang country and western music. Second, she hated men who wore tinted designer aviator lens glasses indoors. "Sez who?"

"Don't play little Miss Innocent with me," Feigl insisted. "Is it, or is it not true that the last time I saw you, you were sneaking out of Marx-Wheeler hospital with a prime murder suspect?"

"No comment!" Jackie answered loudly.

"No? How very interesting that you think you have something to hide," Feigl insinuated. "Maybe you can answer this: Did you, or did you not come to our newsroom in the old building and pretend to be a news writer?"

"I did nothing of the sort," Jackie answered honestly.

Feigl's eyebrows drew closer together. "Do you deny that the very day you came to our newsroom one of our key layabout union technical workers was murdered?"

"I know that it happened," Jackie conceded. "And if you'll recall, I solved the case."

Feigl made a la-di-da face.

"Mr. Feigl," Jackie continued. "I didn't come here to be grilled by you. And I have a dog who is positively going wild in my Jeep."

"I thought I heard howling," Feigl said at once. "It reminded me of that Sherlock Holmes story."

"Please," Jackie said. "Spare me. I am simply here to do Marcella a favor. You have a bone to pick, go pick it with her."

"Bone! Very clever," the crusading reporter sneered.

Jackie used the same tone she employed when scolding Maury. "Mr. Feigl. Do you know where Dr. Linus Munch is—yes or no?"

Feigl immediately heeled, following respectfully behind Jackie as she wandered down the hall of offices. "Yes. He's huddling with Vic Kingston. Why not? Kingston doesn't have much else to do."

What Drew Feigl was referring to was the recent shake-up in the KCIN News line-up, which had resulted in Jackie's friend Marcella being elevated to co-anchor status. Served with a *fait accompli,* Vic Kingston pretended, like all male anchors do in such instances, to be in favor of it, but of course he was actually quietly incensed. After all, what with the sports news and the weather monkey (a chimp named Gooner who could point to blue-screen weather graphics as well as a human being), and the twelve solid minutes of commercials and station promos, there hadn't been much news left to read in the first place. Now Vic Kingston's entire evening broadcast copy could be written on several small Post-its.

"It's murder I tell you!" Kingston's voice thundered.

Drew Feigl pointed, rather unnecessarily, to a large corner office at the end of the corridor. "That's his crib over there. Just stay out of arm's reach of the guy. He may decide that the only way he can get back on the air in any substantial kind of way is to kill someone."

CHAPTER 5

Jackie knocked loudly on the door of the veteran anchor-man's office.

"Come in!"

Jackie entered the smoky corner office, filled with the mementos (everything from autographed photos to a live hand grenade Audie Murphy had given him) collected by Palmer's Vic Kingston in thirty-five years of broad-casting.

The two men, who had obviously been talking heatedly for some time, did not miss a beat as she stepped onto the cigar-burned shag carpet.

"You couldn't be more right, Victor . . ." Dr. Munch was saying.

Jackie noted wryly that the health care professional had a glass of bourbon and branch water in one hand and a fat stogy in the other.

" . . . Young people today don't want to get to the top of the hill. They want to bulldoze half the hill away."

Kingston nodded boozily. "Hell's bells! Some of the people from my generation are still trying to climb the damn thing. You know, I may be sixty-four, but I ain't satisfied." Kingston then puffed on a cigarette which he smoked through a long ceramic holder and took a quick sip of his piña colada. A tough war veteran who, after being stabbed in a crowded Honduran bar, had promptly turned on his attacker and beat him to death with a bottle of basket-wrapped rum, Vic Kingston didn't care if people thought his way of drinking or smoking wasn't sufficiently masculine.

"There were journalism awards I haven't won. There are conventions I'd like to cover. Old as I am, I would love to have a Sunday morning interview show. Hell's bells. I would love to be the most respected man in America— like that damn fruity-voiced Texan used to be."

Munch nodded and murmured, "With all due respect, Victor, the idea that the most respected man in the United States is some phony baloney news jockey with fake hair, capped teeth, and the ability to read words written on cue cards by someone else appalls me. Again, no offense."

"Quite all right, Linus," Kingston replied, waving his hand. "With the exception of yours truly and the late great John Cameron Swayze, anchormen are pond weasels. And incidentally, we don't read 'em off the cards anymore. We got a teleprompter. It looks like a TV basically. Hell's bells. With the little copy I get to say anymore, I'm thinking of going back to writing on those stupid pieces of paper they have you hold. What the hell? If all I'm gonna say from here on in is, 'And here's Marcella Jacobs to tell you all about it,' I can memorize that."

Munch suddenly sat bolt upright on his couch. "Tell me about this Miss Jacobs, Victor."

"Do I have to? Don't I talk enough about this dame?" If Vic Kingston was sorry about offending Jackie with his language, he was apparently apologizing telepathically.

"Please, Victor," Munch urged. "I'm serious. Is she a ballbreaker?"

"Hell," Victor replied, reaching under his desk. "I've still got mine."

That was enough for Jackie. "Excuse me, *gentlemen.* Dr. Munch, I am here to take you over to the Rodgers campus."

"Yes, yes," Munch said impatiently. "I'll be with you in a moment. Just wait outside."

"Uh, Dr. . . ."

"Take that bag too," Munch said, pointing. "Don't put it in the trunk. It's fragile. It has plastic bags of serum in it. Place it carefully on the back seat. I will carry it on my lap."

"I'm afraid I'm not really up for taking your bag, Dr. Munch." Jackie's blood pressure was starting to rise and her peaches-and-cream complexion was reddening.

"What?" Munch said in amazement. "It's an extra charge? Do it. I'll pay you what you want. Write it on the bill."

Kingston was impressed. Men of his generation, even fabulously wealthy individuals, were notorious for their stinginess. "You on an expense account, or something?"

"A fabulous expense account," Munch confirmed with an expansive wave of his arms. "I get grants from the government."

Kingston slapped his desk. "Damn you, Linus. You lucky dog. I have been trying to elbow my way to that particular sugar tit all my life. What I wouldn't give for some big fat juicy tax-exempt government free ride? Hell's bells. I make two hundred and eighty grand a year and I don't net what you and some of your research buddies pull down."

Munch smiled modestly. "Yes, it is a terrific boon to us, Victor. No question. But . . ."

"That's it, Linus," Kingston slurred, pouring himself another drink from his two-quart cocktail shaker. "I'm cutting you off. You're mumbling like an old stewbum. Why just to illustrate, when you said 'boon' just now, you were so drunk you forgot to say 'doggle.' "

"Hah," Munch responded drunkenly. "There's no need to be jealous of me much longer, Victor. It's just a matter of months before they throw me out on my ear."

"You? Pshaw."

Although quietly despising both men, Jackie was fascinated by their conversation. She had no idea people still said things like "pshaw" any more.

"No, it's quite true," Munch elaborated. "I am a relic, Victor. Like yourself, I'm afraid."

"Hey, I resent that!" Kingston roared.

At that moment, Ruben Baskette, still nervously holding a small child and escorting a group of visitors, pushed through the half-open door. "Vic? Are you decent?"

"Decent?" Kingston roared. "No, I'm not decent. I'm half-drunk and I'm about to take an empty bottle and beat the hell out of this old fart here for saying I'm a dinosaur."

"I did not say you were a dinosaur, Victor," Munch said thickly. "I said you were a relic."

"I know what you said, damn it," Kingston roared.

The baby giggled delightedly at the smelly old newsman and grabbed his finger.

"Coochy-coo, you little rug rat. Besides," the craggy old newsreader continued. "Everybody likes dinosaurs these days. Right?" He turned to the visitors and indicated the baby still clinging to his index finger. "Well, what are you waiting for, boys? Here's your picture."

The gentlemen exchanged looks, then the lead man turned to Ruben. "I see that we have come at a bad time for Mr. Kingston. We shall wait in the corridor for you, Mr. Baskette."

"You idiot!" Ruben hissed as he tugged the baby away from the crusty anchorman.

"Screw you, Charlie," Kingston growled. "This is my office. You don't have any right to barge in here with a bunch of tourists while I'm trying to have a little drink with an old friend."

"Tourists? Did you say tourists, Vic?" Ruben screeched, upsetting the baby. Jackie immediately began to cuddle and coo over the squalling infant, and eventually got her quiet.

"For your information, Mr. Big Shot," the irate producer continued, "those gentlemen are from the conglomerate that just happens to own this network. I told them you were unhappy with sharing an anchor role with Marcella. And they were sympathetic, Vic." Ruben turned to Jackie. "Pardon me for speaking bluntly, miss."

He then turned back to Kingston. "If you could have managed to be even civil to them, you may have helped yourself big time. Instead, you may have just signed your resignation letter, buddy. And if you think I'm going to go out there and beg for your job, you're crazy."

Taking great care to slam the hell out of the door, Ruben Baskette left the room.

"Do you want me to help you pack your bags, Victor?" Munch finally said.

"Ah, let the kid take his shot," Kingston growled. "It's just like the time they made me cover the atheists' parade and I said I didn't know why people were marching for something they didn't believe in. The bottom line here, Linus, is that like me or hate me, every year I sell a lot of fish burgers for these people. *Media personalities* like Marcella Jacobs are good at running down to Marx-Wheeler Medical Center every time . . ."

"Marx-Wheeler . . ." Munch laboriously pulled himself off the sofa and exclaimed, "Why that's where I'm lecturing tomorrow. This makes no sense to me whatever. Why not interview me here this afternoon, and then cover the lecture tomorrow? What sort of backward nonsense is this? Today she's at the hospital when I'm not there to lecture and tomorrow—what? She'll be here when I'm not here to be interviewed?"

Kingston growled, "You're not the only man in the world, Linus. You're not the only news event either. In fact, you aren't a news event at all. We're making you one out of the goodness of our hearts."

"Thank you very much, I'm sure," Munch replied, reaching for his coat and hat.

"You're welcome," Kingston said, getting to his feet. "And for your information, Marcella Jacobs is at Marx-Wheeler to cover a staff slowdown."

"Slowdown?" Munch scoffed. "Whoever heard of a slowdown in a hospital? These people are already moving so slow you could document their entire working day with a still camera."

Even Jackie had to chuckle at that one.

"There's no denying that," Kingston agreed. "I thank the Good Lord that whenever I'm sick I have the money to get on a plane and jet on down to Texas. I stay in one of those VIP joints with the catered meals and a private room as nice as any hotel suite. They give you a little silver bell and if you want anything from a pain pill to a hooker, you just ring and they come running."

As Jackie listened to the increasingly boorish Kingston, she lost whatever small degree of respect she might have had for him.

"Well, I'm going down there!" Munch announced.

"I figured you would," Kingston replied. "And I'm going with you. If I'm out of here, I might as well go down with a microphone in my fist. I'll let you and Marcella go off and talk somewhere and while you're gone, I'll snoop around and see if I can sniff out a story. Hell's bells. I may not be able to get another anchor job, what with my handicap of being a white male and all, but maybe one of those cheapo news programs will hire me as a reporter."

Kingston then turned to Jackie. "What are we going to do with this young lady? She stands there in the corner much longer, we're gonna have to put some cigars in her hand."

"Please, Victor," Munch begged. "Do not treat this young woman as a wooden Native American. I'm sure by now that's some sort of hate crime."

Kingston grabbed his hat. "No doubt."

"You, young lady," Munch addressed Jackie with an air of doing her a favor. "We're very sorry to keep you waiting so long, but I want you to drive me to the hospital now."

"Dr. Munch." Jackie had to ball her fingers to keep from striking the old medical researcher. "You are one of the most inconsiderate people I have ever met."

"What?" Munch, drunk as he was, was absolutely floored by her attack. "What is this? What are you saying? What sort of preposterous thing is this? I'm being verbally assaulted by a . . . taxi driver?"

"I would have thought, *Dr.* Munch," Jackie raged, "that by now you have lived in this country long enough to know that even a taxi driver has as much right to express herself as a former Nobel Prize winner. But as I've been trying to tell you, I am not a taxi driver."

"All right then," Munch waved his hand contemptuously. "A limousine driver, although what passes for a limousine in this town would not pass for a taxi in . . ."

"I am not a limousine driver either," Jackie blazed.

"All right then," Munch replied, putting his hand over his left ear. "You don't need to berate me like a fishwife. My hearing aid isn't built for industrial use, thank you very much. If you're not a driver, what are you?"

Vic Kingston, now starting to realize what had happened, answered, "She's a writer, Linus."

"A writer?" Munch considered Jackie with a mixture of fear and loathing. "Not a newspaper writer, I hope against hope."

"No," Jackie replied. "And you're lucky. If I were a newspaper reporter, I would just love to write this story. How the nightly news gets made. I guess it's like sausages—if you like them you shouldn't watch what goes into them. But I am appalled. Absolutely appalled. And I am further appalled by *you,* Dr. Munch. Here you are, being feted by the town, or at least by your old buddies, as a hard-working humanitarian hero, when you are really a self-serving, foul-mouthed opportunist who's only pretending to be a saint in order to keep his fabulous expense account."

"All right, lady," Kingston growled. "You had your say. I hope you got it all off your chest—which isn't bad, by the way, for a skinny girl. Wouldn't you say, Linus?"

Clearly the doctor had already given the matter some thought. "Yes, yes. Quite impressive."

Jackie by now resembled the thunderstorm icon used on the nightly news weathercast.

"But take it from an old newspaper dog, lady," Kingston continued. "You could write that story good enough to win a Pulitzer Prize and it would never see the light of day. You see, your editor, whoever *he* might be, or your publisher, whoever *he* might be, has a lot more in common with me and Dr. Linus here than he does with you and the rabble-rousing college lefties who want to read that kind of bilge. You'll forgive me if I crow about one of the few places left in this country where we still get to win every now and again."

"I don't understand any of this conversation," Munch complained. "Are you a newspaper writer or not?"

"No, I'm a screenwriter," Jackie answered disgustedly. "I happen to work at Rodgers University, where I instruct filmmaking in the Communications Studies Department. As a favor to Marcella, who *used* to be my friend, I was willing to take you over to the college and walk you over to the Science Department, and point out John Brooks to you."

Linus Munch ran his hands through his thinning gray hair in confusion. "But I know John Brooks already. He was one of my favorite research assistants."

"Fine," Jackie said, heading for the door. "Then you don't need me at all."

"But what about our ride?" Munch wailed.

"Take it easy, Linus," Kingston rasped, slapping his pal on the back. "I got my car."

"But you're drunk," Munch pointed out.

"Well, la-di-da," Kingston yelled. "You want to take a bus, sport?"

"No, of course not."

"I didn't think so. I'm driving. Either way. What do you say? You coming or not?"

"*Ja, ja,*" Munch decided resignedly. "What does it matter anymore? If I died in a car wreck, I'd be treated better than I'm getting treated now."

Kingston drunkenly tried to slick down his hair with the back of his tortoiseshell brush. "Never had an accident in fifty years of driving."

"But, Victor," Munch protested. "You're only sixty-four. That means you were driving illegally for four years when you were a teenager."

"So what?" Kingston roared. "Haven't you ever heard the expression, 'practice makes perfect'?"

"Try using that defense at a surgery malpractice board hearing," Munch mumbled. "And for that matter, I clearly remember you cracking up that old Studebaker you used to have when you ran into that fellow who used to own the paint company."

"That wasn't an accident," Kingston sniffed. "I meant to ram that cheap, welching, son of a . . ."

"Goodbye, *gentlemen!*" Jackie said loudly.

"We're right behind you," Munch announced, reaching for his suitcase. "Oh dear, Vic. These cases are so heavy. You're a much younger man than myself. Would you?"

"I'd love to, Linus," Kingston lied. "But this rheumatism of mine has got me knotted up like a pretzel. That's why I drink so much," the old crime beat reporter improvised. "To help me work through the pain."

"Balderoot!" Munch inaccurately yelled (as with many transplanted aliens, the good doctor still prayed and cursed in his native language). "At least take *one* then, you worthless old layabout."

Kingston held up a finger. "Don't make me file an age bias suit against you, Linus."

"Hah! Fire away, youngster," Munch responded.

The doctor then yelled to Jackie as she returned from the nursery, having dropped off the baby. "Miss . . . whatever your name is!"

"Walsh," Jackie replied.

"Like the old spitball pitcher," Kingston said, belching.

"Would you do me a favor, Ms. Walsh?" Munch asked in his most humble voice.

Jackie turned indignantly. "You really do have a lot of gall, Dr. Munch. What possible reason could you have for thinking you've earned a favor from me?"

"Please. I am an old man."

"Too old, if you ask me."

"You wound me, Madam," Munch pouted. "I implore you. Help me out and I will dedicate the next human life I save in your honor. The next three, say. Ach, I don't like to haggle. The next five!"

Kingston laughed hysterically.

"I don't happen to think that's funny!" Jackie snapped.

"Ptah," Munch expectorated. "So you don't like my jokes either. Well, then if you won't do me a favor, do this anchorperson friend of yours a favor."

"I think," Jackie retorted, "I've done Marcella enough favors for one day."

"And I would agree with you, dear lady," Munch quickly conceded. "But you know this modern generation of yours. The fact that you expended so much effort will mean nothing. The mere fact that you did not do exactly what you were asked translates into the fact that you did nothing, and therefore no gratitude will be in order."

Jackie thought long and hard about that one. Reluctantly she had to admit that he was probably right. And Marcella's gratitude was all-important now. "All right. What's your favor?"

"It is the smallest favor in the world," Munch averred.

Jackie tapped her foot impatiently. "Yes?"

"Simply call or drop in on Mr. Brooks."

"Dr. Brooks," Jackie corrected. "He's a Ph.D."

"Of course he is," Munch effused agreeably. "Tell him, if you would, that I am at this hospital. If it's convenient to him, he should meet me at this Marx-Lenin . . ."

"Marx-Wheeler!" Kingston corrected.

"Whatever!" Munch roared. "Tell him I'm going there and ask him if he can meet me. Whenever it's convenient. Thank you."

Jackie reluctantly nodded and walked out to her Jeep.

It was gone.

Jackie looked around and then saw it, thirty feet away, in the TV station's award-winning flower bed (which had once spelled out KCIN in tulips).

Maury had apparently thrown himself against the sides of the vehicle until he had turned it over. The new, sturdier roll bar (which Jackie had installed after Maury had done something like this once before) had allowed the Jeep to roll completely over and back onto its wheels again. In all the excitement the enormous tongue-wagging puppy had explosively thrown up.

Jackie looked at the puppy (guiltily trying to clean up after himself), then looked at the sides of her eighteen-month-old Jeep. The windows were scratched, the red paint was partially scraped off, and the soft metal alloy sides were pocked with gravel and other debris. Jackie was pissed. Not at the greedy Palmer steel magnates who had closed the local foundry, throwing many of the town's blue-collar workers out of a job, and taken their business overseas, where both the labor and the quality were markedly cheaper. She was mad at her miserable, despicable, good for nothing pet!

Hello, Mistress! Maury slobbered as she got into the car. *What kept you? You've been gone for a long time,*

*right? Wait a minute. I forget now. Did you go out?
Where are we? Are we home yet? Where's the kid who
always feeds me? Wonder if he's got any more of those
meatballs? They were good. Boy, they slid right down. I
bet I could eat a whole boxcar full of meatballs.*

"Maury!" Jackie yelled, grabbing the dog's shaggy ears.

The big dog looked up adoringly at his lovely, good-
hearted mistress. *How did she know his ears were itchy?*

Jackie squeezed ferociously.

That felt great! Maury tried for a sweeping tongue kiss
and his breath nearly caused Jackie to fall over backward.

"Maury! Please!"

The dog sat up attentively. When she said *please,* it
was time for him to beg for Dill Doggie Nibbles. He
didn't remember much from obedience school, but he
sure remembered that one.

Jackie waved her finger. "You can . . . not . . ."

Maury, initially a little hypnotized by the dancing digit,
finally gave Jackie's finger a little nip. He did it gently,
though, with scarcely enough pressure to snap a canary's
back.

"Ow!" Jackie shrieked.

Suddenly a loud beep from behind startled her. It was
the joy boys, Laughing Linus Munch and Slick Vic
Kingston.

"Watch where you're going, why don't you?!" yelled
Kingston.

"Yes!" Munch called out to her. "You'd think from the
way you slaughtered those poor flowers that you were the
one who was drunk." Whooping like endangered cranes,
the two celebrities then careened down the road.

Jackie was already so mad that when she pulled out of
the flower bed and heard her front bumper fall off, she

could do nothing else but laugh, albeit bitterly. Routinely going through her collection of curse words under her breath, Jackie wrestled the bumper into the back seat, noting with annoyance that it stuck out the rear window on the left side.

"I better not," Jackie said, after considering a moment. She could see the police pulling her over and fatuously claiming that the four inches or so of the piece of bumper sticking out constituted a menace to other drivers.

Rearranging the bumper so that it now stuck four inches out of the right rear window, Jackie got back into her Jeep, glared at Maury (who was happily sniffing the bumper to find out where it had come from), and pulled out of the TV station parking lot.

Jackie was no more than thirty feet down the Woody Hayes Turnpike when she saw red flashing lights in her side mirror. "Foo!" she said explosively.

Maury, although he didn't have the slightest clue as to what was going on, barked.

A few moments later, Officer Patricia Watson, a wide-hipped, pleasant-faced highway patrolwoman with short blonde hair, strode up to Jackie's driver's side and demanded, "License and registration, please."

Mistressing with difficulty the urge to put on an Inspector Clouseau performance (confusing the request for her driver's license with a question about the dog's license, then confusing the word "please" with a question as to whether her mastiff had fleas), Jackie responded calmly. "Is there a problem, Officer?"

Patrolwoman Watson gave the rote snappy answer most favored by the Ohio State Police. "There will be, Ma'am, if you don't let me see your license and registration."

"Is this about the bumper sticking out four inches?" Jackie asked.

"Ma'am, if I have to ask you for your license and registration one more time, I'm going to put you under arrest and impound your car."

So much for the claims that female highway patrol officers go easy on members of their own sex, thought Jackie.

Jackie reached out to her glove compartment but Maury quickly grabbed her wrist in his huge mouth. *Playtime!*

"No, Maury!"

Yup, yup, yup. It was time to play and show the nice lady who smelled of Old Spice outside the window that he was the best damn dog any mistress ever had, and a heckuva lot of fun to boot.

"Maury!"

The big dog's snickering could be heard as far away as Wardville.

"Maury. Let me get into the glove compartment."

No, no, the big dog chuckled. *This is a game. I can't give it to you. You gotta win fair and square.*

Feeling Watson's eyes boring into her (indeed Jackie could imagine that there were now two staple-like holes in her neck, resembling those of the poor little boy's mother in the movie she had intended to show in her film lab the next day, *Invaders from Mars*), Jackie reached into her bag and pulled out the last little Doggie Gobble.

"Get the treat, boy," she said, flipping it over her shoulder. Of course, Jackie figured that while Maury scrambled around for it, she would have time to open the glove compartment and get her car owner's papers.

What the film instructor had not counted on was the fantastic telescoping properties of her puppy's massive neck. A blur of shaggy teeth and fur, Maury caught the doggie treat in mid-air, chewed, swallowed, and whirled around just in time to catch Jackie's arm as she reached toward the glove compartment.

Despite herself, Jackie was impressed. "Wow!"

"Having troubles, Ma'am?" Officer Watson asked.

"Uh, yes," Jackie admitted. "I am. I'm afraid he won't let me into the glove compartment."

"Is this *your* dog?" the officer asked, reasonably enough.

"Yes," Jackie responded, a little nettled to be accused of dognapping. Did the policewoman actually think that she was stupid enough to go out and *steal* a dog this aggravating?

"Do you need some help?" Watson offered.

"I would love some help," Jackie admitted.

Officer Watson slowly walked around the front of the car and approached the passenger's side.

Maury, his mistress' arm still gently but firmly locked in his jaws, watched as the pretty policewoman made her way around. *This was going to be great! Two players! He was looking forward to tasting this new lady—big time!*

As Patricia Watson opened the passenger door, she didn't notice Maury's eyes lighting up with malicious mischief. Officer Watson then reached for the glove compartment. Maury let go of Jackie's wrist and in a moment had Watson's wrist instead.

"Hey!"

Yum. Delicious, Maury thought. And the leather sleeve of the young lady's motorcycle jacket added a delicious flavor of beef.

Jackie shook her arm a couple of times, then reached again for the glove compartment. Maury, in his turn, released Watson's arm and grabbed his mistress'. The film instructor reached again and Maury extended his neck, grabbing Jackie's arm without letting go of the police officer's appendage. The two women looked at each other, now both trapped in the mouth of the big dog.

Maury snickered so hard he almost pulled a rib muscle.

"Maury!" Jackie yelled.

Maury, finally bored of the game, released the two arms and turned around to investigate that big pole in the back seat again. It reminded him of a favorite children's crossing pole he used to sniff extensively whenever he went on a walk in his old 'hood back in LA.

Jackie then reached into the glove compartment and the moment she did, a bottle of Tango Apricot liqueur fell out and shattered, filling the car with the smell of cheap booze.

"This isn't your day, is it?" asked Patrolwoman Watson.

Suddenly Maury pushed the bumper completely out of the window. It hit Watson's motorcycle, which crashed to the ground.

Jackie winced but the stoic officer didn't bat an eye. "I'm going to let you go with a warning this time . . ." Officer Watson looked at the driver's license and said, " . . . Jackie. But I think it's only fair to warn you, that dog license renewals are not automatic. If your beast keeps destroying public property, he may have to do some public service."

"Thank you," Jackie replied, smiling. "And I . . . I won't keep alcohol in my glove compartment any more."

"That's a good idea," Officer Watson confirmed. "Although frankly if that were my dog, I'd drink too."

CHAPTER 6

Fortunately the motorcycle wasn't damaged too much and just to make it up to Officer Watson, Jackie had given her the tip that if she wanted to run in someone who was really driving drunk, she should hie on down to Marx-Wheeler, where a thoroughly soused Vic Kingston could probably be found driving into inanimate objects in the parking lot.

Officer Watson was thrilled by this little tidbit. She knew that if she were lucky enough to catch local celebrity Vic Kingston driving his car, even marginally inebriated, she could count on a detective's shield for sure.

It didn't matter a whit if the TV station squelched the indictment with a little sugar so that Kingston would get off without so much as a ticket. It didn't even matter if Officer Watson drove by a dozen grievous crimes in progress in her zeal to hustle Palmer's biggest celebrity downtown to the drunk tank. As long as she could get on TV, with her hair done by professionals and her tailored police blouse open just enough to show some cleavage, and on the cover of the *Herald* or the *Daily Chronicle* as well, and perhaps be picked up on the network feed by some of the big-city news stations, giving Palmer a national spotlight, Officer Patricia Watson's route to the top was assured.

Jackie didn't care. She was still mad at Maury. "If you don't behave, I'm going to tie you to the back of a westbound train and send you back to your mommy in Los Angeles."

Maury looked chastened for a change. Jackie couldn't tell whether he didn't want to go back to his mother, a huge mastiff bitch named Straussey and her handler, Sergeant Hippolito Lavan of the LAPD, or whether he was frightened of the idea of being tied to one of the cross-country trains, which had been crashing recently with alarming frequency.

Jackie drove into the faculty parking lot of Rodgers University and waved hello to the new campus security guard, "Friendly" Mickey Farrow.

Across town, at the Marx-Wheeler Medical Center, Marcella Jacobs, newscaster, looked with great disdain at the lethargic, disorganized shuffling that passed for a union strike action.

It was pitiful.

Only a few had signs, and they were filled with misspellings. None of the singing of colorful old union songs was on key, and of the entire group (most of whom could be characterized at best as peeved), the only one actually shaking his fist at the penurious ivory-tower management had completely ruined the effect by holding in that shaking fist a caramel apple.

"Listen, you candy asses," Marcella cried at last, unable

to stand another moment. "Is this a strike action or a company picnic?"

"I wish it were a picnic," moaned one grossly obese nurse. "I'm starving."

This gave Marcella an idea. "You guys want to have lunch at the best restaurant in town on me?"

"Yes!" the hospital workers yodeled, genuinely excited for the first time that day.

Marcella clapped her hands. "All right then. You listen to me. Do exactly what I say. You put on a good show for the cameras and I'll guarantee you not only free eats"—like many people in show business, Marcella was under the impression that most people could be bought for the price of a not-all-that-expensive meal—"but a quick resolution to your strike. What do you say?"

"Yea!" the cheer went up.

"We'll do it!" shouted an otalaryngologist.

"We're behind you all the way!" yelled a proctologist aide.

"Thank you," Marcella growled, reaching for a pack of cigarettes. "Now, stand in line where I can see you."

Marcella looked over the motley collection of health care providers and shook her head in horror.

"All right, people. Listen up!" Marcella said. "We are going to do some protesting here. Not whining. Not mewling. Not stamping our feet like sunburned children who've had their Kool Aid party suddenly canceled by their mommies and daddies."

"What's Kool Aid?" asked a maintenance man.

"Never mind," Marcella snapped. "Just pay attention. Since this is going to be for TV, we're going to do a little retouching here and there. Tina, my makeup lady . . ."

Marcella referred to Tina Dokae, a petite Salvadoran cosmetologist with the cheekbones of a top model.

" . . . And Andre, my hairdresser . . ."

Marcella's hairdresser, Andre Zormandie, was a French troubadour of the tresses who resembled *The Beauty and the Beast* TV show's Vincent, without the testosterone.

" . . . will pass among you, making you beautiful."

"That's gonna take more than makeup and a comb job," yelled a comic urine lab technician.

"No doubt," Marcella agreed, snapping her lighter a couple of times, failing to get any kind of flame. "But we don't have the time or the money for plastic surgery. Anyone got a light?"

A secretary in the pulmonary department gave Marcella her own cigarette to effect a jumpstart.

"Thank you. Now," Marcella coughed. "Without any intention of offending anyone, I'm going to have to do some recasting. You, miss . . ."

Marcella pointed to the overweight obstetrical nurse, Donna Lee Botz.

"Yes?"

"I'm going to give you a headstart on dinner."

"Oh, boy."

"Ask my producer over there . . ."—Marcella pointed to the irate young head of the nightly news who had finally managed to pay one of the union technicians (a big fellow named Mashie) a staggering bribe to take over as nursery monitor—"for a credit card and find a nice big table near the back, big enough for everyone."

"Which restaurant are we going to?" Nurse Botz wondered.

"Make it the Juniper Tavern," Marcella decided on impulse.

The Juniper, once a greasy cheeseburger joint, where policemen and city employees congregated to compare procedures and illegally drink alcohol on duty, had slowly

but surely changed. Thanks to the marketing genius of
Reg White, the Juniper became Palmer's answer to Planet
Hollywood and the Hard Rock Cafe by the simple expedi-
ency of buying props and posters from the hit animation
series, *Teen Skater,* affixing them to the walls and ceil-
ings along with witty sayings and nonsensical aphorisms
carefully selected to make it seem like the restaurant had
a unique sort of philosophy besides, "Get 'em in, get their
dough, and get 'em out quick!"

"Great!" the broad-beamed nurse enthused.

"And," Marcella added, "as long as you're going . . ."

"Donna."

"Debbie . . . take uh, Ms. . . . I'm sorry, what is your
name, Madam?" Marcella addressed a distinguished looking, carefully coiffed, middle-aged burn ward nurse standing almost at the end of the line.

"Virginia. Virginia Horsey," the long-time nurse and
regular at the Palmer dog shows answered.

"Good. Take Ms. Horsey with you."

"Just a moment," the older nurse protested mildly. "I
won't stay if it's counterproductive, but would you mind
informing me why I'm being replaced? Is it my age?"

"No, no," Marcella said impatiently. "Old is good.
Especially if you've got gnarled fingers or gray hair
or . . ."

"Lots of melanin," suggested a diplomatic dermatology
receptionist.

"Exactly," confirmed Marcella. "You, Madam, no offense, look like some rich man's wife who volunteers two
afternoons a week to push the bookcart or sit in the lobby
and sell stamps."

"Very well," Nurse Horsey conceded.

As the two nurses with the most experience in hospital
work piled into a Taurus and drove out of sight, Marcella

turned to her cameraman and said softly, "Chris, call your wife . . ."

Marcella referred to Iliana Ngadiman-Compton, a gorgeous Filipino model, who the cameraman had snared while doing freelance fashion photography work in Chicago.

" . . . and tell her to come down here. Right away. She has a nurse's outfit in her wardrobe, doesn't she?"

"Hell, yeah," the balding bearded technician leered. "I bought her one myself."

"Good. Tell her to bring dance pumps. It's a four-hour call at the usual wage."

"Hot damn!" As the underworked union cameraman dashed off to his Mercedes to make the call, Marcella turned to Sandy Carlisle, her beautiful red-headed assistant (and, not so oddly enough, the daughter of famous television actress, and former star of the hit show *CopLady,* Margo Diedrickson).

"Sandy, get a nurse's outfit and . . ."—Marcella noticed that the young assistant had inherited at least a couple of hundred thousand of her mother's famous million dollar legs—" . . . uh, make sure the skirt is good and tight."

"Right away, Marcella," the unpaid Ivy League student (who always spent her summer vacations hanging out with fellow nepotism beneficiaries, learning the cool jobs they would be handed on silver platters the day after graduation) dashed off, giggling with excitement.

"You!" Marcella bellowed, pointing to the fellow who rented hot televisions to bedridden patients. "Can you play a guitar?"

"No," Kevin Erlanger answered.

"Can you look like you're playing a guitar? Do you know how to handle one, at least?"

The ruggedly handsome rip-off artist scratched his head

for a moment. "Well, I know the strings are supposed to face out."

"Good start! Someone get this man a stool. No, better yet, some realistic . . ." Marcella started looking up and down the line for a technician type. "Who's in charge of fixing things in this hospital?"

The employees laughed heartily.

"Well," a balding Italian gentleman in a three-piece suit volunteered sheepishly. "I'm the one who collects the check for the position anyway."

"You'll do," Marcella decided. "Can you find an old spool somewhere? Something that may have some wire on it?"

"Sure," the maintenance engineer replied. "We got a lot of crap like that stored in one of the rooms where they used to let the patients go and smoke."

"Good," Marcella rasped, lighting a new cigarette from the stub of her old one. "Get one. And as long as you're up there, get me an ashtray."

"You got it." The maintenance engineer started to run for the executive elevator.

"Wait a minute! Uh . . . ?"

"Anthony. Anthony LoBrusso."

"Anthony. Can you exchange the Armani for overalls?"

"Jeez," the maintenance engineer pulled at his chin. "I don't have nothing like that. I got it. Maybe I can run across the street and borrow one from the guys at the muffler shop."

"Do it," Marcella ordered. "Send somebody else up for the spool and ashtray."

Anthony snapped his fingers and his brother Lucas (the maintenance engineer's fifty thousand dollar a year "do all the real work" assistant) rushed to carry out the errand.

"Now," Marcella clapped her hands and put a whistle on a chain around her neck. "We're going to work on a little simple choreography. Nothing fancy. Like doing the Alley Cat or the Hokey Pokey at your sister's wedding."

There were good-natured laughs from the striking employees. Marcella wasn't the most informed anchor-person they had ever heard deliver the news, but she sure was chock-full of personality.

"All right. Now stay with me. Mr. Ben-Faisl here"—Marcella motioned toward her Libyan soundman—"will play a little music on his DAT machine."

The hospital workers looked enviously at the expensive sound machine. Every day at least one of their members heroically intervened to save a human life and yet, most of them still had cheap little cassette players and radios.

"It's peppy aerobic-type music that's fun to move to."

"For you maybe," grumbled a diener (which was what autopsy technicians had been called since the days of Dr. Frankenstein's Igor).

"All right. Thank you, sir," Marcella quickly decided. "You can knock off for the day."

As the dead-handler departed, the remaining employees straightened up and started taking the whole affair more seriously. With the economy the way it was, no one could afford to be laid off the job action line and lose forty dollars a day strike pay.

Marcella took a telescoping swagger stick from her shoulderbag and snapped it loudly against her leather hip boots. "All right. Give me four lines. Tall people in back. Short people in front. Second row, dancers or singers who can move. Third-row people—I want you to make up what you lack in talent with oodles of personality. Fourth row, try not to fall down. If you do feel yourself going, fall backward so you don't take out someone who really can dance in front of you."

The people reluctantly moved into the proper line, then Marcella, popping a herbal energy pill, yelled, "Now I'm going to show you the first set of movements and then you imitate me. Ready? Music, Rory. Five, six, seven, eight . . ."

A techno pop hit started blasting.

Marching in place, Marcella yelled, "Unfair! Say it with me."

"Unfair," the hospital workers responded petulantly.

"Again. Louder. Unfair!"

"Unfair."

"UNFAIR!"

"Unfair!"

"Good. Now march the way I'm doing."

"Which foot do you put down first?" the billing supervisor asked.

"The right one," Marcella yelled. "Pretend you're stepping on a cockroach in the operating room."

The employees laughed at the clever reference to this familiar, everyday activity.

"Swing those arms."

The employees tried to oblige. However, some were unable to march, instead acting as though they were slogging through another unpleasant hour on the Stairmaster. Others could march after a fashion, but not in place.

"Come on, people!" Marcella exhorted. "You can do it. Think of *The Music Man!*"

The newscaster was met with a rain forest of blank looks.

"All right," Marcella conceded. "Never mind that. Think of . . . the monorail episode of *The Simpsons*."

The hospital employees nodded their heads like they

were big and on springs. This was something they could relate to.

"Okay. Better. Much better," Marcella lied. "Now again, after me. Shout like a UFO just landed in your backyard and you want grandpa to bring the video camera."

The employees rocked with merriment.

"Unfair!"

"Unfair!"

"Not right!"

"Not right!"

"We want a raise or we're gonna fight!"

"We want a raise or we're gonna fight!"

"UNFAIR!"

"UNFAIR!"

"NOT RIGHT!"

"NOT RIGHT!"

"WE WANT A RAISE."

"WE WANT A RAISE."

"OR WE'RE GONNA FIGHT!"

"OR WE'RE GONNA FIGHT!"

"Good!" Marcella yelled, taking a swig from a flask of Tango Apricot she always kept in her shoulderbag for such emergencies. "Now let's add a little choreography. First row march to your left. Not in place. Cover ground with long strides. Good. Unfair!"

"Unfair!"

"Good. Move those arms. Not right!"

"Not right!"

"Good. Second row," Marcella ordered. "March to your right. We want a raise."

"We want a raise!"

"Keep it loud now," Marcella urged.

"We want a raise, or we're gonna fight!"

Marcella blew her whistle again. "Terrific. We're on our way to Broadway."

Just then Iliana Ngadiman-Compton, the beautiful model, showed up.

Her nurse's outfit was more Frederick's of Hollywood than Acme Uniform Supply, but that suited the young anchorwoman just fine.

"Where do you want me, Marcella?"

"Right up front," Marcella directed. "Between the first and second rows."

"We want a raise, or we're gonna fight!" the small crowd continued chanting.

"Good. See the way it works now, folks?" Marcella asked. "Okay. Try doing it without me directing traffic."

"Unfair!"

"Not right!"

"We want a raise, or we're gonna fight!"

"Good. Men, give the gorgeous model a little breathing room. Women, don't try to trip her as she goes by. We're all on the same side here, honest."

Marcella accepted a Goodwillie water bottle from her producer and drank quickly. "Thank you. How are you doing for petty cash, Ruben?"

"Well," Baskette responded. "I have my weekly salary in my pocket, if that's what you mean."

"Good. We'll need some drinks for the strikers."

"Yeah, and some salt pills, from the looks of them."

Marcella gave her young producer a wry look. "Well, Ruben. What do you expect?"

"Unfair!" The voices of the hospital workers were growing louder.

"Picketing is a lot harder than sitting in the visitors' lounge . . ."

"Not right!"

" . . . complaining that the patients' howls of agony are keeping you awake."

At that moment Anthony LoBrusso returned, proudly wearing a soiled muffler and transmission specialist's overalls. "How do I look?"

"Great," Marcella responded approvingly. "But what's that under your eye?"

"Grease," the maintenance expert explained. "You know—like I've really been working."

"Great. Next time," Marcella suggested, "put some on your hands, why don't you? The way things stand now, you look like someone who would rather switch than fight."

"Huh?" responded her perplexed producer.

"Forget it, Ruben," Marcella advised. "An old TV commercial. Before your time."

"Where do I go?" LoBrusso asked.

"Second row. In the middle. Lady with the knee brace!" Marcella then yelled.

The physical therapist stopped shouting at the mention of her brace. "Yes?"

"You're off picket duty," Marcella informed her. "Anthony, you take her place."

Marcella then turned to her producer. "Ruben, give this woman fifty dollars."

"Ma'am. I want you to go to the Piggily Wiggily." Marcella raised her voice over those of the strikers. "Get some liquid refreshments for your fellow workers out here."

"Get a quart of bourbon," someone from the chaplain's office yelled.

"Later!" Marcella replied. "Come on. Keep shouting. You're not on a break yet."

"Unfair!"

"Louder!"

"NOT RIGHT!"

"Good," Marcella clapped her hands. "I want those heart-less misbegotten misers who run the hospital board to look out their windows and turn ruby red from shame."

"How about," a hospital publicist suggested, "we yell, 'Shape up you mugs, or we'll pull the patients' plugs'?"

Marcella considered for a moment. "That's a little hard-boiled for this strike. Keep it simple."

At that moment, Lucas LoBrusso came running up with the spool. "Sorry I took so long. Somebody stole a patient's watch, and I had to come up with an alibi. Where do you want this?"

"Put it over there," Marcella pointed.

Marcella then shielded her eyes from the setting sun and called out, "Where's the folksinger?"

"Here I am!" the hunky TV renter called out, walking up the driveway.

"Did you get the guitar?" Marcella asked him.

"Yeah," Erlanger answered dourly. "I got it from one of the nuns in the Catholic day school across the way."

"Any trouble?"

"A little. They said they trusted in God, but I'd have to leave them a forty-dollar deposit."

"Pay the man, Ruben," Marcella instructed her pro-ducer.

"I don't suppose," Baskette groused, "you bothered to ask one of the sisters for a receipt?"

At that moment, Sandy Carlisle, Marcella's unpaid intern, returned in a borrowed nurse's outfit. "What do you think, Marcy?"

"All right." Marcella started to clap her hands one more time, but decided the miserable no goodniks in front of her weren't worth getting chapped skin over. "While you weasels wet your whistle, I'm going back to my trailer for about ten minutes. Tina! I'll be ready for makeup in two. Andre! I'll need hair in five—and do me a favor. Would you take a bottle of white wine out of my little fridge, open it up, and let it breathe?"

"Of course, Marcella," the big French-Canadian responded.

Marcella looked at the departing man and shook her head with regret at what might have been.

Meanwhile, Jackie Walsh, fuming to have wasted so much of her day doing favors for her seldom-grateful friends, wrestled Maury (mildly restrained by a stout lead) into the Isaac Asimov Applied Science Building at Rodgers University.

She walked straight up to the receptionist and noted with mounting fury that the science chairman's secretary was none other than her old nemesis, Polly Merton.

"Well, well. If it isn't Ms. Walsh," the teutonic secretary greeted her with a smile that to Jackie seemed to reek of superciliousness. "What brings you to our lonely outpost?"

Jackie gave the blonde, bee-hived secretary a suspicious look. Normally, whenever Jackie came upon the former tyrant of the supply closet, the ageless secretary pretended to be in the middle of a phone conversation or deep in concentration on some word processing document so as to have an excuse to keep Jackie cooling her heels for five minutes. Today, the Mata Hari of secretaries was casually running an emery file over her perfectly polished vanilla-colored fingernails. This was odd, to say the least.

"I'm here to see John Brooks. Is he in?"

"Just a moment," Polly said pleasantly, "I'll check."

As Polly Merton pushed buttons on her futuristic switchboard, Jackie looked around at the lobby displays. Every time she visited they were almost completely different. Out of curiosity, Jackie pushed a panel next to the picture of a well-dressed Massachusetts Institute of Technology professor. She was startled backward as the brilliant linguist's voice blared out.

"The reason for the Japanese businessman's success is no secret. We were obsessed with the military while they were obsessed with making money. We made computer chips that could withstand a nuclear explosion. The Japanese simply made computer chips that worked . . ."

Polly Merton turned off the volume with a knob on her control board. "Dr. Brooks will see you now."

Jackie looked around in confusion at the new doors which had seemingly sprung up everywhere.

Polly, snorting at the film professor's helplessness, pointed contemptuously to a corridor behind Jackie. "Take the first left."

"Thank you."

As Jackie walked along she thought about Vic Kingston and Linus Munch. One thing struck Jackie about the way they talked and joked. These men were not only cynical but also malicious. They had been hurt so often they were determined to get even. Or perhaps they were so tired and disgusted that they no longer cared.

Jackie had sensed all this, not so much in what they said, but how they said it. How they had looked at each other with twinkles in their eyes that carried no hint of humor. How they had exchanged mirthless smiles and laughs that came not from their bellies, but from a very dark part (perhaps the *substantia nigra*) of the mind.

As Jackie meditated, she took the left turn Polly Merton had mentioned, then an immediate right turn, which she had not expected. Jackie wondered if Vic Kingston would consider doing the interview (after all, as Dr. Munch had pointed out, Marcella wasn't acting like she was thrilled to have been given the assignment), which would let Munch make a case for his research, using figures Vic knew weren't accurate.

The issue had come up once before, Jackie remembered. Just last year, a science writer for a weekly science fiction magazine had written an article sharply critical of Dr. Munch's grant proposal (which his son, an AIDS activist, had supplied him with), in which the writer pointed out that the doctor had deflated even the most conservative figure of people with full-blown AIDS and had arbitrarily inflated the most generous figure of people with any form of Alzheimer's to make the point that the number of AIDS victims was smaller than that of those afflicted with Alzheimer's.

The critique had been quite scathing, and Munch's friends had demanded that he respond, but, taking advantage of the fact that the science writer suddenly died after the article appeared, the distinguished researcher had announced he would let sleeping dogs lie.

Would he go on TV now and repeat his challenged figures, the way Ronald Reagan had continued to repeat the story of the Chicago woman who collected a dozen welfare checks, even after numerous reporters showed him copies of the actual records proving that the woman he was thinking of, twice-widowed, had never received more than three checks at once?

After all, what did Vic Kingston care if a once-effective researcher continued to draw research funding that he had lied to obtain?

Her mind still churning furiously, Jackie came to the end of another corridor and hesitated as to whether to take a left or a right. It was taking her forever to get to John's office. Where was he located now? In the basement? Had she been going down a series of gently inclined ramps? Had the science wing expanded again? Would there be any virgin forest left in Palmer?

Jackie then tried a door marked "Door." It was a solid wall. She turned right and walked the length of the corridor to a panel with a light shining under it. This was a solid wall as well. Jackie was about to start screaming when all of a sudden a seemingly solid panel opened up.

It was John Brooks. "Ah, here you are."

"Where am I?" Jackie asked, minutes away from breakdown.

"The Psych Maze," Brooks replied. "She usually only does this to naïve, unsuspecting graduate students. My apologies." The fatherly former professor took her hand and shook it warmly.

As they walked through the cool blue corridor to the chairman's office, Brooks apologetically went on to say, "It's not a big thing, and don't feel personally responsible, but I think this is the last straw. We obviously need someone with less of a wry sense of humor than Ms. Merton."

"Has she been a problem?" Jackie asked, checking herself out briefly in a large mirror at the end of the corridor. The black wool Valentino suit she'd chosen for the funeral, with its brass buttons and short skirt, still looked okay, but her panty hose and suede slingbacks had mud on them.

"Don't spend too much time preening in front of that mirror, Jackie," Brooks warned.

Jackie struck a sexy attitude and asked him in her best husky Lauren Bacall imitation, "What's the matter, John? Am I driving you frantic with carnal desire?"

"I'm sure you would, eventually," Brooks replied. "But

the fact of the matter, Jackie, is that there's a hidden camera behind that panel and right now the second-year psych class is studying your every action for a class on vanity."

Jackie practically dived out of view. Although she was fairly happy with her body lately, Jackie was painfully aware that, despite the inexorable march of the years, she still broke out occasionally, and on this particular day she had a spectacularly gruesome pimple on the left side of her chin.

"Besides," Brooks continued, as if nothing out of the ordinary had happened. "I don't think I will be lusting after any young ladies right now."

"Well, you wouldn't be lusting after me," Jackie mumbled. "My hair is a mess. It probably has white stuff in it."

"That's nothing to be ashamed of," Brooks replied warmly. "I'm starting to get a little gray at the temples myself."

"No, no," Jackie responded, becoming more embarrassed all the time. "It's stuff . . ."

Brooks, in his quest to be understanding, kept making things worse. "Oh, you went by the founder's statue? They really should do something about those pigeons."

"John!" Jackie interrupted. "I'm talking about my Jeep. My stupid dog took a bite out of it and now it's leaking, I don't know what. Some sort of asbestos, I suspect."

"No, no," Brooks grinned amiably, clapping his hands to turn his office lights on. "That space filling is protein-based. It would be as harmless to eat as a bag of Spicy Pete Cheese Clouds, and about as equal in nutrition, I'm afraid. Heh, heh."

The lights failed suddenly and the former structural engineer had to clap his hands several times to restore them. "No, that stuff is utterly harmless." Brooks chuckled again, settling into an old rocking chair. "Eventually, it'll break down into some gross-looking gooey white strings."

"Great!" Jackie groaned. "People are going to think I have head lice."

"No, no," Brooks smiled, stuffing a pinch of mint snuff in his cheek. "We're talking two or three weeks before that would happen. And that's the most optimistic prediction. You know those manufacturers lie like sailors to the EPA. I assume you would have washed your hair at least once or twice in the interim."

Jackie hesitated in front of the chairman's private bathroom. "I'm tempted to wash it right now in your sink."

"Please sit down, Jackie," Brooks urged. "What I started to say is, as a family man, with a wife I adore and two beautiful new daughters . . ."

"Oh, yes." Jackie sat down, her hands between her knees. "I'm sorry. For a minute there, I forgot all about it. How did it go?"

"Without a hitch," Brooks smiled. "I suppose my attorney bribed someone down at City Hall."

Jackie lifted her eyebrows. Knowing John's lawyer, Nate Northcote, somewhat intimately, she didn't doubt for a moment that this had indeed been the case.

"The judge was sober," Brooks continued. "The clerk wore a tie. It had rolling dice on it, but it was a tie. They winked at the fact we brought a cake into chambers. And they winked at the fact that we had a religious person, Father MacMurrie of Judges' Episcopalian, there to bless our new daughters."

"It sounds like everything went smoothly," Jackie commented.

"It was really something," Brooks agreed. "It actually

made me think for once that not every penny we're all paying in real estate taxes is going straight down the plumbing or into the poke of some crooked politician."

This last phrase reminded Jackie irresistibly of the mayor of Palmer, a former civics teacher at Rodgers University. "Was Her Honor Jane Bellamy there?" The canny mayor, up for re-election, loved photo ops.

"No," Brooks commented. "She had a fundraiser."

"Huh. Well, God bless our community-minded mayor," Jackie said.

"Indeed," Brooks agreed. "We brought Lea and Mia back here for a little party. Milly did invite you?"

Jackie nodded her head in embarrassment. "I tried to get here, John. Honest. Things just kept conspiring against me."

"Well, stuff happens," the science chairman temporized. "Millicent was a little troubled, I must tell you."

"I'm so sorry," Jackie apologized.

"Well, she gets this way when she doesn't eat. You know about her low blood sugar, of course?"

"Hypoglycemia," Jackie nodded.

"Winn's Hypoglycemia," Brooks clarified. "A rare condition. I think that's why the living science instructors agreed to have an engineer serve as chairman. It would give them an opportunity to study my wife."

Jackie made a face.

"Anyway," Brooks said as he thumbed through his calendar, "the condition doesn't keep poor Millicent down too much of the time. Except when she becomes emotionally overwrought, of course. Then stress causes her to consume blood sugar at an alarming rate."

"She was overwrought—Milly?" Jackie asked, knowing the answer would only make her feel worse.

"I should say so," Brooks answered at once. "You

should have seen her mood ring. It was like a thunderstorm in an old Universal horror film."

This particular analogy really hit home and Jackie felt terrible. "I'm so sorry."

"Land o'Goshen, Jackie. It's not your fault, entirely, that my wife didn't eat."

Jackie grasped at straws. "Well, of course she had a busy day—what with everything happening. And that may have contributed to her being overwrought and all."

"But her fingers and lips turned blue at one point," Brooks blurted out suddenly.

"My goodness!" Jackie exclaimed.

Brooks nodded his head sadly. "She wanted to wait to serve the food until you arrived. We begged her to change her mind of course, but she was adamant. Right up to the point where she passed out. The ambulance people came and started the glucose drip into her arm. She revived in oh . . . forty-five minutes or so. It cast a bit of a pall on the party, I'm sad to say. Her lying stretched out in the middle of the floor like that absolutely let out dancing."

Jackie finally caught on. "You . . . rogue, you. You were just teasing me. You actually had me believing all that."

"I did, didn't I?" Brooks smiled quietly. "I'm sorry we didn't get as far as me telling you about having to give the spoiled food to the poor radioactive lab animals on the seventh floor."

"No, no. You did quite enough. Thank you," Jackie responded. "You're wasted here, John—you should be in theater. Now how are they really? Milly and your children, I mean?"

"I have the best family in the world," Brooks swore.

"Good," Jackie said at once. "I know you're probably anxious to get home to them but Dr. Munch wants you to meet him at the Marx-Wheeler Medical Center."

The toothpick-thin chairman's face fell. "He does, does he?"

"Sorry," Jackie apologized. "I guess you know Dr. Munch better than I do, and, well, he seems pretty difficult. I tried to explain to him, but . . ."

Brooks shook his head sadly. "I know. I do know, Jackie. You must feel very put upon."

"Well," Jackie started to deny it, simply out of politeness, then decided, why bother?

"I wish you could have known the man in the sixties," Brooks continued. He walked to his bookshelves and withdrew a red leather photo album. "Look at this."

"The Nobel Prize ceremonies?"

"No," Brooks grinned. "Just the professor with me and a couple of other science nerds."

Jackie gazed at the faded kodachrome of a younger Linus Munch, intently describing a chemistry problem to a group of earnest, adoring young students, including a heavily bespectacled John Brooks.

"It wasn't," the new contact lenses-wearing chairman continued, "just us students who respected him. Every major scientist would pay him a courtesy call if they were in town. Christian Barnard, Jonas Salk, Albert Schweitzer. I met Mother Teresa, Carl Sagan—all through Dr. Linus. He introduced me to Ram Kossovsky, the Los Alamos metallurgy engineer who got me interested in the study of the effect of foreign substances in the human body, which later decided me to change my major."

Jackie nodded. She knew it was men like John Brooks and medical doctors like Nir Kossovsky (Ram's son) who finally succeeded in alerting the public to the injurious effects of silicone in the human body (especially in breasts).

"I lost touch with Dr. Linus for a while," Brooks went

on. "Everyone said he was slipping. Becoming more iras-
cible, less patient, less flexible, more vocal about his
views . . . and prejudices . . . and resentments."

"But you still invited him to speak," Jackie pointed
out.

Brooks nodded. "He knows his stuff. In the past, Rodgers
University has invited Robert Heinlein to lecture on science
fiction, Red Barber to speak on the importance of team
sports, and Ray Kroc to lecture the students on entrepre-
neurship. You wish all speakers were heroic people with
warm hearts and progressive thoughts on every subject,
but that's not the way things work out sometimes. What's
Dr. Linus doing over at Marx-Wheeler?"

"He's talking to Dick Bellamy," Jackie replied.

"Hm." Brooks puffed thoughtfully on his pipe. "I wonder about that."

"What's the matter?" Jackie asked, curious despite herself.

"Well, there's some talk, mostly from Dr. Linus himself . . ."—as always John Brooks spoke in a measured
tone, but Jackie could tell, by the way he fiddled with
the contents of his desk, and repeatedly tapped his can of
mint snuff, that he was seriously upset about something.

" . . . that he has some sort of AIDS vaccine he wants
to try out here. It's just . . . well . . . unimaginable to me
that he could actually have such a thing. He's stayed out
of the chase for so long. It's hard to believe that while Dr.
Linus was damning every AIDS researcher in the world
he was simultaneously keeping up on the literature—and
there's a flood of it—at least well enough to know what
was being tried in the vaccine field.

"None of the people who have been calling me—my
old friends, his former students—knew anything about
it. And it strikes me as very strange that if Dr. Linus

were working on AIDS-related vaccines that he would
fail to mention it to the research fellows who turned
him down precisely because they wanted to get involved
with something along those lines. Why would he fail to
mention it to any government people? Even the biggest
blockhead in Washington knows that it will eventually
lead to bad publicity to treat a distinguished scientist
like Linus Munch this way. If they had a straw like
this to grasp—that Dr. Linus was finally admitting the
importance of AIDS research and was doing some work in
the field himself—well then, they could continue funding
Dr. Linus and everyone would be happy."

"It does seem odd," Jackie agreed. "Could it be that he
wants to check it out first? To experiment . . . ?"

"On unwitting human volunteers?" Brooks's measured
tone grew harsher. "I would hate to think, Jackie, that such
a thing was happening. But I would prefer even that to the
alternative."

"Which is?"

"That this is all some sort of cynical stunt," Brooks
replied bitterly, "to show the folly of supporting AIDS
research."

"Is he capable of that?" Jackie asked.

"I don't know what he's capable of, Jackie," Brooks
responded. "The gifted aren't like ordinary people. Ordinary people slow down with age. They get dull—tire
easily—maybe become a little bit forgetful. Geniuses
like Linus Munch don't just fade away. They crack like
imported crystal and shatter into a thousand pieces."

CHAPTER 7

By the time Jackie got back to the tree she had left Maury tied to, quite a crowd had formed.

The pizza that Communications Studies student Khalil Moore had ordered was gone. Indeed most of the cardboard box that once surrounded it was gone too. All that remained, in fact, of the Red, White and Blue Pizza Special was the little plastic flag on an island in the middle that kept the boxtop from sticking to the melted cheese and toppings. The young lad who had tried to deliver the pizza was shaking in horror.

"What happened here?" Jackie asked. Others—students, teachers, college cafeteria employees, and various onlookers who had rushed over to watch the deliveryman's misery—began to shout answers, but Jackie, like the host of a game show, waved them quiet and indicated that she would accept an answer from one source and one source alone.

"The dog . . ." the chubby-cheeked young man sobbed.

As he tried to wipe his tears away Jackie recognized him as Chubb, the son of Max Greenway, the renowned businessman who owned McKean Soda.

"He took your pizza, didn't he?" Jackie sympathetically filled in.

The young deliveryman's chins wiggled as he nodded his head. "He grabbed my putt-putt . . ."

Chubb Greenway referred to the motor-driven three-wheeled vehicle with a big tin box on the back, which had been supplied by the Red, White and Blue management. "He flipped me over. Licked me a lot, then ate my pizza. I tried to climb the tree like the cats . . ."

Chubb pointed to five different kitties perched tremulously in the loftiest branches of a stately maple.

"But he'd chewed off all the lower branches . . ." Chubb then pointed to a bunch of gnawed limbs neatly stacked like firewood.

"Bad dog!" Jackie barked quite unnecessarily.

Maury gave a little Gallic *c'est la vie* shrug, then went back to his task of digging up an underwater sprinkler.

"Who's going to pay for the pizza?" Chubb moaned.

"Well, Chubb . . ." Jackie replied sadly. "Doesn't Red, White and Blue have a policy that if the pizza doesn't get there in thirty-five minutes, there's no charge to the customer?"

"Well . . . yes."

"And was Maury here the customer who ordered the pizza?"

"Well, no . . ." Chubb answered miserably. The principal reason Chubb was miserable was because Maury had by now succeeded in sinking his teeth into the flimsy plastic waterpipe, causing a thick spray of water to douse the large crowd.

"Then I guess *you'll* be paying, Chubb," Jackie commiserated, while opening the folding umbrella she always carried in her shoulderbag with a snap of the wrist.

"Yeah . . . just like all the other times," Chubb blubbered. "Mom and Pop made me get this job so I would learn some responsibility. And all I've done so far is cost them money."

Jackie briefly considered hugging the needy teenager, but then, because he was wet, didn't. "There, there, Chubb. After all, your parents can probably afford it better than most."

"Oh, I don't know," Chubb replied, whimpering gratefully as the water finally stopped. "Most of the other delivery guys are in the same boat. Meyer Klingelhoffer, Joey Buzone, Little Petey Dill."

Jackie considered this new piece of information with amazement. These were indeed the sons of some of the richest men in town. "That's kind of interesting. You know, Chubb. You may actually be able to turn this embarrassing moment to your advantage."

"How so?" he asked politely.

"Did you see that man over there?" Jackie pointed to Charles "Bingo" Allen, the Stetson-hat wearing roving reporter for the *Herald* who was standing in front of the faculty building.

Reporters, Jackie knew, were frequently spotted around campus lately. Without the shrewd protective Dean of Faculty, B. Crowder Westfall, to watch over them (the Latin scholar and master of diplomacy had recently been felled by a massive coronary), the faculty had made one error after another in terms of offending the student body.

First, some of the history professors had insisted on flying American flags, despite the university's refusal to add the flags of Puerto Rico, Nicaragua, the Dominican Republic, Haiti, Zambia, Iritrea, the Sudan, Syria, Quebec, and Guam to the pole at the front gates of the university (the sobriety-challenged acting dean of the university, Algernon Foreman, had been perfectly willing, of course, but the janitor, Mr. Packer, had finally been the one to nix the idea—pointing out that the flagpole would simply bend over and all the international banners would be dishonored by being dumped on the ground).

Next, several English teachers had been caught correcting several students' spoken grammar or pronunciation, causing them humiliation and embarrassment (and simultaneously showing a prejudice for American-born English speakers).

Last, but most grievous of all, an unfortunate older law professor had accidentally spoke aloud his true feelings and personal political opinions during a lecture on the First Amendment of the United States Constitution.

The offending educators had been thoroughly disciplined of course.

Bingo Allen had shown up to interview the poor teachers—but they were avoiding him.

"Go over to that man wearing the ten-gallon hat," Jackie repeated. "And tell him your story. Tell him that I think there's a scoop and a half here. A *Sixty Minutes*–type exposé."

"Wow!" Chubb exclaimed.

As the crowd scattered (unhappy not to see someone, anyone, getting hurt) and Chubb drove his wobbly wheeled putt-putt across the street, Jackie unleashed Maury.

"How was your pizza, boy?" she asked.

The big dog thirstily drank from the muddy puddle in front of him.

"A little salty? Well, now you and I are going over to the Communications Studies building where you're going to be a good dog and not do any more *bad* things that will land your mistress in civil court for the rest of her natural life."

Maury agreed by lolling against Jackie's new pair of panty hose until they too were shredded and caked with mud.

You bet, Mistress, he seemed to respond. *Whatever you say.*

CHAPTER 8

As Jackie entered the Communications Studies building, she redialed Marcella Jacobs's number.

"Yes, yes? Who the hell is this?"

Jackie could tell from the co-anchor's gruff manner that Marcella must be in the no-smoking section of the hospital. "Marcy, Jackie. How's it going?"

"Terrible!"

"Terrible? The strike story's petering out?"

"The strike's settled!" Marcella barked in her harsh, grating, off-air voice. "Management caved in as usual. What else? Especially when it knows it can pass on the costs to the patients, plus a little extra. These poor patients, sick as dogs . . ."

"Speaking of dogs . . ." Jackie dived in.

"Oh, my puppy!" The newscaster's voice suddenly softened as she remembered her new cuddly pet. "How is he? Are you taking good care of him?"

Jackie threw her umbrella at the big dog who dodged

it easily. "Of course I am, Marcy!"

"Has he been a good dog?"

Maury turned around and passed gas.

"I've never seen him better behaved," Jackie replied honestly.

"That's wonderful."

"When can I bring . . . ?"

"Well, do you mind meeting me at the hospital?" Marcella asked disingenuously.

"Not at all," Jackie said at once. To rid herself of Maury, she would crawl the length and breadth of the Sahara, even if it were covered with broken glass. "Why are you still there if the strike is over? Isn't that the story you went there to get?"

"Yes, but the whole thing was so pathetic, I gave the story to KOPY."

"Those clowns?"

Jackie was amazed to see such cooperation between Palmer's most heated competitors. For years the two local TV affiliates had undergone a cut-throat competition.

KCIN's style had been to hire the best small-market talent, the youngest and brightest, and most energetic producers, and the best veteran newswriters (who were being laid off left and right by news bosses who thought that their highly paid talent, like so many stand-up comedians, could write their own material). Despite the fact that their program was constantly being whittled down to make way for more and more commercials, KCIN consistently did a good job presenting the news.

KOPY, on the other hand, unable to hire the best and brightest because its cash was largely tied up in the enormous salaries paid to legions of network vice presidents, now simply had its trucks follow around the KCIN ones. The KOPY cats would patiently wait until the KCIN crew had rounded up the story, then they would tap the satellite feed, interview some of the same witnesses, and then scoop KCIN every time because their show aired one hour earlier.

"Well, to be honest, Jackie," Marcella continued, "I had a conflict of interest. Like a fool, I started whipping those losers up by choreographing their strike routine."

"I thought all the network shows did that," Jackie responded.

"Most do," Marcella agreed. "I kind of went over the line this time, though."

Jackie pulled hard on Maury's chain to keep him from defiling the lobby's potted plant, then climbed the stairs with him to the second floor. "That's too bad."

"Yeah, well. Life isn't all warm hugs and Godiva chocolates," Marcella responded. "But now I have a new story."

"What's that?" Jackie asked automatically. Her attention was divided as she critically watched Maury dig through the garbage outside the cubicle of her neighbor, Mark Freeman. Jackie knew from experience that there would be a lot of food wrappers, but that the somewhat overweight animation instructor was not likely to have left any tasty morsels, and so hoped that her big dog would not react badly and start kicking the garbage can around.

"Your friend and mine," Marcella resumed, "Linus Munch, is about to publicly inject some of the patients here at Marx-Wheeler with his new vaccine."

"Is he there now?" Jackie asked edgily.

"No, he's still upstairs with the hospital administrator."

"And is Vic Kingston there too?"

"Vic? Here?" Marcella asked irately. "No. I mean, I haven't seen him. Is he supposed to be here?"

"I don't know," Jackie replied, watching helplessly as Maury turned the garbage can on its side, then fell on it, squashing it flat. "I saw him earlier today, and he was going to give Dr. Munch a ride to the hospital."

"That son of a gun. He's trying to scoop me, isn't he?"

"I don't know," Jackie replied, opening her cubicle and slipping inside, hoping Maury, busy swatting the flattened garbage can down the hall, wouldn't notice for a moment. "Listen, Marcella. Before you get off, I really do want to dump off . . ." The film instructor hesitated about mentioning her pet's name for fear this would summon him.

"Maury, do you mean?" Marcella asked loudly.

The big dog burst into the room, wondering who was talking about him.

"That's right," Jackie said nervously. As she talked, she kept one eye on Maury—now sniffing her wall poster of Mae West—and at the same time tried to read the electronic messages left for her on her office computer. "You know, I was talking to John Brooks. He has some, well, very troubling things to say about what Dr. Munch's reasons for doing this inoculation thing may be."

"So?" Marcella's tone betrayed immediate interest. "Give. I'm not busy at the moment."

"Well, that's the thing," Jackie responded. "I am. In fact, I have a hundred things to do, and I keep getting new assignments all the time. However I am going to drive John Brooks over to the hospital."

"Really?"

"Yeah." Jackie finished a long memo from Arne Hyverson, her teaching assistant. There were good comments on her lecture notes for the upcoming semester and a few paragraphs on some of the students and the problems they were having. Jackie sent the document to print and as she did, felt waves of guilt wash over her. Perhaps she was wrong, but Jackie couldn't help but feel that her kids wouldn't be having so many problems if she didn't miss class so often. "So you'll get a chance to interview him and then you can decide whether you still want to run the story."

Marcella laughed. "You don't understand, Jackie. If we find out that a story isn't exactly what it seems, that doesn't mean we kill it. Just the opposite, in fact. If we can show that Nobel Prize winner Linus Munch is acting like St. Francis of Assisi for the cameras and undercut it with some pictures of an important Palmer scientist saying he's a hypocrite, a liar, and a fraud, that's not only a go-one lead story, that's a submission to the Peabody Award committee."

"Well good," Jackie commented absently as she watched Maury drink a half-cup of coffee she had left earlier, and wondered if it were possible that the dog would become even more hyper. "I'll be there as quick as I can."

"Great, Jackie. Thanks."

As Marcella signed off, Jackie grabbed Maury and wrestled him away from the potted cactus her boyfriend, Ronald Dunn, had given her for her thirty-sixth birthday. Of course the present had been carefully chosen with the idea that this was the one thing her pet buffalo would not destroy. Poor Dunn however had not counted on Maury's capacity for enduring pain while having a good frolic.

As Jackie emerged into the corridor, she decided on impulse to call her long-distance lover. Jackie was having a beastly day and the low soothing bedroom voice of her new boyfriend always made her a little happier.

"Hello," said one of the more famous voices in American adventure television.

"Hi, Duke," Jackie said shyly. "It's me."

"Jackie . . ." Ron's voice poured out of the phone like a soothing syrup. "How are you, darling?"

"Eh," Jackie replied. "I'm not waking you, am I?"

"It's six o'clock here, Jackie."

"You told me you retire early when you're shooting."

"By that I meant midnight, darling," Dunn replied. "The silent film stars in the Motion Picture Actors Retirement Home are still awake at this hour. Even our former president and distinguished Warner Brothers alumnus is reasonably coherent."

"How is . . . ?"

"The Governor? That's what people out here call him. He's fine. Still telling funny stories like there's no tomorrow. He keeps trying to tell me the one about the time he did a live TV show about a group of Trappist monks and how one young knothead played the entire program with a bunch of lipstick imprints on his cheek. Not only does he keep forgetting that the young playboy priest was me, but on top of that he keeps telling people that the smooch marks were on my right cheek, when any schoolgirl knows it's my left cheek the ladies adore."

"Have you been faithful to me?" Jackie asked suddenly.

"I've always been true to you, darling, in my fashion," Dunn replied glibly.

"So this is what it feels like to date Howard Keel," Jackie remarked.

"Hey," Dunn joked. "If I could sing like Howard, I wouldn't be making goofy TV movies. I'd be playing Daddy Warbucks or the King of Siam in some Dallas Civic Mall Theatre."

"How is the goofy TV movie going?" Jackie asked.

The film in question was a reunion film of the cast of

CopLady, a modest hit television show from the seventies, which Jackie and her partner Celestine Barger had worked on. After a series of similar revival films, the network had easily gathered together the mostly semi-retired survivors of the old show to do *CopLady: Back with a Vengeance.*

The producers had uncharacteristically come back to Jackie and Celestine to write a script for the new version, not out of loyalty or sentiment (Fred Allen once said, "You could stuff all the genuine loyalty and sentiment in Hollywood into a flea's navel and still have room for two caraway seeds and a producer's heart"), but because they wanted to use, as the basis of the script, a ninety-minute teleplay the pair had written (and had been paid for) many years before. Because of the illness of one of the show's stars at the time the teleplay had never been filmed.

Ronald Dunn, who had not been on the original show, was playing one of his justly famous H. R. Haldeman–type villains in the film. And, although he and Jackie had started dating before the movie project had come together, the time she had spent living with him in California had certainly cemented their relationship.

"Eh," he said, in conscious imitation of Jackie's earlier evasion.

"That bad, huh?"

"I don't know," Dunn replied. "I've seen worse, but this shutting down the production and changing the script, or re-casting the guest villainess or having Legs Diedrickson and Hal Erhlichman (the film's two leads) go back to Sassoon's for new color jobs, is getting pretty old. On *Heaven's Gate,* the joke went, they planted grass and waited for it to grow. I think Stan Gray has planted a bunch of redwoods."

Jackie started to say something, but held her tongue. Stan Gray was the telemovie's director. Stan was the lone principal of the old *CopLady* show to go on to much bigger and better things, and this particular project was a big comedown for the once Academy Award–nominated motion picture director.

After many years of making funny films with big stars (mostly adaptations of Neil Simon–type hit Broadway plays, but very funny Neil Simon–type Broadway plays), Stan Gray had lost his touch. Or perhaps he had simply lost his hold on the American consciousness.

With Broadway no longer coughing up three or four sure-fire stage-to-film smashes anymore, Stan Gray was now scratching for material. The stars of his yesteryear hits were generally pretty loyal to their old director, but they too were no longer in fashion. And the public had shown, by the way they voted with their pocketbooks, that to the extent that their rapidly aging public was willing to support them at all, it was only to see them do good, serious work, in good, serious films which were really about something.

Or course Stan Gray had no idea how to make films like that. He didn't really stand for anything and didn't really understand anyone who did. And so, his agents, as a face-saving gesture, got a couple of TV producers to option *CopLady* and to hire him (sending a signal throughout the TV industry that Stan Gray would now consider such work) as director of *Back with a Vengeance.*

The project had started very well, but as time went on, Stan Gray had become more and more trouble-some, balking at the intensive TV shooting schedule, complaining that he did not have his usual crew, and grousing about having to play second fiddle to stars whom he considered second bananas and has-beens.

Although Stan Gray and Jackie had not been particularly close, they had gotten along a lot better than would Stan and Celestine Barger.

When Jackie returned to Palmer to resume her teaching (and take care of Peter, her son), Celestine Barger had taken her place. The fiftyish director, who remembered the young Celestine as being an appealing, dumb, and beautiful Gracie Allen type (an obvious act even then, but not too obvious for old Stan apparently), did not like the fact that the still-attractive (but in a mature, confident way) screenwriter did not want to flirt with him. He also didn't like the fact that she didn't want to hear his ideas on how each scene should be written to reflect Stan Gray's philosophy (which of course was irrelevant to the story). When Celestine did not play along, Gray exploded and tried to get her fired. Unable to win the battle, Stan Gray had been reduced to foot dragging, fit throwing, and picking fights with cast and crew members. Now, rumor had it that Stan Gray, anxious to leave the Hollywood scene, where he was increasingly despised and unappreciated, was politicking with the Rodgers University Board for the job of chairman of the Communications Studies program, should it become available.

" . . . But we'll get through it," Dunn concluded.

"I know you will, Ron," Jackie answered.

"Then he's your problem."

"Don't even joke about that," Jackie demanded. "When am I going to see you, you terrible man?"

"Next month, if we're not still shooting. I have a booking for my *An Hour and Sixty Minutes with Jack Benny Show* on the eighth in Wardville."

"Why, that's just a hop, skip, and a jump away."

"It is indeed," Dunn rumbled. "And I thought we'd spend the holidays together."

"That would be lovely," Jackie agreed at once.

"And of course I have a very special Christmas present for you," Dunn purred.

"Are you talking dirty to me, you sexy man?" Jackie asked, blushing.

Maury, bored with being good, knocked over Jackie's Betty Boop garbage can and swatted it the length of the room.

"Well, I guess I should go."

Hearing the crash and guessing who the culprit was, Dunn queried, "I thought you were going to unload that behemoth?"

"I've been trying all day. Honest." Jackie then nudged (some would say "kneed") Maury out into the corridor, and locked the door of her cubicle.

As she did, Marcus Baghorn, one of the two deputy chairmen of the department, passed by. "Aaagh! What's this? I thought Jumbo the Elephant was dead!"

Jackie spoke into her Fona-Dict. "I've got to go, Ron."

"Parting is such sweet sorrow . . ."

"Call me tomorrow?"

"If I can. I love you passionately, Jackie."

"Me too, Ron." Jackie broke the connection and then saw Marcus feverishly feeding Maury some Reese's Pieces candies he happened to have in his pocket.

"Is it all right, Ms. Walsh, that I feed your dog candy?"

"It's all right," Jackie allowed. "But he hates it when you stop."

"Oh, oh." Baghorn looked down at his rapidly emptying hand. "Are you serious?"

"No," Jackie smiled. "How are you, Marcus?"

"Terrible. How do you think? I live in a city that can't make a pizza. Can't make a bagel. With Mr. Big Shot Famous Director Chairman Ivor Quest sunning his tootsies in Florida, I'm doing all sorts of administrative work. What do I know about paperwork?"

"Is Ms. Zweiback helping?"

"She's tried." Baghorn let go of the unpainted sasafrass root cane he called his "third leg" and made a dismissive gesture with his hands. "But the woman thinks she's Julia Child. Always cooking. The filing stacks up, the typing doesn't get done, the phone rings like we've got a dead receptionist, and whenever we go looking for Ms. Zweiback, she's in the kitchen cooking something."

Jackie shook her head sadly. She had questioned the advisability of hiring the decidedly eccentric secretary of the former Dean of Rodgers University, Henry Obermaier, but knowing that the opening had only occurred because Marcus had married the last department secretary, Jackie considered it politic to hold her tongue.

"She's a good cook," Baghorn continued. "If that matters. But she always brings me lunches that are designed to embarrass me."

"Really?" Jackie asked.

Baghorn put his hand on his chest, as if crossing his heart. "I may be paranoid, but that's the way it seems sometimes. You may not have been able to tell from just looking at me, but this blinding set of choppers I hold in my jaws are not my own teeth. They look good, but at chewing they are at best fair. So what does Betty Crocker the secretary bring in—caramel apples, salt water taffy, and pan-glazed yams."

"I'm sure it's completely unintentional," Jackie said, suppressing a smile.

"So I transferred her."

"Oh, oh."

Baghorn nodded happily, taking the note of alarm for a pat on the back. "I came in this morning, found a big slab of rock candy on my desk, and said, 'Miss Zweiback . . . Martha . . . our department cannot properly appreciate your skills and achievements. We are transferring you to Life Skills, where you may terrorize students and teachers with sound teeth.''

"Who's going to replace her?" Jackie asked at once.

Baghorn shrugged. "I called the personnel office and begged for them to send us someone good this time, but they said we'd have to take whoever was available. It's not fair, darn it. Why can't we hire someone we want, instead of just taking any schlepp who walks down the road? If I had any hair under this cheap toupee, I'd be tearing it out. I guarantee you."

"You do have my sympathies, Marcus," Jackie remarked, edging past him.

Baghorn would not allow Jackie to detach herself so easily. "It's a tragical situation here. I'm up to my surgical socks in paperwork and I'm helpless without a *secretary*. For twenty-five years, I used the same pencil. Maybe once every ten years I would even have to sharpen it. Take it from a man who knows, this is an impossible situation."

"Well." Jackie gave the real-life Damon Runyon character a sympathetic pat on the shoulder. "If anyone can solve the impossible, it's you, sir. I'll be seeing you, Marcus."

Baghorn hobbled after her as quickly as he could move, hollering, "You wouldn't by chance be going to the Groucho Marx-Bert Wheeler Medical Center, would you?" the old publicity man asked.

Jackie looked at him in some amazement. "Yes, I am, as a matter of fact. Why?"

"Could you give an old Hebrew a lift?"

"I suppose so . . ." Jackie hesitated.

"Don't worry," Baghorn said at once. "I'm just going for a flu shot. A man gets to be my age, he's usually dead. If he isn't, he's got to take precautions."

"Okay," Jackie agreed, somewhat reluctantly. "I have to walk by the science building first and pick up John Brooks. If that isn't a problem?"

"All my problems should be so horrible," Baghorn averred, linking his arm with Jackie's. "It's a beautiful evening for a walk. Isn't it, Godzilla?"

Maury turned back to Baghorn and gave him a hug, almost knocking the old man over.

"Maury. Be good," Jackie instructed.

"So, what sort of murder are you investigating this time?"

"Actually, I'm hoping I'm out of that line of work," Jackie answered, as they left the communications building and started across the slick cobblestoned courtyard.

"Why?" Marcus asked. "It sounds exciting."

"So does alligator wrestling," Jackie responded. "But after four or five times, most people are ready to move on."

"You know what I'm afraid of," Baghorn volunteered. "I'm afraid that someday, some nutcase who you helped to put in jail will come back to the school and try to get even with you by planting a bomb in your lunchbag or something."

"Pleasant thought," Jackie managed.

"It would be bad enough to lose you," Baghorn joked. "But if we had to do capital repairs with what little we've got left in our budget, it would mean the end of us."

"Really?" Jackie asked. "I thought Chairman Quest had gotten a lot of Hollywood types to donate money to the center."

"He did," Baghorn agreed. "But it comes in and goes

out, like airplanes on a secret Arkansas landing strip. Fred and I aren't fundraisers. I'm afraid they're going to hire some horse's ass like Stanley Gray to come here to take Ivor's place."

"Oh, dear," Jackie responded. "Does that look like a strong possibility?"

Baghorn shrugged. "I don't know what else they're going to do, Jackie. I'm too old to do the chairman's job, even if I wanted it, and I don't. Management isn't Fred's cup of tea either."

Jackie grimaced. "I have a feeling if Stan Gray did come here, it would mean a lot of changes."

"A lot of heads would roll, you mean," Baghorn nodded. "Yes, I think so too. We're living in a changing world, Jackie."

"Yes, we are," the young filmmaker agreed. "Marcus, would you do me a favor?"

"Anything within reason," Baghorn said at once.

"Would you go up and buzz John Brooks to come down? I'll get my Jeep and meet you both here in a few minutes."

"All righty."

As the former publicist walked off, Jackie phoned her home.

The phone rang ten or twelve times, then a sleepy voice picked up. "Hello?"

"Peter, this is Mommy."

"Who?"

"Jackie Walsh," Jackie repeated. "Do you remember, Pete? Your mother?"

"Oh, yeah. Hi."

"Hi. How are you?"

"I don't know."

"When will you have some idea?" Jackie persisted.

"When are you coming home?" Peter asked. "I'm hungry."

"Where's Merida?" Jackie asked. "I thought she was going to cook dinner for you."

"I don't know where she is," Peter grumbled. "And I'm starved. Guess what, Ma?"

"You love me dearly?" Jackie fished.

"No," Peter answered with some disgust. "I had practice today."

"I know, darling," Jackie responded, pulling Maury away from the remains of a possum that someone had backed over in the parking lot. Jackie felt sad for a moment, as she pictured how badly she would feel if her own slothful son had been similarly tire-crunched. "Don't you feel great to get back to exercising regularly again? All you did was lie around and watch TV all summer."

"I did not," Peter protested. "I helped you, remember."

Jackie considered for a moment. Had Peter helped her at all? It seemed like an unusual enough event that she would remember it if it had actually happened.

"What did you help me with, Peter?"

"I took out the garbage, remember?"

Jackie smote herself. How could she have forgotten? Once a week, with only a maximum of reminding, scolding, and complaining, she managed to get Peter to carry the garbage out to the big recycling bins that took up half of her backyard. "Now that you remind me, Peter, that's right. You did help me. Thank you again. Now how did practice go?"

"Good. We skated three laps around the rink and then we scrimmaged and Isaac Cooks got hit in the head with a puck and we got to sit down while they cleaned up the blood."

Jackie shook her head. She had enrolled Peter in the

Downtown Arts High School, hoping a nascent spark would ignite his interest in drawing or playing a musical instrument. Instead, the chunky little twelve-year-old had only become more obsessed with hockey, and at the moment was the only starting defenseman to still have all his own teeth.

"Great. Well, you make sure to call Isaac later and tell him you hope he feels better."

"Mom!"

"Don't tell me," Jackie said in her best "outraged mom" voice, "you can't be bothered to call your best friend after all the times his parents have given you dinner, and let you spend the night, and tell him you're sorry he was hit in the head with a hockey puck."

"I didn't tell him not to wear his helmet."

"Peter!"

"He's not even home. He's in the hospital."

"Marx-Wheeler?" Jackie asked.

"I guess."

"All right. Go around and knock on Ms. Green's door and . . ."

"She's already here."

"Where?"

"In the kitchen."

"In the kitchen making dinner?"

"I guess."

"I thought you said she . . ."

"Well, she's taking a long time," Peter explained. "Why can't she just use the microwave like I asked her? I'm hungry!"

Jackie counted to ten and then said, "Peter. Go in the kitchen and give the phone receiver to Ms. Green. Tell her I want to speak to her."

"I just got back from the kitchen," Peter complained.

"I appreciate you making this effort, darling," Jackie responded. "Just give the phone to Merida and then you can go back to bed and brood about your problems."

Muttering how unfair was his lot, Jackie's son trudged off to the kitchen without bothering to put the receiver on hold. Jackie winced as she listened to her awkward son bouncing into various inanimate objects as he descended the stairs of their duplex and shuffled off to the small kitchen.

Having investigated the possum to his satisfaction, Maury came bounding over to smear Jackie with the gore he had managed to get on his snout and paws.

"Stop!" she yelled. "Maury!" Jackie tried again. Then, seeing that her mastiff had no intention of stopping, Jackie dropped her Fona-Dict and ran up the stairs to the field house. Maury, dripping like a stunt double for Cujo, ran after her.

Getting through the door, Jackie flashed her faculty badge and warned the security guard, "Mickey, there's a dirty dog right behind me."

"There is?" he chuckled. Not willing to take a woman as pretty as Jackie seriously, Farrow turned slowly and went over like a tenpin when Maury barreled into him.

Jackie ran into the women's locker room, looking for a damp towel to clean up her annoying pet. Turning the bolt to keep Maury outside for a moment, Jackie scouted through the maintenance closet and found some old swim towels which were now being used as cleaning rags.

Wetting one of them in the work sink, Jackie reflected on how long it had been since she had been in the building. An inveterate swimmer, Jackie had once used the Olympic indoor field house pool at least four or five days a week. Unfortunately, the fact that a real estate saleswoman Jackie knew had been found murdered in the pool had cast something of a pall on the activity. That, and the fact that the former Palmer Steel Foundry near her apartment had been turned into a community center complete with an outdoor pool, had kept her out of the field house for the better part of the past six months. Now that it was getting cold, she supposed she would start using the university pool again. It would be tough to swim past the memories however.

A banging and scratching on the locker room door awakened her from her reveries.

"Just a minute, Maury. Please!"

Jackie covered herself with rags, held out the towel, and opened the door. Maury burst in, skidded on the tile floor, and crashed into a table holding magazines and hairdrying equipment. The cheap piece of furniture broke into a dozen pieces and a hairdryer switched on, making Maury bark furiously.

"Maury!" Jackie shouted. "Bad dog!"

"What's going on?" asked a voice from the showers.

Ever alert, Maury hipchecked Jackie aside and went charging inside to flush that female attacker who was yelling at his beloved mistress.

"Help! Help!" the person yelled.

Jackie staggered inside to see Sylvia Brown, a part-time aerobics instructor in the Physical Culture Department, standing on a bench near the showers as Maury slid back and forth on the wet floor, tremendously enjoying his newest game.

"Who let this . . . dog in?" Sylvia demanded.

Jackie smothered the impulse to laugh hysterically. Although she had been angry at Sylvia for the past six months for stealing her former boyfriend, Homicide Lieutenant Michael McGowan, the film instructor would not wish a frenzied Maury on anyone.

"What's going on?" Sylvia yelled.

"Help me!" Jackie urged. "Wrestle him into the handi-capped shower."

So a soaked and towel-draped Jackie and a nude and outraged Sylvia managed to drag Maury inside and shower him down good. Maury howled like a stuck pig, not because he didn't want to rinse off (he actually found the sensation invigorating) but because he remembered that his former owner, Sergeant Hippo Lavan, always sang in the shower, and figured that this was the thing to do.

"Ms. Walsh! Ms. Walsh!"

Jackie finally heard Mickey Farrow above the clamor and handed her towel to the fitness instructor. "Sylvia, I know this is crazy, but I better go out there before Mickey comes in. Would you finish toweling him off and then put something on? I'll make it up to you . . . somehow. How about if I buy you a dinner sometime?"

Sylvia brushed her wet blonde hair away from her eyes and looked at Jackie. Remembering that they had once been friends, and a little contrite that her desire for the handsome policeman had ruined that closeness, Sylvia was glad to have an opportunity to bury the hatchet. "Sure, Jackie. Go ahead. I'll try to get him halfway dry, then send him out to you."

"Thanks, Sylvia," Jackie said fondly. "I appreciate it."

Then, hearing a strange hissing noise, Jackie turned and ran for the locker room.

When she got there, she saw a blood-streaked Mickey putting out the electrical fire with a chemical fire extinguisher. "Oh my goodness."

"It's okay. It's out."

"Great. Thank you. I'm terribly sorry . . ." Jackie started.

"What are you going to do?" Mickey said cheerfully.

"When you have a big dog, he calls the shots."

"I'm giving him away tonight, honest," Jackie swore. "I hope this means we'll never have to deal with him again. The only thing is . . . if his new owner hears about this . . ."

Mickey put his finger to his lips. If there was one thing this cheery Irish-American, a former button man for a Philadelphia mob, could do, it was keep a secret. "Don't worry, Ms. Walsh. My lips are sealed."

"Thanks, Mickey," Jackie said warmly. There was no doubt about it, if he wasn't a paroled murderer and she wasn't already attached, Jackie would definitely consider Mickey a contender.

"No problem." The former tough, now on the bright and shiny path to an honest life, grinned, wiping his hand over his fashionably stubbled jaw. "I tell you, though. I ain't taken a beating like that guy gave me in quite a while. Maybe if you can't unload him with your pal, you should consider giving him to the university as a guard dog."

"Oh, no," Jackie said. "Remember, I own a security dog, and for a job like that you need one that combines brawn with brains."

"I guess so," said Mickey. "Still, I wouldn't mind having a dog like that. He'd sure keep you in shape."

Jackie smiled wanly and hung up the damp towels she was still holding in the maintenance closet. "He does at that. The problem is paying for all the stuff he damages. Can I give you ten dollars to have your uniform dry-cleaned?"

"Well, normally I wouldn't ask but . . ."

Jackie nodded. She knew that the university was taking advantage of the fact that the ex-convict needed a job to pay him only the minimum wage, and quickly extracted a ten-dollar bill from her fanny pack. "Thanks, Mickey."

"Ollie ollie dog come free!" Sylvia yodeled as she approached with the now damp but fairly dapper Maury. "Ready or not, here comes the Beast from Ten Thousand Fathoms."

Mickey laughed good-naturedly and Jackie made a mental note to show that film to her lab. "Thanks, Sylvia. Mickey, do you know Sylvia Brown?"

Mickey politely checked out the trim athlete, now dressed in a sleek, blue-striped exercise suit and sneakers.

"She teaches aerobics here at the college," Jackie explained. "Sylvia, Mickey Farrow. He used to work for Morton Slake."

"Actually, I worked for Bill Curtis," Mickey politely corrected Jackie. "I was hired to keep an eye on Morty. Which is kind of not the same thing."

Jackie shrugged and it was clear Sylvia didn't particularly care either. Gangsters, former or otherwise, were kind of passé these days, and one politician was just as crooked as another in the eyes of most Palmer citizens.

"Hi."

"Well, if you'll excuse me," Jackie interrupted. "I have someone waiting. And you," she said, addressing her big dog. "If you don't stop acting up, I'm going to brain you."

Maury wiggled, delighted to be the center of attention again, and gave his mistress a friendly head goose from behind, just to show her how much he loved her.

CHAPTER 9

Having a beer and a cigarette in the Mexican rathskeller that the hospital had installed, Marcella Jacobs was startled to see Stuart Goodwillie sitting across from her, chowing down on the free nachos.

"Mr. Goodwillie!" she exclaimed. "What are you doing here?"

The elderly bottled-water baron didn't even look up. Clearly he had completely forgotten the young woman who had interviewed him several times, both as a print reporter and later as a television personality.

Instead Evan Stillman, the seedy former Palmer police captain and current head of security (which included duties as Chairman Goodwillie's personal bodyguard), stood and stuck his hand up, trying to block her off as if she were Jack Ruby trying to kill Lee Harvey Oswald.

Marcella easily slipped by and plunked herself down on the seat next to Palmer's crankiest millionaire.

"Great," the thin, bald plutocrat mumbled into his Shirley Temple. "The tavern trollop."

Marcella grimaced and pulled down the hem of her skirt. "I am wearing a lot of makeup, Mr. Goodwillie, because I am the co-anchor for the KCIN *Nightly News*."

"Save your tawdry stories for your twelve-step cronies," Goodwillie wheezed. "I mind my own business, why don't you?"

"Because I'm a reporter," Marcella said proudly.

Stuart Goodwillie turned his long, thin turkey neck to look at Marcella for the first time, then spit the pit from an olive into her glass.

"Bartender!" Marcella shouted, completely undaunted. "I'll have a refill. In a clean glass, if you will. And some more free eats for Palmer's richest man."

"Inaccurate as always, I see," Goodwillie grumbled. "Thanks to the influx of our little brothers from across the sea, I am no longer in the top five, Miss Nosey Parker. You've heard they're already considering going bilingual in the schools . . ."

If it were Jackie, she would have said, "Food for thought," but Marcella cut straight to the point. "Here to meet Dr. Linus Munch, Mr. Goodwillie? Planning to stick a bottle of Goodwillie Goodwater in his hand so he'll be forced to give a spot endorsement?"

Goodwillie's beady little eyes lit up. "Actually I'm just here for a flu shot, but that's a corking good idea. Stillman!"

"Yes, sir?" The former policeman jumped to his feet.

"Insert a Tic Tac or two in your mouth, then run out to the car for a couple of 1.5 liter bottles of my water."

"Yes, sir. Will you be all . . . ?"

"I think I can defend myself for a few minutes." Goodwillie distastefully removed the comic stirrer from his nearly finished drink and snapped, "If anyone tries to assassinate me, I suppose I can fend him off with this pink plastic monkey. Now hop to it, man."

As Stillman left, Goodwillie turned to Marcella and confided, "Just once in my life I would love to have a bodyguard who didn't move like someone had nailed the soles of his shoes to the floor."

The scabrous millionaire then turned to the bartender. "You! Draughtmaster! Stop mentally undressing that scrub nurse and sprint over here with our refills. You may put this woman's last drink on my bill. Providing it is under five dollars of course."

Marcella mockingly put her hand to her chest. "Why, Mr. Goodwillie. You flatter me."

"No, woman," Goodwillie rasped. "You flatter yourself. Consider our interview ended."

"Not so fast," Marcella protested.

Just then Georgiana Bowman, the distinguished former motion picture director turned part-time instructor at Rodgers University (thanks to Jackie), motored into the room in her top-of-the-line wheelchair.

"Good gravy!" Goodwillie exclaimed. "Who is that vision of loveliness?" The besmitten millionaire turned desperately to Marcella. "Do you know who she is?"

Marcella nodded.

"Can you introduce me to her?"

"Sure," Marcella replied easily, sensing a story was developing before her weary eyes. "Miss Bowman!"

The impervious director, her hair recently blue-rinsed to bring out her flashing eyes, turned toward the duo.

"You remember me, Ms. Bowman? Marcella Jacobs, the television reporter?"

"No," Georgiana snapped. "I haven't watched a TV newscast since Chet Huntley retired."

"A woman after my own heart!" Goodwillie simpered. He impatiently pushed past Marcella and took Georgiana's hand. "Pardon my impetuosity, dear lady. May a humble admirer request the honor of an introduction?"

"Georgiana Bowman," Marcella said. "May I present Stuart Goodwillie?"

The bottled water baron removed his yachting cap and bent low, kissing the veteran film pioneer's hand. "*Enchanté,* Madam."

"I know you," Georgiana responded at once, giving him a frank, appraising look. "You're the fellow who dumped all the psychedelic chemicals in the reservoir and had people wandering around for months like they were in some ghastly fifties soap opera."

"It did happen on my watch," Goodwillie responded as contritely as he could manage on such short notice. "Mea culpa, dear lady."

"What?" Georgiana asked, sipping her Lynchburg Lemonade. "Did you pollute the reservoir so you could hustle a few more cases of your bottled water?"

"No, alas," Goodwillie responded with a deprecating wave of his pale liver-spotted hand. "I wasn't smart enough to think of that one until a few weeks after the big cleanup. Then I was caught in the act—curse my luck."

Georgiana sipped her drink. "And you were supposed to give lots of money to the citizens of Palmer, weren't you? As part of your settlement for staying out of jail?"

Goodwillie quickly went into his poor me routine. "Well of course, good woman. But you must understand that my current fiduciary situation is such that . . ."

"You intend to welsh on that commitment, don't you, Mr. Goodwillie?" Georgiana asked pointedly. "I'll wager dollars to donuts you don't intend to pay the city of Palmer another thin dime."

Seeing that Georgiana was clearly amused by it all, Goodwillie dropped his mask and cheerfully admitted. "To be perfectly frank, dear lady, that's exactly what I intend to do. My philosophy is 'Accidents happen.' I paid plenty to clean the water. Even the water I didn't foul. And now the free ride is over. Those losers had their chance to put me in jail or attach my assets and they chose not to do so. That time has now passed. You snooze, you lose."

"Well, you're certainly a man with gumption," Georgiana commented. "I admire that."

"And I, dear lady, if I may be so forward as to tell you this, deeply admire your feminine charms." Goodwillie quickly clapped his yachtsman's cap back on his bare scalp and held out his arm. "Would you grant an elderly tycoon a precious boon and consent to having a beverage with me?"

"Well . . ." Georgiana allowed, as she cooled herself with an ivory fan she had been dying to use for the past thirty years. "I've already got a drink. But you can buy me a Mexican dinner if you want to."

"Olé!" cried Goodwillie. "Say the word, dear senorita, and I'll have these slugabeds toss the rest of the riffraff into the parking lot and we'll have a cozy candlelit dinner just us two."

Georgiana smiled her Barbara Stanwyck smile and turned around again.

Goodwillie immediately signaled the bartender to take his drink to Georgiana's table, then simply plucked his umbrella off the end of his chair, and prepared to join the object of his affection. "I don't suppose, Mr. Goodwillie . . ." Marcella started.

"Suppose away, Madam," Goodwillie replied. "Publish whatever the hell you want. That's why our Founding

Fathers invented libel courts. Now, if you'll excuse me, I hear the siren call of romance."

While the pharmaceutical tycoon made his move, Jackie apologized to Marcus Baghorn for keeping him waiting.

"Quite all right," Baghorn replied, holding up Jackie's Fona-Dict, which he had picked up off the ground. "I called my honey and talked dirty to her for five minutes. The filly still expects to have my children. Can you believe it? I'm old enough to be her grandfather. Well, God loves an optimist."

"I should say," Jackie agreed. "John Brooks didn't come down with you?"

"No. I never found him. Got involved with some damn maze and just managed to retrace my footsteps. Let's hope your friend is all right and we don't have yet another body on our hands."

"Marcus!"

"I'm sorry! Oy gevalt!" Baghorn complained, "You'd think with all the death and drama that's struck Rodgers University that we could at least have a sense of humor about it."

Jackie frowned. She didn't hold to that view at all. Sure, even she had laughed when she saw the student T-shirts that Lynn Bigbee, a student, was selling in her spare time—some bearing a skull and crossbones saying "Jolly Rodgers U—Learn or Die," others saying, "Com. Studies Graduate Program—Ph.D. or R.I.P." Jackie however tried not to lose sight of the fact that the half-dozen people who had met a bitter end were real human beings who deserved, even the worst of them, a far better fate.

Baghorn turned to the dog. "What about you, schnorrer? You liked my joke, right?"

Maury obligingly licked Baghorn's hand, causing the elderly publicist's non-waterproof watch to stop.

"Okay," Jackie replied. "We'll let it go. Let's change the subject. How's Fred Jackson? I don't think I've seen him around."

"Actually, I think he's still in traction."

"Traction?" Jackie was scandalized. She had always thought of old Fred as a veritable Hercules. "What happened?"

"He was demonstrating some exotic camera to the kids."

"A steady cam, do you mean?"

Jackie had heard through the grapevine that Stan Gray had persuaded KidVid Studios in California to donate some obsolete equipment to Rodgers, probably as a subtle form of bribery to help him win the job he wanted.

"Terrible thing," Baghorn nodded. "You'd have to be a weightlifter to carry that contraption around all the time."

"Absolutely," Jackie agreed.

"Anyway," Baghorn kvetched. "Fred was trying to be Mr. Macho Fella, and show the kids how it worked, and he threw out his back. We should stop by and see him when we finally get there."

At that moment John Brooks arrived. "Sorry to keep you, folks. I had to make a call."

"Okay," Jackie replied. "If we're ready, let's go. Oh, Marcus Baghorn, John Brooks."

"Hello, Doctah!" the transplanted New Yorker greeted him.

"How did you know John was a doctor?" Jackie asked.

"I don't know this man from a hole in the wall," Baghorn replied. "I call everybody doctor."

Brooks held out his hand. "Well, I'm actually an engineer, Mr. Baghorn. Pleased to meet you."

"I'm charmed to my orthopedic socks," Baghorn said graciously.

As they walked to the parking lot, Jackie led a much quieter Maury on his leash.

"He seems a little mellower," Baghorn commented. "What'd you do, slip him a Mickey Finn?"

"Sort of," Jackie admitted. "Sylvia Brown had some Tryptophan in her purse and we got him to eat a half-dozen pills by mashing them up with some ice cream."

"Ice cream?" Baghorn exclaimed. "I missed out on ice cream?"

"Not real ice cream," Jackie explained. "Some sort of dehydrated hiking food Sylvia carries around for when she goes hiking."

"Speaking of hiking," Baghorn complained. "When are we going to get to this Jeep of yours?"

"It's over there," Jackie pointed. "I couldn't park it near any other car because of Maury."

"He pees on the tires, you mean," Baghorn surmised.

"I'm afraid so."

They reached the battered Jeep and Jackie unlocked the passenger door first. "Get in, Maury. Get in the back, boy."

Giving Jackie a dirty look, Maury reluctantly obeyed. Baghorn then got into the passenger's seat and Jackie closed his door for him. As she started to open the door on her side, John Brooks said something to her in an undertone.

"I'm sorry, what?" she asked, pulling the seat forward so he could get in the back.

"I said, do you remember what we were talking about earlier?"

Jackie got into her seat, looked at Baghorn, and decided, "I think we can talk in front of Marcus."

"You can shout your heads off. I'm an old Jew with a hearing aid. You want privacy, I'll just cut it off."

"No," Jackie replied, turning the key in the ignition. "It's just that John is . . . well, suspicious of the motives of a doctor friend of his. I don't know whether you've been following the news, but Dr. Linus Munch, the vaccine researcher, is coming to Rodgers to guest lecture for John."

"Good idea," Baghorn said approvingly. "You should milk the publicity for all it's worth, if you don't mind me saying so. Print up flyers. Get it on local TV. Then you can use it for recruiting next spring."

"I had sort of planned to do that," Brooks replied. "Now I'm not so sure."

"No?" Baghorn asked, meeting Brooks's eyes in the rear view mirror. "Why not?"

Jackie made the turn out of the parking lot and sighed, "Tell him everything, John."

"Well, to make a long story short, I've heard that Dr. Linus is going to inoculate some patients at Marx-Wheeler with his new AIDS vaccine. It probably won't do any real harm, but my sources, the people who have been working with Linus Munch for the past few years, are convinced that this is some sort of stunt. They are positive that he hasn't been working on anything of the kind, and think that this is either being done to mock the real AIDS researchers, or to trick funding agencies into giving him money under false pretenses."

Baghorn nodded, unsurprised. "Sounds like the Linus Munch I know, all right."

Jackie turned to him, somewhat surprised. "You know the doctor?"

"I worked for him," Baghorn disclosed. "Years ago. Doing publicity for him. An egomaniac, our doctor. And not a nice person. I've worked with both in show business so it was nothing new, but it left me with a bad taste in my mouth. No question. Actors, you know, except for a few phonies, don't pretend to be holier than thou. And the public doesn't care if they raise a little hell, or fall asleep the minute the conversation isn't about them—as long as they keep it within reason of course.

"The problem with Dr. Linus was that he was just as bad, or worse, and really disappointed a lot of people who felt that doctors should be warm, friendly, modest Robert Young types. His making passes at ladies young enough to be his daughter—and acting like he was the only one practicing medicine who was any good—turned off a lot of fellahs.

"Before he left, he was kind of sniffing around, trying to get a teaching and research gig in New York. I told him flat out it would be the biggest mistake of his life. If he wanted to keep any kind of respect at all, he should go back to the woods and practice his charm on the chipmunks and raccoons."

"I'm sure that didn't go over too big with Dr. Linus," Brooks commented.

"No, it sure didn't, my friend," Baghorn replied at once. "The big goof attacked me."

"Really?" Jackie asked.

"Absolutely. In forty-five years of running my own agency, I've been slapped, I've been kicked, I've had people throw drinks in my face and trash my office, but no one ever physically tackled me and tried to bash my head against the floor. If a client with jaws strong enough to chew bricks hadn't picked him up by the scruff of the neck and thrown him across the room, the son of a gun would have killed me."

Brooks and Jackie were stunned for a minute.

"Listen," Baghorn finally said. "Maybe you want me to stay out of this, and if you do, I will. But maybe, just maybe, it would help the cause if I talked to him before he starts making an ass of himself. I know him for what he is. He knows I know him for what he is. Maybe I can scare him into not doing something he shouldn't be doing."

"What if he tries to strangle you again?" Jackie asked.

"I'll go with you," Brooks offered. "My jaws aren't strong enough to chew bricks, goodness knows, but if it's true that Linus plans to take advantage of my trying to do him a good deed by turning this into an unpleasant publicity stunt, then, I'll tell you here and now, they'll need someone to pull me off him!"

CHAPTER 10

Not having anything else to do, Marcella went into the corridor to check in with her cameraman. She had a beeper and knew that Chris Compton would signal her when Dr. Munch finally came down, but she was restless.

It was nearly 8 P.M. now. Marcella had been at the hospital since a little after one. She had long ago sent away her makeup and hair people, meaning she would now have to do her piece off-camera and cut in intro and reaction shots later.

Ruben Baskette had left just a few moments ago, threatening that if Munch didn't come down by ten o'clock, she would pay for wasting so much of his time.

Marcella was on the spot and she knew it. Her decision not to go with the strike story they had so expensively staged had infuriated Ruben. In addition, as things had worked out, both she and Vic Kingston had missed the broadcast. Luckily, there were filmed segments in the can, which could be aired, but from all accounts, the sportscaster, Biff Mayberry, had not appreciated doing the entire newscast alone with no one to talk to but Gooner the Weather Chimp.

For hours the plucky young newscaster had been trying to get up to the administrator's office, but it seemed impossible. The medical center's security guards were eager young brutes who liked nothing better than throwing a reporter or a grieving relative down a flight of steps to show how tough they were.

In addition, Dick Bellamy, the hospital's administrator and the husband of Palmer's diva mayor, Jane Bellamy, had a personal bodyguard, Dannen Jeffreys, provided by the city, who made sure that no unauthorized person ever came within five feet of the doctor in chief.

Marcella had tried flirting with the gruff Tae Kwon Do instructor, but he hadn't shown even the slightest interest. This convinced the young newscaster that either he was gay or his kevlar vest extended down low enough to cover his libido.

Not able to think of anything productive to do, Marcella stopped into the TV rental office, sat on Kevin Erlanger's desk and asked, "May I use your phone?"

"Sure," Erlanger replied. "Who you calling? Your station?"

"Actually, I was going to order a pizza," Marcella informed him.

"Push asterisk seven."

"Like pizza, do you?"

"Not a lot of places are willing to deliver out here late at night."

Marx-Wheeler Medical Center was located in the unfashionable Old Town district of Palmer. All around the hospital were the slums and 9–5 government buildings that became the property of tramps, indigents, and panhandlers after dark. Wags were wont to say that if you weren't badly hurt, it really wasn't worth it to go to Marx-Wheeler after dark. Because if you did, you might end up getting hurt worse!

Marcella pushed the two buttons and almost immediately an adenoidal young counterperson picked up. "Red, White and Blue Pizza. May I help you?"

"I'd like to have a small number seventeen pizza delivered to me at the Marx-Wheeler Medical Center please. My Lucky Red, White and Blue discount card number is 33115."

"Okay, Ma'am," the counterperson replied, keying the information into Red, White and Blue's computer. "Would you like some soda, or pepperoni-flavored breadsticks?"

"No, thank you," Marcella answered. "Just a moment. Kevin? Would you care to join me in a little snack?"

"I'll have a slice," Erlanger allowed, while running a pocket comb through his heavily pomaded hair.

"Great. Soda?"

"Nah," Erlanger replied.

Marcella nodded and uncovered the mouthpiece of the phone. "Make that a medium pie and give me a 1.5 liter bottle of the McKean All Spice Pop."

"Yes, Ma'am. Where in Marx-Wheeler Medical Center should we make the delivery?"

"The TV rental office," Marcella answered. "Just down the hall from the Mexican rathskeller."

"All right, Ma'am," the voice wheezed. "We'll be there in thirty-five minutes or the pizzas are on us."

Marcella put the receiver back in its cradle and flirtatiously brushed her hair back from her face. "Well, you're working late."

"So are you," the sulky TV renter responded.

"This isn't New York or Los Angeles," Marcella said.

"If I don't get the story, I don't get paid."

"Yeah, well same here," Erlanger sneered, utterly unimpressed. "This is strictly a cash-and-carry business, you know. If I'm not here, I don't get paid."

"You must make a good living," Marcella flattered, knowing that complimenting a man's earning skills was as flattering as whistling at a woman's legs.

"I do all right."

"Do you supply TVs to everyone in the hospital?"

"Everyone who's got a tube gets it from me."

"Does that include the hospital administrator?" Marcella asked.

"I guess 'everyone' includes 'everyone,' don't it?"

"I guess it sure does," Marcella forced out, checking her impulse to boot the pouty provider of Panasonics in the back of his tight blue jeans. "What sort of TV does Dr. Bellamy have? I mean, it is a wide-screen?"

"He's usually too drunk to watch TV," Erlanger retorted. "But he's got three monitors up there, which he can use to watch TV or monitor security feeds, or call up patient data on the hospital computer."

"And he can switch any one of them into each of the three modes?" Marcella asked knowledgeably.

"Yeah," Erlanger reluctantly conceded, running his comb through his hair again. "Pretty much."

Marcella dropped her voice to a husky, Eartha Kitt growl. "Is there any way I could persuade you to take me up there with you while you check a connection, or something?"

"You want me to pretend," Erlanger clarified, "that there's something wrong with the boss's TV so you can burst into Doc Bellamy's office like Mike Wallace and do one of them ambush-style interviews?"

"Something like that," Marcella admitted. "But my target is actually Dr. Munch. And I'll play it by ear just how rough to make it on him. All I really need to know is whether he's going to do this inoculation stunt tonight or not."

"Well, that don't sound too bad," Erlanger conceded. "And I wouldn't mind stretching my legs—after we have that pizza of course."

"Of course," Marcella said at once.

"But like I said before," Erlanger repeated, "when I'm not in this cubicle, I'm not making any money."

Marcella nodded. She had fully expected something like this. "Of course I understand that, Kevin," she said disingenuously. "How much business do you think you would lose while you're doing this public-spirited little errand with me?"

"Couple of hundred dollars," Erlanger said easily.

Marcella bit the inside of her lip. She had been sitting with Erlanger for fifteen minutes and not a soul had called or wandered by. In addition, it was obvious to her, if not to everyone, that the evenings did not figure to be periods of great money making and she was surprised that Erlanger thought they would be. After all, most inpatient admissions are made during the early part of the day. Clearly, if TVs were desired, they would be ordered then. Anyone who came into the hospital after four P.M. would come in through the Emergency Room. If they were sick enough to merit instant admission, chances were they wouldn't be all that interested in TV. But Marcella took out the Spanish coin money clip Ral Perrin had given her (for getting him occasional work as a cameraman) and counted off five twenties. "I'll give you a hundred dollars."

"Done," Erlanger said at once.

Giving the young grifter a look, Marcella handed him

the money, then proposed, "What do you say we head up now?"

"I don't mind," Erlanger replied, sticking the wad in his blue jeans. "But what about the pizza?"

"I'll leave some money with the nurse at the reception desk."

"Works for me," Erlanger responded, picking up a long pendulous connection wire. "Let's go."

Outside, having let the men go on ahead, Jackie stopped to visit a moment with another Thursday night poker player, Bara Day.

"Hi, Bara. What brings you here?"

"Flu shot," the white-haired, African-American woman answered. "Better safe than sorry."

Jackie nodded, knowing that the former private-duty nurse was a great deal more health conscious than most women of her mother's generation. "How's Scalia?"

"Better, thank you." A matter-of-fact woman, Bara Day enjoyed talking about her passion, a sixteen-foot female African python, far more than she enjoyed disclosing revelations about herself. "We're hoping, your mother and I, that the fact that Scalia's running a slight temperature might raise her interest in romance."

Jackie knew that Bara, with her mother's full cooperation, was trying to get her pet impregnated by Frances Costello's male, sixteen-foot South American python, Victor. "That may do it."

"Let's hope so," Bara responded. "I've been feeding Scalia shellfish for the past few weeks."

"Do you think that will help?" Jackie asked, negligently giving Maury a little more slack.

"I've got a notion it will," Bara responded, suddenly becoming more animated. "They say fish, particularly pregnant mommas, are aphrodisiacs the world over. Cows and horses fed pregnant fish have more foals. Pythons in the wild . . ." Bara produced a thick, colorful *Long Snake Fanciers* magazine from her shoulderbag as if to supply documentary evidence. "See here. Pythons eat fish and various amphibians in their natural habitat. And what does that tell you?"

"Don't drink the water?" Jackie guessed, sneaking a peek at Maury who seemed to be stalking something near a toolshed just around the corner from the Emergency Room entrance.

"No!" Bara barked. "It means we're all doing it wrong. No wonder snakes are very seldom born in captivity. We're cutting off their mood enhancers. I defy you to name three zoos or reptile houses in the entire country that feed their pythons live eels or frogs or even softshell turtles. And that's zoos that have the resources and supposedly know what they're doing.

"Pet owners like your mother and me, well, we wouldn't even think to do that. I've had snakes for fifteen years. I've fed them bugs, mice, piglets, and now these tasty South American beavers that all the pet stores are carrying, but never once did I think to vary Scalia's diet with a little seafood."

"Live and learn," Jackie said philosophically. "I guess I always assumed that snake matings were rare because the breeders did what a lot of dog breeders do—damaged the reproductive organs of the pets they sell, so that the owners will keep having to come back to them when they want a replacement."

"I don't even want to think about that," Bara said, shuddering.

"It is horrible," Jackie agreed. What Jackie didn't tell

the former nurse was that she had herself donated several thousand dollars to Thalia Gillmore's Canine Rights Lobbying Organization in order to bring pressure on the major offenders in the dog world to stop. Jackie did not like to think of any dog being treated in this fashion, but she also had a personal reason for donating.

Her favorite dog Jake, a brilliant, almost human German shepherd that had once worked as a police dog, was also a very valuable commodity. There are actually very few purebred German shepherds left in the United States. Jake's stock contained the best blood of his French-German ancestors, the small, fleet, black-and-brown Alsatian and the best blood from the American "German" shepherd, a larger, stronger, smarter dog that was better with children. The dogs that came from this strain were perfect for police work and as Seeing Eye dogs for the wealthy. Therefore, Jackie reasoned, as the price for each of these dogs climbed into the thousands, the breeders might be tempted to neuter dogs like Jake before selling them. This would insure that a police department buying a half-dozen dogs could not start its own little stud farm and thus drive down the breeders' price.

"What are you doing here?" Bara inquired.

"I'm dropping off Maury over there with his new owner," Jackie answered. "A braver woman than I, I'll tell you."

The two women looked over to where Maury was convinced he had trapped a field mouse. Elephant mastiffs of course are great mousers because they were first bred to guard and lead elephants, and, as everyone knows, pachyderms and rodents don't mix.

"I see."

As the two women watched, Maury dug frantically at

the cement slab in front of the toolshed, covering the cesspool.

"I thought you might be here for the AIDS vaccine."

"Me?" Jackie asked.

"Well, don't get offended. If I were sexually active, I would take a shot."

"You would?" Jackie asked, amazed.

"Sure. As long as there wasn't any real risk involved. Why the hell not? You never know when you're going to get knocked down by a bus and be taken to a hospital for a blood transfusion and end up with some tainted blood."

"Please," Jackie pleaded. "I thought they got a handle on that."

"In the big hospitals," Bara agreed. "Some of the smaller hospitals just don't have the time or the money to buy all the screening equipment and do all the tests. Palmer gets three-quarters of its blood through Red Cross blood drives. A plasma pack or two from every batch is screened, but not every single drop of blood."

Jackie made a face and forced herself to ask, "So there are people inside waiting to be given the AIDS vaccine shot by Dr. Munch?"

"Oh, yeah. Ten or twenty of 'em. And most of the people in post-op care want him to come around and give them the shot too, since a lot of them are still getting blood."

Jackie started to say something, then decided to hold her tongue. There was no reason to start alarming everyone. If John Brooks and Marcus Baghorn couldn't persuade Dr. Munch not to give his shots, or if they were unable to convince Richard Bellamy not to let it take place, there was probably nothing anyone could do. A private citizen calling the famous Dr. Munch a charlatan not only would probably not be listened to, but also get her sued, and maybe fired from her job.

Still, Jackie, even without Jake to back up her instincts, knew that there was something bad about these inoculations. But what to do? What to do?

While his mistress pondered, Maury hopped. Again and again, he threw his weight onto the thin slab of cement, finally causing giant cracks to form on the surface. Given a purchase for his nails, Maury started tearing chunks of concrete out of the slab.

"Maury!" Jackie yelled. "No!"

There was no stopping him now. Convinced that he was inches away from locating the miserable rodent who was tormenting the medical center's elephants, Maury's giant scoop-like paws dug down, down, down, and finally through.

"Arooof!" he yelled, falling headfirst into the septic tank.

Jackie, whose arm was nearly dislocated as she held onto the chain, was dragged across the parking lot. Bara Day managed to catch hold of her, and, together, the women were able to hold their ground for a moment. Then, slowly but surely, the force of gravity and the struggling of the big dog started to pull them closer and closer to the cesspool.

Suddenly, an elderly, stooped, pot-bellied Lone Ranger, Cyril Plum, another of Jackie's fellow instructors in the Communications Studies program, dashed out the Emergency Room door and grabbed onto Bara Day.

"Cyril!" Jackie exclaimed gratefully. "Where did you come from?"

"I'm here for a flu shot," he panted. "I saw you out the window and was about to come out and say hi, when I saw your dog go down. What the hell is he doing?"

Jackie shook her head. "God alone knows."

"You know what I can't understand," Bara said in her turn.

"What's that?"

"Who would be crazy enough to want to take this dog home with her?"

CHAPTER 11

Marcella Jacobs, warily following behind Kevin Erlanger, boarded the executive elevator and watched as he fitted a special key into the floor panel and turned the elevator on.

"Why did the administrator let you have a key?" she asked.

"To be honest," Erlanger answered, "he loaned me a key when I installed the current setup. He wanted the key back and I knew there would be a lot of adjustments to make over time. So, I made myself a copy."

The two stood silently for a moment. Then Erlanger gave Marcella a probing look. "You got something to say on that subject?"

"No," Marcella said quickly. "Seems perfectly sensible to me."

The elevator lurched to a stop.

"Penthouse. Everyone out."

Moving swiftly down the paneled hall, they reached the

end of the corridor, where, under a giant oil painting of a benevolent Mendel Marx, the walnut-stained double doors to Richard Bellamy's office lay.

While Marcella watched puzzledly, Erlanger reached up to a squawk box on the wall down the hall from the administrator's office. He threw a switch, cutting off the announcements calling emergency resuscitation teams to the intensive care unit and urgent pleas for Dr. Michalowski to please remove his Rolls-Royce from the ambulance lane. He then attached to it the length of cable he had brought up from his office.

"What are you doing?" Marcella whispered.

"You'll see," Erlanger said quietly. He stretched the cable down to a picture frame containing a heavily retouched portrait of the Marx-Wheeler medical staff.

Observing closely, Marcella saw that the left corner of the frame covered a small hole where a female connector from another cable lay waiting.

Moistening her lips, Marcella watched as Erlanger inserted the male end of his cable in the female hole and suddenly the voices of Linus Munch, Victor Kingston, Richard Bellamy, John Brooks, and Marcus Baghorn were heard. When the hubbub caused by too many people talking at once settled down, Marcus Baghorn could be clearly heard.

"Linus, listen to an old man."

"Pah," the doctor immediately responded. "Why should I listen to you? You're a Broadway flack, Marcus. This is strictly a medical decision."

"I am not a Broadway flack any more," Baghorn said with dignity. "I'm a teacher, and maybe you can learn something from me."

"I think not."

"Come on, Linus. Don't play high and mighty with me.

Twenty-five years ago you paid me to get you glowing tributes in the glossy magazines, bookings on interview shows, and invitations to events where rich people and busty starlets could fawn over you. You trusted me then. You can trust me now. I may have slowed down some, but I haven't gotten any stupider after another quarter-century in the business. This thing you're doing is crazy."

At that moment the sound cut off and Marcella saw that Erlanger had disconnected the sound cable. "Ready?" he asked.

Marcella was startled. "We're going in. Just like that?"

"We can, if we're quiet," Erlanger whispered. He inserted his key and slowly depressed the crank handle on the door. After removing her high heels, Marcella followed.

They slipped into the administrator's office. Immediately crouching in a shadowy area near the coat closet, Marcella saw that the men were actually seated around an enormous, oak conference table in an adjoining room.

Erlanger tiptoed over to a panel next to Bellamy's framed, North Dakota School of Medicine diploma and flicked a couple of switches. Suddenly, the face of Marcus Baghorn appeared on one of the three TV screens on the wall next to Marcella's head. She jumped as she heard Marcus Baghorn's voice coming at her from two directions at once.

"I don't understand what you're trying to do," Baghorn continued. "Testing this vaccine of yours here, tonight?"

"I should think it obvious," Munch answered portentously.

Marcella finally saw Erlanger signaling her frantically to turn down the volume. The newswoman found the lever and quickly depressed it so the words only came from one direction.

"I have been quietly working on a vaccine that may save some of these poor unfor . . ."

"Never mind the rhetoric, Linus," Baghorn snapped. "I ask you from a publicity standpoint, Dr. Munch, why tonight?"

"There is no real plan to my action, Marcus," Munch claimed disingenuously.

"Fiddlesticks!" Baghorn snapped. "You could have found as many willing volunteers in Colorado as you could here in Palmer."

"Very likely," Munch shrugged, "but I had to come here to lecture for my good friend John here at the university."

"Why here, Doctor?" Baghorn repeated insistently. "Why here? Why tonight?"

"Why not tonight?" Munch said finally.

"Where are the newspapers?" Baghorn demanded.

"The *Daily Chronicle* is on the way," Dick Bellamy answered.

"And I'm handling the TV coverage," Vic Kingston slurred.

Marcella bit her lip to keep from crying out. Of all the nerve! Not only was Vic Kingston going out into the field for a story, something he shouldn't have been doing without Ruben Baskette's okay (which Marcella knew he didn't have), but on top of that he was doing it in her face. Kingston had declined the opportunity to interview his old buddy initially, sticking Marcella with an assignment she hadn't really wanted. Then, as soon as the puff piece interview became a real story, Kingston had swooped down like a great gray gooney bird.

Kingston knew darn well that she was already on the scene. He could have known, if he had bothered to call the office, that Marcella had already passed up a story she had in the bag to do this one. Worst of all, Kingston hadn't even bothered to call her to gloat and tell her to go home, that he had the inside rail. It was almost as if the craggy old newsman wanted Marcella here for some reason. Marcella could only assume that it was to rub her face in it. Perhaps this would be Kingston's swan song—get one last story over the new kid, then quit—or retire.

If Kingston had come to her and asked for this one shot, Marcella would have gladly stepped aside. She would have even agreed to keep quiet and let others whisper that Kingston had outsmarted her. But no, this was a slap in the face, and she fully intended to stay where she was and maybe get in a few slaps of her own.

"I don't believe you," Baghorn snapped. "If you're here to cover the story, where's your camera crew? Why are you drunk?"

"Hell's bells," Kingston growled. "I've covered more stories drunk than you've got teeth in your head."

"I'm an old man, Mr. Kingston. If you're talking about real teeth, that's not saying much," Baghorn cracked. He had been trying to stay serious, for this really was a serious matter, but after a lifetime spent making wisecracks, it wasn't surprising this one slipped out.

"I'm an old man too, Baghorn," Kingston growled. "How about cutting me a break here? I've got one foot in the grave and another on a banana peel career-wise. If you must know, Dr. Linus offered, with a little bit of unsubtle prompting by me, to do this thing tonight and give me the story."

"That's not the only reason, Baghorn."

"No, Doctor?" the old publicist taunted him. "You have another top-secret reason for curing patients in the dead of night? Please, share it with the rest of us."

"You know, I resent your tone," Munch exploded. "Who the hell are you?"

Munch now addressed the other men in the room. "Who the hell is this man to come in here and question my motives? The man is a broken-down Broadway press hack."

"And you, sir, are a broken-down Nobel Prize winner," Baghorn replied.

"The last time this man was heard from," Munch continued, "he was telling the national press that the new play *Moose Murders* would run forever. Then, when he couldn't get another job in New York he came out here to Lower Slobovia to teach."

"I guess this is where all washed-up professionals come to teach then. Eh, Linus?"

"I resent that!"

"And I'm supposed to kiss your ring in gratitude for doing the same to me? The heck with you, buddy!" Baghorn said loudly.

Marcella smiled and checked the little recorder on her belt to make sure it was recording. Yes, indeed.

"You want to insult me for getting fired?" Baghorn continued. "What about you, Doctah? Isn't what's happening to you the same thing? I read in the papers that the government is cutting all programs it finds redundant or unnecessary. Which of the two are you, Dr. Munch? Redundant or unnecessary?"

"All right, all right," Richard Bellamy said as he pounded his desk with a bronzed rib paperweight, given to him by the head of pathology many years before at his bachelor party. "We said this would be a discussion—not a shouting match. Great Lucifer's horns, people. If I wanted to watch a shouting match I'd turn on *Tag Tream Wrestling*. Or go home to my wife."

Many of the men chuckled at this gratuitous swipe at the administrator's notoriously shrewish wife.

"Now, Mr. Baghorn, you have to understand that Dr. Munch is here as my guest."

"All right, all right." Baghorn threw up his hands. "Just answer my last question, Mr. Kingston. If you're here to film Dr. Munch's miracle demonstration . . . if this really is your last hurrah, where is your camera crew?"

"Well . . . downstairs," Kingston improvised glibly. "The tall, blond, seedy-looking fellow. He's my cameraman."

"Come, come, Mr. Kingston," Baghorn protested. "I have worked with your 'co-anchor person' and her crew on a half-dozen occasions. That man downstairs is Marcella Jacobs's cameraman."

"You come on," Kingston responded harshly. "Mr. Compton is an employee of KCIN. He works with *Miss* Jacobs because she is usually the first one out in the field. But he doesn't sleep in her drawer."

Bellamy guffawed at what he assumed to be a sexual allusion.

"When someone else needs him, he is assigned to other reporters. On a special occasion, like this one, an old duff like me can commandeer whoever the hell I want to help me get the story."

This last statement gave Marcella pause. While, under other circumstances, Vic Kingston would have trouble actually getting away with such a thing, tonight it was possible. With Ruben Baskette mad at her and needing to justify the day's expenditures, it was very possible that her cameraman could be stolen away from her. Unless . . .

Marcella stole over, clamped her recording device in an inconspicuous place as near to the conference room door as possible, then signaled Erlanger it was time to go.

Relieved to get out before he could be discovered, Erlanger held the door, locked it after they were both in the corridor and then walked briskly toward the executive elevator with Marcella. "Did you find out what you wanted to know?"

"Just that there is definitely a story here, somewhere," Marcella responded. "Could I use your phone again?"

"I guess. Who are you going to call?"

"The night shift," Marcella replied.

At the same time, outside in the Marx-Wheeler Emergency Room parking lot, Jackie, glowering madly and reeking of sewage, hosed down her big dog and muttered curses. Bara Day and poor Cyril Plum stood nearby with towels rented (at no little expense) from the hospital laundry.

"What are we going to do when we're finished with him?" Bara asked. "We stink almost as bad as junior here."

"I know. You could take off your clothes," Plum proposed. "I could hose you both off."

Bara responded with a look of feigned shock, and then a laugh.

"Cyril's a real ladies' man. You should read his books, Bara," Jackie commented as she turned off the hose. "*Joshua of the Jungle.* Just chockablock with steamy jungle sex."

"Where can I get these wonderful books?" Bara asked at once.

"Well, of course the barbarians have let them fall out of print, but I would be more than happy to give you an autographed original from my personal hoard if you care to stop by the old manse."

Bara and Jackie exchanged looks.

"Let's not beat around the bush, grandpa," Bara said, narrowing her eyes. "Are you coming on to me, or what?"

"I am indeed," Plum replied cheerfully. "Am I completely out of line?"

"Hell, no. You ain't no Ted Danson, but I ain't no Whoopi Goldberg so we're even. How's about Wednesday night?"

"I'll clear my social calendar. May I fix you dinner?"

"Can you cook?"

"My grilled shish kebab are spoken of with hushed reverence across two continents."

"No onions."

"They shall be permanently banned from my larder!"

"You got a deal, Jack. Hell, I'll even bring a bundt cake, if you want."

"I desire nothing more dearly."

Bara turned to Jackie. "He's kind of cute, ain't he?"

"Adorable," Jackie agreed.

"Ah, then," Plum teased. "Then you'll consider the idea of submitting to a good rinse."

Jackie laughed. "It might be a good idea. If we all had a change of clothes."

"Couldn't you borrow some scrub garments from the hospital?"

"We could try, I guess," Jackie answered dubiously. "Wait a minute. You know, I never did talk to Merida."

Bara and Plum exchanged blank looks.

"Never mind," Jackie responded quickly. "She's my neighbor who's looking after Peter. I started to talk to her before, but we got cut off. I better call her back so she won't worry. Would you dears do me another favor? Would you start toweling off the monster there? I know he doesn't deserve pampering, but I just want him to look good so Marcella will take him off my hands."

• • •

While Jackie went to look for her Fona-Dict, Marcella sat in the TV rental office and spoke on Kevin Erlanger's phone.

"I'm sorry to call you at the last minute like this, Ral. Listen. Do you want to make a few bucks as my cameraman?"

"Always," the perpetually impoverished young cinematographer responded.

"Good. Get down to Marx-Wheeler Medical Center as quick as you can. Meet me in the Emergency Room area. If you see Chris Compton, get the Panaflex from him. If you don't see him around, ask directions to the TV rental office. It'll be waiting inside for you."

"We're not going to film some car accident victim getting a baboon liver transplant, or something, are we?"

"No, I think we're just going to be filming some old fraud of a doctor giving people inoculations that are completely worthless."

"Sounds easy enough. Let me get my wheels."

"Ciao." Marcella slammed down the phone and gave Erlanger a look. "How do you like your first close-up view of the wacky world of TV?"

"It's . . . interesting," Erlanger allowed.

"Do we seem like horrible leeches feeding off innocent people's pain?"

"Not today, anyway," Erlanger replied.

"Good. Would you do me a favor? Would you stay here and help me coordinate things? I'll be glad to reimburse you."

"Sure. What the hell?" Erlanger commented. "It's a lot more exciting than renting TVs."

CHAPTER 12

Unable to persuade Linus Munch not to give his inoculations, and unsuccessful in their attempt to persuade Richard
Bellamy to cancel the publicity stunt, John Brooks and
Marcus Baghorn sadly followed the three inebriated Mus-
keteers into the executive elevator.

As the elevator descended . . .

. . . Outside, by the Emergency Room entrance, Jackie
picked up her Fona-Dict. She coded her own number and,
just as Merida picked up, an ambulance, sirens wailing,
pulled up.

Trying to get away from the noise, Jackie ducked into
the Emergency Room entrance. As she did, the loudspeaker started blaring, "Code 99, Coronary Care Unit.
Code 99, Coronary Care Unit."

Jackie stepped aside as a mustachioed central supply
technician started wheeling a squat code cart (which resembled somewhat a safe, with a series of drawers fastened

tight with plastic ties) out from behind the Emergency Room reception desk. He ducked into the page room and asked the dispatcher, "Where we going?"

"Mendel 512!" the page operator yelled out. "Mr. Westfall. The Latin teacher."

"Again?" The technician shook his head. "Too bad. Wonder if he knows how to spell *Requiescat in Pace?*"

Jackie approached the technician as he waited for the slow elevator. "Excuse me . . ." Suddenly she recognized the technician as someone who, pre-facial hair, had once been a regular fixture at the university. "Emilio? Emilio Donaldson?"

The tightly muscled technician looked up suspiciously. "Yeah, who are you?"

"Jackie Walsh." Seeing the man's uncomprehending look, she explained, "I teach at Rodgers. In the Communications Studies Department. I used to work with your friend Jonathan."

"Yeah?" Donaldson relaxed a little. "You didn't climb with him, did you? I never saw you out at the cliffs."

"No, we were just in the same department." Jackie didn't bother to explain how their association had ended, figuring it wouldn't endear her to the man's good friend. "I'm sorry to interrupt you. I know you're going on a code run, but did I hear you say you're treating Dean Westfall?"

"Yeah," the technician cautiously answered. "You know him too?"

"He's the dean of faculty at the university. Is he in really bad shape?"

"Well . . ." Donaldson indicated the code cart which did, after all, speak for itself.

"I see. Would it help if I donated blood or something?"

"Couldn't hurt," Donaldson replied noncommittally.

"He's not going to make it, is he?" Jackie asked, feeling guilty that she had never stopped in to visit him and now it might be too late.

"Guy's got a bad heart," Donaldson answered unsympathetically. "You never know, though. I've seen guys have five, six heart attacks and still walk out the door. They might have dropped dead a week later, but they wasn't complete invalids. Excuse me."

The elevator came and Donaldson wheeled the cart on. As the car whisked up out of sight, Jackie turned to see Marcella emerge from the TV rental office.

"Marcella!" she called out.

"Jackie!" the co-anchor called out. "I'll be with you in a minute!"

As the newscaster made a beeline for her sleepy cameraman, Jackie resumed her phone conversation. "Merida? Oh, hi. I'm sorry, dear. It's been a madhouse. How are you? Writing? Oh, good. Listen, can I ask you another in a whole series of terribly big favors? Okay, I owe you big time. Listen, I'm in a real fix. No, I'm not in jail—not yet, anyway. I'm at Marx-Wheeler. No, I'm okay. I've just been trying to pass off my crazy puppy to Marcella all day, and I've finally caught up with her. Problem is, he fell into a cesspool. It's a long story. We'll get drunk later and I'll try to do it justice. My favor is, will you go into my bedroom, and get me a change of clothes? Something casual. Then come meet me in the Emergency Room. Yes. No, I'm okay, honest. Just smelly.

"What? Oh, you don't have a car. Right. Well, call a cab. No, better yet, call Milly Brooks. Tell her John's stranded and needs a lift—which is sort of true. Because with you and Peter with me, there won't be room for John and his guest. Just between you and me, I am heartily sick and tired of doing favors for John's guest.

"Who is it? Dr. Munch. Linus Munch, the big shot from Colorado. Yes, I know he's supposed to unveil his magic formula tonight. Everyone's down here in the lobby now, lining up for it. Okay, Merida. Yeah. Gotta go. Bring a couple of old sheets too, will you? Thanks."

As Jackie signed off, Marcella tapped Chris Compton. Clearly thrilled to be dismissed, he shook Marcella's hand and split for the parking lot.

"I've never seen a guy so happy to go home to his wife," Erlanger commented.

"Maybe you've been hanging around the wrong married people," Marcella answered tartly. She pointed to the camera Erlanger held in his arms. "Do you really think you can operate that thing until Ral Perrin gets here?"

Erlanger's first response was a disgusted look. "I think I can manage, Ms. Jacobs. I did work my way through high school filming weddings, after all."

"Work your way?" Marcella asked, amused.

"I went to a private school," Erlanger said unapologetically.

"So did I," Marcella conceded, a bit of wistfulness creeping into her voice for the first time all evening. "A posh girls' school on the Main Line in Philadelphia. Didn't learn a thing, except," Marcella arched an eyebrow, "certain bedroom arts. How about you?"

"Just what are you asking?" Erlanger asked, surreptitiously raising the camera.

Marcella blushed. "I mean, did you ever learn anything in your private . . . boys' school, was it?"

"Boys' school. Yes. We went in boys and came out boys. And no, we didn't learn anything terribly practical." Erlanger then raised the camera to his eye and started shooting close-ups of the still slightly pink news-caster.

"What do you think you're doing?" she asked, half-turning away.

Erlanger reached out, lightly cupped Marcella's chin in his big strong hand, and gently turned her face back toward him again. "Practicing."

"Shoot some doctors," Marcella responded. "Or nurses. Or patients."

"I'd love to," Erlanger said at once. "But if I'm going to film somebody, it might as well be a knockout TV star like you."

"Stop," Marcella protested softly, pulling away. "I don't have any makeup on. My hair's a mess."

"And you look gorgeous," Erlanger said easily.

"You . . . shouldn't be flirting with me," Marcella claimed.

Erlanger let the camera droop. "Why not? Am I out of my league? The sexy TV princess would never consent to date the common little stable boy?"

"No, silly," Marcella responded, reaching out to gently touch Erlanger's hand. "I think you are very sweet, and very sexy, and I would love to go out with you sometime, but . . ."

"But?"

"I'm working," Marcella said simply.

"And you've got to put on your ice queen act to do your job efficiently?"

"I'm afraid so," Marcella answered directly. "If men can wear protective masks and clothing to do their jobs, why can't women?"

"I never looked at it that way," Erlanger admitted. "All right. Do your schtick. I'll be 'Kevin the Cameraman' until my relief gets here."

"Thank you, Kevin." Marcella looked fondly into Erlanger's face for a moment, then suddenly her expression changed.

"What is it?" he asked.

"It's your look," Marcella said critically.

"What's wrong?" Erlanger asked. "It's not right for a network cameraman?"

"No, just the opposite," Marcella responded. "You look just right. And that's a problem."

"It is?"

"Yes! Any second now Vic Kingston is going to come through that door and he's going to spot you and commandeer you on the spot."

Erlanger smiled uncomprehendingly. "Well, if he does, obviously I'll refuse."

"Of course you can refuse," Marcella said impatiently. "You don't work for the station. But then I've got to explain why I gave you the station's camera! No, we need a disguise so you look like you're just some camera nut recording the moment for posterity. Hm." Marcella considered for a moment. "You don't have a kimono, do you?"

"No, sorry. Wait a minute," Erlanger said suddenly. "I've got it!"

"What?"

"When the last chaplain quit, he left some stuff behind. I've got it in my office closet. Suppose I wear a cassock?"

"Perfect!" Marcella exulted. "Hurry!"

As Erlanger rushed off, Marcella turned and spotted her friend.

"Jackie!"

"Marcella!" The two women hugged as if they had never been so glad to see another person in their lives.

"How are you?"

"Miserable! And you?"

Marcella dropped her voice. "I think I'm in love."

"Really?" Jackie beamed, genuinely glad for her friend. "Who's the lucky fellow?"

"Gooner the Weather Monkey," Marcella replied straight-faced. "What's that terrible smell?"

"Me," Jackie admitted. "We had a little accident before."

"Yes . . . skunk?"

"Even worse," Jackie said.

"I should say," Marcella exclaimed, taking a step backward. "Do you know what you smell like?"

"The ladies' room at the bus station?"

"Even worse," Marcella replied. "More like the boys' room at a rowdy bar on Beer Night."

"How would you know?" Jackie grinned.

"I was a wild teen." All of a sudden, Marcella spotted Maury. "Oh, no. Look who's here."

The elephant mastiff pranced into the waiting room as if he were a dancing Austrian stallion.

"He's beautiful," Marcella exulted, turning to Jackie. "You washed him. You combed his hair."

"Heck," Jackie joked. "I'm even turning him over to you with a full tank of gas."

As if on cue Maury released a little love burst and Marcella fanned the air with her hand. "So you did."

At that moment Cyril Plum and Bara Day pressed closer.

"And here's the rest of the dog-grooming squad," Jackie said, by way of introduction. "May I present Bara Day, the famous python fancier, and Cyril Plum, the superstar-pulp-scribbler turned writing-instructor at Rodgers."

"Pleased to meetcha," Bara said at once.

"Charmed, dear lady," Plum said in his turn, tipping his straw boater.

"Nice to make your acquaintance," Marcella said automatically. "Uh, no offense, but I take it you guys are all wearing the same scent."

"That does it!" Bara said loudly. "Cyril!"

"Yes, dear lady?"

"Come with me!"

"To the ends of the earth. But where specifically?"

"Any bathroom will do. You and I are going to get this stink off our bones, then find some clothes to change into."

"Do you really think so?"

"Come on!"

As Bara and Plum left, Marcella opened her shoulderbag (which she had retrieved from Erlanger's cubicle) and handed Jackie a bottle of cologne. "Here."

"Thanks." Jackie started dousing herself. "I hope this isn't the real expensive stuff I'm splashing on. Maybe I would be better off just dabbing a bit of Lysol behind each ear. Thank you very much."

"No, thank *you*," Marcella corrected, bending down to hug her new pet. "For the most wonderful dog in the world."

Maury, delighted by an unaccustomed spasm of love (up to now he thought humans were only capable of fear, loathing, and disgust), licked Marcella with a warm drippy tongue.

"Aren't you cute?" Marcella asked.

Maury's vote was in the affirmative. Jackie, not wanting to queer the deal, held her tongue.

"You and me, big guy, are going to be a team from now on," Marcella announced. "What do you think about that?"

Maury barked so loud, every head in the waiting room turned. Maury smiled and winked at his new public.

"And from now on," Jackie contributed, "Marcella will be your mistress instead of me. All right, boy?"

Maury gave Jackie a blank look as if he were trying to place her face.

"Good dog!" the two women said together.

Just then, Erlanger returned in his cassock. Marcella noted with approval that the outfit fit the young TV technician very well. "Jackie, Kevin Erlanger. He's been nice enough to help me out."

Jackie, noticing the glance that passed between them, checked out Marcella's new love interest. She noted with approval Erlanger's strong resemblance to a young, dark-haired Dennis Quaid, and gave her friend an approving wink.

"I'm the guy who rents TVs here at the hospital," Erlanger introduced himself. And as Jackie took his outstretched hand, he added, "And you must sell perfume."

"No," Jackie smiled, giving the bottle back to Marcella. "I'm just a lady delivering this big galoot to his proud new mistress."

Marcella and Maury exchanged smiles. The newscaster's pupils actually dilated slightly as if she were beholding a baby. The dog stared back with goofy adoration.

"Well, I hope you're getting a good price for him," Erlanger commented. "He certainly is a handsome dog."

This compliment was almost more than Maury's great heart could bear. He immediately rose up on his back legs to his full six-foot height and prepared to give Erlanger the tongue kissing of his life. Unfortunately, Maury never got that far. Afraid the camera would fall, Erlanger withdrew. At the same time, Marcella grabbed her dog's paws and pulled him in her own direction. Adjusting quickly, Maury put his big mitts on Marcella's shoulders and gazed adoringly into her eyes. *Gosh, he sure loved his mistress! Could any dog be more loyal to any human being? No siree. Spot . . . !*

Jackie, trying to save a potentially embarrassing situation (and not wanting to get the blame for bringing a big dog into a hospital), came up with an inspiration and yelled, "Look, everyone. They're dancing!"

Patients, staff, and flu shot seekers alike all turned and laughed like loons.

Anxious to seem a good sport, Marcella started singing. "When we're out together—dancing cheek to cheek . . ."

The Emergency Room rocked with laughter, so much so that when Dick Bellamy made his announcement introducing Nobel Prize winner Linus Munch, no one heard a word he said.

The grumpy, half-in-the-bag researcher, as if nothing out of the ordinary was happening, pushed his way in.

"All right, everyone," the doctor announced. "I have only so much serum, so I will inoculate on a first-come, first-served basis. Line up, everyone. Don't be shy. No one ever died getting stuck with a little needle."

Taking advantage of Munch's appearance to distract everyone else, Jackie nervously helped Marcella lower Maury to the ground. He would have likely stood right back up if someone all of a sudden hadn't entered, shouting his favorite word.

"Pizza!"

As Maury bum-rushed poor Chubb Greenway, the air was rent with a shrill, sudden scream. It was Bara Day, and she didn't scream often. Bara only screamed, in fact, when she saw a Nobel laureate lying on the floor, after having been stabbed in the back.

No one saw it happen. All they saw was the blood staining the starched white back of the doctor's lab coat.

It seemed so unreal somehow—to see someone famous die before their eyes. As unreal, perhaps, as a dancing dog eating pizza, slice by slice—after first carefully removing every single anchovy.

CHAPTER 13

Officer Patricia Watson was the first on the scene. One of the reasons for this was that Richard Bellamy had cut off all outgoing telephone service (although this would not become apparent for quite some time) in order to keep patients and employees from phoning the tabloid shows to exploit their proximity to the place where a great man had been murdered.

Another reason for Patrolwoman Watson's entrance onto the scene was that she was just arriving in order to see if she could catch Victor Kingston in the act of speeding. It wasn't her fault, after all, that her motorcycle kept stalling and then finally died completely a good half-mile away from the Marx-Wheeler Medical Center. And so, panting and grimy from her effort, Patricia Watson finally burst into the waiting room and was confronted at once by Jackie Walsh.

"You!" she said. Had Officer Watson been French, likely she would have substituted, "*J'accuse!*"

"Officer Watson!" Jackie replied. "Here you are. Great. There's been a murder."

"There's going to be two murders in a moment," Watson growled, giving Maury a paralyzing glare.

"I'm serious," Jackie said earnestly, taking Watson by the elbow and leading her over to the body. "See for yourself."

Watson suspiciously followed Jackie to the cubicle where Munch had been setting up to give the inoculations, and finally spotted the sprawled physician, lying with his head toward the window, with a blue cap now placed over his face.

"Who put the shower cap on his face?" Watson asked at once.

"Dr. Bellamy," Jackie answered.

Watson looked around, taking in the Emergency Room cubicles, each screened with a shower curtain-like arrangement and asked, "Dr. Bellamy's on the staff of this hospital?"

"He's the chief administrator," Jackie answered, pointing to a flattering oil portrait of the doctor.

If Officer Watson felt any sense of shame that she didn't know the name of the millionaire supervising physician, she concealed it magnificently. "And someone called him when this fellow . . . ?"

Jackie avoided a blood spot on the tile floor and cheerfully supplied the victim's name, "Dr. Linus Munch. The Nobel laureate."

Watson nodded, again unimpressed. " . . . when this Dr. Munch was killed?"

"No," Jackie replied, careful not to brush against the nearby tray. She was amazed, as were most people who passed through the Emergency Room, at the way doctors and nurses left sharp blades and needles, some undoubtedly contaminated with a dire disease, lying on the flimsy plastic tray that could be easily bumped into or overturned. "They didn't have to. Dr. Bellamy was standing about five feet away."

Watson nodded a third time and then reached into her back pocket for her notebook and pencil. "You saw this with your own eyes?"

"Yes, Ma'am," Jackie responded. She wondered, idly, why police officers always took notes in pencil. Was it, she mused to herself, so that they could go back and erase incriminating evidence on the rare occasions when corruption hearings were held? "I don't suppose if I quickly told you everything I saw and everything I know, that you would let me just go home?"

Watson gave her a look. "No, Ma'am. No effing way."

Jackie nodded. It was just as she expected. "Worth a try anyway."

Watson looked around again, noting the lack of air circulation (which, she suspected, wasn't a great idea for a room full of sick people), and said, "Before I waste a lot of time—did you see who, uh, killed . . . ?"

"Stabbed, looks like," Jackie offered.

Watson irritatedly rubbed out the word with her eraser and snapped, "You a coroner?"

"I've seen stab wounds before," Jackie remarked.

Watson was more impressed than dismayed. "What, you in the war?"

"Researching stories for a TV series," Jackie elucidated.

Watson made a face. This interested her less. "What, *America's Most Wanted?*"

"*CopLady*," Jackie answered tersely.

Watson smiled slightly, dragging her memory back to the golden days when the air was clean, Nixon was president, and she was a size six. "I used to watch that show."

"It had a forty share in 1975," Jackie said automatically.

Watson gave Jackie a humorless glare. "I don't know what that means."

"It was a popular show," Jackie translated.

"Who gives a . . . ?" Watson caught herself just in the nick of time. Sensitivity training, now mandatory for police officers, had taught her that lashing out with an insult or an open-handed slap in the mouth was no longer considered appropriate in circumstances where perps or witlesses (as the police cheerfully referred to them) refused to stay with the issue at hand. "Never mind, Ma'am."

"Jackie," the film instructor reminded her.

"Jackie. Listen . . ." Watson grabbed a towel out of a bin and patted some perspiration off her neck. "I don't mean to be rude. Honest. I'm just tired and I want a few answers."

Jackie offered Watson a tissue, which was cheerfully accepted. "I understand."

Watson blew her nose and then asked, "Do you?"

"I not only wrote about cops," Jackie informed the cop. "I once dated a cop. For almost two years."

Watson, immediately competitive, asked, "You ever make him homemade donuts?"

"Do homemade cookies count?"

The officer shook her head with derision (an act, really, since Pat Watson liked homemade cookies as much as any policeperson), and commented, "Maybe that's why it didn't work."

Jackie shrugged. "Well, you set my mind at ease. I always thought Michael was fooling around because he wanted a woman with a better build."

"Hey, there's no secret to a better build," the overweight

but strong Officer Watson counseled. "You just gotta eat right and hit the gym five times a week."

"Can I hit the gym now?" Jackie asked.

"Don't be a wisenheimer," Watson warned. "My question was did you see the actual stabbing of Dr. Munch here?"

"No, I didn't," Jackie responded.

"But you were close enough to see where Dr. Bellamy was standing?"

"Yes, Ma'am."

As Watson continued her interrogation, she looked through the open drawers of the instrument cabinet, as if trying to find the murder weapon. "Where's this Dr. Bellamy now?"

"I think he went to his office," Jackie answered.

Watson wheeled to face her. "Do you know where that is?"

Jackie was absolutely unruffled. For once she was happy to let the police handle the investigation of a murder case. "I think it's right off the elevator on the fifth floor."

Watson, who had begun to take notes, pointed her pencil at the set of patient elevators to the right and opposite the Emergency Room entrance.

"No, actually there's a special elevator through that entrance"—Jackie pointed to her left and Watson carefully noted the fact—"and around the corner by the lobby florist's."

"Okay," Watson said wearily, shutting the drawer of the instrument cabinet, snapping a delicate ear-examining instrument in half. "We'll go there together after I get some statements from the people in the ER."

Jackie was a little taken aback. "You want me to go with you?"

Watson gave her a "what else?" look. "You know the way, right?"

"There are hundreds of people who could lead you to the administrator's office," Jackie reasonably pointed out.

Watson, having stowed her notebook, folded her arms and got a little huffy. "I don't know hundreds of people, Jackie. I know you. Plus, it's standard procedure when you're interrogating VIP's to bring along a witness. It cuts down on the lying, slightly."

"Okay, if you think it will help," Jackie agreed.

"Listen, Jackie," Watson began. "I know this is an imposition, but this is my first murder case."

"Congratulations," Jackie commented.

"Thanks for nothing," Watson replied, but not ungraciously. "Let's hope this is the last murder that ever occurs in Palmer so that none of us have to become involved again."

"Amen," Jackie said at once.

While Officer Watson was sealing off the crime scene with adhesive tape and ordering nurses to find a working phone (not realizing that Jackie had her Fona-Dict with her), Marcella Jacobs and Kevin Erlanger were outside, hiding by the toolshed around the corner from the Emergency Room entrance. While his mistress cowered, Maury took advantage of the opportunity to roll around in the grass, pick up some new scents, and, at the same time, give himself a good scratch.

"What are we doing now?" Erlanger asked. "Shouldn't we be inside, telling the police what we know, or investigating the murder or something?"

"In a minute," Marcella responded. "Look at those people over there." The newscaster pointed to a group of civilians heading for their cars. "They shouldn't be leaving now."

"Ah," Erlanger replied, unconcerned. "I don't think those people are murderers. They probably just came to the Emergency Room to have some problem taken care of and got ignored with all the excitement. They're probably trying to get to another hospital."

"How do you know?"

"Trust me, Marcella. If those people really were escaping because they were guilty of something, would they come out this way? There are eleven exits from the hospital. There's no way the police could have blocked them off already. If this was planned in advance, you got to believe they would have stashed their car somewhere and found another way out."

"I guess so," Marcella conceded reluctantly. "But just to make sure, get their plates as they're leaving. In fact, if you have tape left, get all the plates in this parking lot. It'll make it easier to track people down for interviews later on."

"Okay." As Erlanger walked away, Marcella considered her new big dog. "Maury! Come here, boy!"

The big dog tiredly shambled over.

"What's the matter?" Marcella asked. She put her hand on the mastiff's snout and found it to be warm and dry. "Are you sick?"

All of a sudden, the big dog's tongue rolled out of his mouth like a wide colorful roll of stamps. "Thirsty, huh?"

Maury nodded wearily. He didn't know what his beloved mistress was saying, he just knew he was thirsty.

"We'll get you some water in a minute." Marcella turned as she heard Kevin Erlanger approach. "All set?"

"I think so," the emergency cameraman responded with

a twinkle. "At least I remembered to take the lens cap off. Now what?"

Marcella, trying not to think about how attracted she was to the young man, answered, "Now we wait for Ral to arrive. Wait a minute. Here he is now."

Pulling into the parking lot, Ral Perrin turned off his loud tape deck and yelled, "Hi, Marcy. Am I late?"

Marcella looked nervously over her shoulder. "Well, the police aren't here yet. Kevin, give him the camera."

Erlanger did as instructed.

Maury suddenly banged into Marcella's legs. "Ral . . ."

"Yes, Ma'am," the polite young cinematographer responded (as soon as he had wrapped the camera up in an olive drab army blanket, which had once belonged to his father, and placed it securely on the passenger seat next to him).

"Do you have something to drink by any chance?"

Ral looked around and came up with a plastic 1.5 liter bottle of McKean Super Bubble Seltzer. "How about this? They're giving them away free with a fill-up."

"Perfect." Marcella snatched the unopened bottle away from the young man and immediately handed it to Kevin Erlanger. "Open this and give it to Maury, will you, Kev?"

Erlanger smiled at the casual use of his first name by the young woman with whom he was so smitten.

"We don't have a bowl, do we?" he asked.

Marcella turned back to the cinematographer. "Ral?"

"No, Ma'am."

"Then you'll have to bottle feed him," Marcella decided.

Erlanger looked into Marcella's eyes and pointed out, "After what he did to that pizza, I'm a little worried. He could take my arm off at the elbow."

"Use the left one then," Marcella suggested.

Although flattered that Marcella had remembered that he was right-handed, Erlanger protested, "Hey!"

"Kevin," Marcella teasingly pointed out, "what's the worst that could happen if he takes off your arm? You sue the station, the parent company pays you a million dollars to forestall bad publicity, and you get one of those neat new mechanical arms that does everything your old one does, plus has a cupholder and a secret compartment for quarters or breath mints."

"I hope you're kidding," Erlanger replied.

"I am. Now get to work." As Marcella turned back to Ral. "Now, as for you."

"I take it we're through filming inside the hospital?"

"Right," Marcella responded.

"So where to next?" Ral asked. "You riding with me or am I following you?"

"Actually, Ral," Marcella replied impatiently, "the filming's done. All I want you to do is . . ."

"Oh," Ral said at once, clearly hurt. "You don't really want a cameraman, right? You want me to be your delivery boy."

Marcella at once realized what she had done and apologized. "I'm very sorry, Ral. I wasn't trying to trick you. Honest. When I called you, I was waiting for something to happen and Chris was anxious to leave. I didn't think things would develop until you arrived, but they did and we had to improvise. Kevin ended up helping me out."

Erlanger looked up from where he was pouring soda water into Maury's mouth (a little at a time so the dog wouldn't choke) and nodded.

Ral gave the hospital employee a reluctant nod back.

"It's a long story. But the upshot is the man we were trying to film got murdered."

"On camera?" Ral asked, amazed.

"We don't know," Marcella answered honestly. "We hope so . . ." Then, realizing how that sounded, she explained, "I mean both for us, and for the police. Maybe it will help them make their case."

Erlanger gave Maury a "Yeah right" look and the big dog answered with a short bark before going back to his drinking.

"So what do you want me to do?" Ral asked, still a little grouchy.

"Copy the tape, first of all," Marcella instructed. "Then get the original back here. As fast as humanly possible, Ral. If the police find out we taped the incident, they'll want it right away. If they see an empty camera, I'm in big trouble. This is, after all, a murder investigation."

The reminder of this salient fact sobered Ral up considerably. He knew very well the touchiness the police often exhibited during the investigation of a murder since his father had been murdered the previous year.

"So, although your driving skill will be important," Marcella continued, "that won't be all you're doing. First of all, you're going to be given your full cameraman rate, plus hours earned."

Ral nodded his thanks. As disappointed as he was to have missed out videotaping the big event, he couldn't afford to blow off Marcella completely. The amount of money Ral earned as a cameraman was important because only after he had reached a certain amount would he be able to join the cameraman's union. The number of hours logged as a working cameraman would be important later to set his wage scale and to keep him near the top of the list of people sent out whenever a job came in.

"Okay, thanks." Ral started to turn the ignition on when Marcella grabbed his arm.

"Wait. You didn't let me finish."

"What?"

"After you get back here with the original tape," Marcella continued, speaking quickly, "I want you to go back to the TV station and view the tape. With an editor. Dan Sotkin. You'll have to call him at home. His number's on the contact sheet on the bulletin board—or in the phone book.

"The two of you will do a pre-edit. Presuming that the camera was pointing in the right direction, we should have something, but I don't know quite what. Now when you're looking at the footage, ignore the story that's on the beginning part of the tape. Don't erase it. We may need it later as a backup, or to pull faces and facades. But your main juice is the stuff in the Emergency Room as Dr. Munch comes down and gets stabbed.

"Cut for a 4.5-minute story. Try and find some 'when alive' footage on Linus Munch. Whatever we have in the library for now. Tomorrow we'll try to get some decent stuff from a Colorado station, depending on what I have to trade for it.

"Now understand, what you're doing is very important. Once I go in, they'll probably hold me here, maybe for a few hours, so I won't know what else we need until I talk to you. Maybe nothing will come out of all this, but if the footage is there and this story is aired and becomes a scoop or memorable moment, it will be a lot easier for me to get you some more work with the station."

"Gosh, that's very nice of you, Ms. Jacobs."

"Please. *Marcella.* Now go."

Ral started the car but Maury once more foiled the plan. Now rehydrated to an extent, the big dog regained both his energy and his powerful hunger for snacks. And so, smelling some ancient bit of roadkill on Ral's wheels,

Maury immediately clamped his teeth onto the treads of the right rear tire, causing it to go flat slowly.

Ignoring the barely audible howls of outrage from the parking lot, Patricia Watson passed among the two dozen or so people who still lingered in the Emergency Room.

"Thank you for your patience," she told them.

There were a few scattered titters.

"No pun intended. I know many of you want to go home. I know many of you are still waiting to be serviced here."

Patients exchanged looks at the unfortunate turn of the phrase.

"Those of you who are here for Dr. Munch's vaccine," Watson continued. "I'm afraid that's not going to happen."

"Why not?" asked the first on line, veterinarian Jason Huckle.

"Because, sir," Watson answered a little testily, "we don't know what's in the vaccine. For all we know it's something dangerous and that's why the doctor was killed."

Huckle, obviously peeved to have made the trip for nothing, continued, "Well, maybe we should try it anyway."

Jackie was shocked. "Jason. Really."

"Well, I'm sorry, Jackie," Huckle replied, a little embarrassed to be confronted with one of his clients in this context. "But we of the community are grasping at straws at this point. This isn't the flu, you know. This is a plague."

"Hey, this flu is nothing to joke about," Marcus Baghorn piped up. He had been sitting quietly to one side, waiting to be interviewed.

"Please," Watson said loudly. "We're not here to debate diseases. There is no vaccine. It has apparently disappeared. We are looking for it. If the vaccine surfaces, I will ask my superiors to get someone to test it. Right away. If it doesn't seem to present any sort of immediate danger, we will see if someone else in the hospital wants to distribute it. In the meantime, we are investigating a murder, folks. For all we know, Dr. Munch's murderer doesn't like people who want AIDS vaccines and will try to kill someone else. We can't take any chances until the murderer has been apprehended and put behind bars."

"That'll be the day," someone sang out.

Patricia Watson looked up, ready to read the riot act to some cop hater, when she recognized, standing in front of her, her former partner on the Palmer police force, now proudly wearing the uniform of the Marx-Wheeler security force, Muhammed Sanji.

"Muhammed!"

"Ah . . . infidel Patricia. How are you?"

As the two security professionals embraced, the crowd of onlookers was distracted by the sight of Stuart Goodwillie who stood in the doorway. Beside him was Georgiana Bowman in her wheelchair. Standing just behind his other shoulder was Evan Stillman, the armed-to-the-teeth bodyguard. Goodwillie made his presence known by banging his umbrella against the firebell several times. "Much as I hate to break up this meeting of the Furtive Fondlers Society . . ."

Muhammed immediately broke away from Watson and snapped to attention.

"You're the head of security, aren't you?"

"Yes, sir. Muhammed Sanji at your service, sir."

"Would that it were so. I would immediately order you to commit suttee."

"Beg pardon, sir?"

"Never mind. Bloody . . ." Goodwillie stopped himself just short of saying "wog," then continued, "It seems, *sir,* that one of the gun-happy security louts in your employ is under the impression that no one is to leave this Dickensian charnel house without permission. Are you the fellow who can authorize my leaving this hellhole or should I just spend my few remaining years wandering from one dank dark little office to another, trying desperately to find someone who cares whether or not this bleeding parlor is reduced by my lawyers to a pile of bedpans and moldering bandages? Hm?"

"The security guards are under my direction, yes," Officer Sanji announced. He turned to Officer Watson and heroically informed her, "I have sent someone to phone the station house. And I have put my staff at your full disposal, Patricia." What Officer Sanji did not say was that he fully intended to help Officer Watson solve the case without the bad publicity and interference that would be generated if he really had done what he had claimed and called the police.

"Why thank you, Muhammed," the policewoman beamed gratefully. "I was just circulating a clipboard on which I want everyone to write their names and addresses."

"Good thinking," Muhammed said quickly. "That will be very helpful later."

Goodwillie banged the steel tip of the umbrella on the highly polished floor. "Much as I hate to keep cutting in on your sickening orgies of self-congratulation, I demand to be allowed to go home!"

Officer Watson turned to Goodwillie and said bravely, "I am sorry, sir. I am conducting an official investigation here."

"You're investigating what?" Goodwillie demanded.

"Graft, criminal inefficiency, and corruption? I am sure you will find it everywhere you look. The only question is what took you so long. I fail to see how you're improving anyone's lot by shackling us all to leaky radiators while you fumble through years of hospital paperwork."

Goodwillie fumbled in his pockets for a toffee and was quickly given one by his ever faithful retainer.

"Young lady, let me put this baldly. I am a very important, terribly wealthy pillar of this community. Millions of freeloaders, including the stumblebums and butterfingered incompetents that run this meat factory, are entirely dependent on my goodwill and tax-deductible donations to survive. If I am not immediately given special treatment and allowed to exit this madhouse, I will raise a fuss that will be heard from Fairbanks to Honolulu. I will reduce this institution to a series of tarpaper shacks. I will have your jobs and order my minions to whip you naked through the streets of Palmer with a cat o'nine tails."

"Sorry, Mr. Goodwillie," Watson said, unruffled. "You'll just have to wait your turn like everyone else." She then handed the clipboard to the security chief. "Muhammed, would you make sure that everyone gives us their name and address and telephone number? I'd like to make an announcement over the public address system."

Jackie pointed out the door she had seen Emilio Donaldson enter and exit before. "It's right over there, Officer Watson."

The officer nodded, went in, and grabbed the microphone. "Hello, everyone. This is Officer Watson of the Palmer Police Department. We need your assistance in helping us to investigate a crime that occurred in the Emergency Room approximately thirty minutes ago.

"Everyone—that is, every patient, visitor, staff member—anyone who was in or around the Emergency Room from 8:45 to 9:15 this evening, please come to the Emergency Room right away. We will take your name and number and a brief statement, then let you go on your way. We're sorry for this inconvenience, but if we have full cooperation, we'll be able to wrap this thing up quickly."

"Who are you trying to kid?" Jackie demanded facetiously when Watson re-emerged.

"Everybody," the police officer said with a wink. She then asked loudly, "How's that clipboard coming?"

"Why, now that you ask," Stuart Goodwillie snapped, "I think it's sprouting roots and branches, we've been here so long. If you'll make some little attempt to carry out your duties and start taking statements, you'll find that I'm on top of the list."

"That's only because you had your friend cross out all the names of the people in front of you and write them again on the bottom of the list," Chubb Greenway complained.

"Quit your sniveling, boy," Goodwillie snapped. "Stillman, if this worthless pizza booby addresses me again, backhand him like a tennis ball."

"Yes, sir."

"Just one minute, Mr. Goodwillie!" Officer Watson yelled. "You're way out of line here."

"You better watch your butt, Watson," Evan Stillman warned. "Mr. Goodwillie has powerful . . ."

"Not powerful enough to save your job with the department, Captain," Watson pointed out. "Now, Mr. Goodwillie. If you don't stop your shenanigans, I'm going to haul you downtown as a material witness."

"Please, Stuart," Georgiana added, trying to quiet the bottled water baron. "Why don't you just look upon this terrible calamity as an example of fate giving us some additional time to sit and talk with each other?"

"But, dear lady." Goodwillie's tone immediately became that of the considerate courtier. "I've only been hurrying these clods because I promised to escort you to your door—where I was hoping, I am embarrassed to say, for the tiniest of goodbye kisses."

"Sit, silly." Georgiana, more like a schoolgirl than she had been in seventy years, went on to explain, "It doesn't matter now, dear. The nursing home won't allow any comebacks after nine P.M."

"What? The dastards!" Goodwillie fumed at the cruelty of his beloved's keepers. "Do you they think the moment a person becomes sixty-five he or she must be treated like a child again? Why shouldn't a resident be able to stay out late and raise a little hell every once in a while?"

"Now, Stuart," Georgiana smiled indulgently. "I assure you, most of my fellow tenants are more than ready for bed by nine P.M."

"That's because they've been brainwashed," Goodwillie snapped. "Drugged to the teeth, bored silly—put a chainsaw in their hands and they'd hack off their own limbs if told to. But take those same people, give them something to do, let them go out at night and see a show or attend a nightclub. They'd live years longer. And it's not as if the nursing homes are doing you any favors. You're paying for twenty-four-hours-a-day service. Why shouldn't you get it?"

"You're a very sweet man," Georgiana pointed out. "Do you know that?"

"Yes, I do," Goodwillie smiled. "Those people who think I'm a crochety old tyrant don't know the real me."

"Oh, Stuart."

"Say the word, dear Isolde, and I shall buy the place and fire those jailkeepers. Good gravy. What am I saying? Firing's too good for them. We'll rig some sort of negligence suit. Yes, that will do nicely. My professional witnesses can convince a jury of anything you might want to name. We'll take them for every cent."

"You do know the way to a woman's heart, don't you, Stuart?" Georgiana said, hugging her ardent suitor's arm. "Why don't we talk about it later? After all, I have to find a hotel room now."

"Nonsense," Goodwillie exclaimed, adopting a heroic Woodrow Wilson attitude. "I have the largest mansion on the lake. You may have any one of thirty-seven bedrooms. Needless to say that number includes my own."

"Stuart, really," Georgiana said, discovering that her blushing mechanism still worked.

Taking advantage of the distraction that had most of the Emergency Room occupants eavesdropping on the elder couple's every word, Patricia Watson grabbed Muhammed Sanji's arm. "Listen, Lion."

Muhammed smiled from ear to ear. He loved to be called "Lion."

"You have some kind of security camera system, right?"

"Of course," the Indian security chief nodded. "The average patient is worth seven hundred dollars to us. We can't have them just running out the door without paying. The cameras aren't in that great a shape, though." Muhammed pointed to a corner camera, thick with dust and dappled with small spider webs.

The Palmer policewoman (originally from the Bronx in New York City) nodded and looked around. "You don't have . . . let's see . . . Jackie, would you do me a favor, hon, and move to where Dr. Munch was standing when he got stabbed?"

"Sure," Jackie said agreeably. Like Stuart Goodwillie,

she was trying to finagle an early send-home from this murder, which, for once, she had absolutely no interest in trying to solve.

When Jackie was in position, Watson turned to the hospital security chief. "Is there a camera that covers that spot there?"

"Hm." Muhammed took a small folder from an inside jacket pocket and flipped through the schematics. "No, it appears not."

"All right. Take me to your surveillance area. I'll tell you what angles I want and you pull the tapes from that half-hour period."

"Delighted to help, Patricia," Muhammed said at once.

As the former partners started to leave, Watson yelled to the security man being left to guard the Emergency Room exit, "You!"

"Hidalgo Rojas, Ma'am!"

"Mr. Rojas. No one in or out until I get back. When I return, I'll start seeing the witnesses, one at a time, starting with Jackie Walsh."

The film instructor turned to the glass door opposite where she was standing to give herself a secret, grinning thumbs up. Then, all of a sudden, she saw—now locked out of the hospital—her son Peter, her neighbor Merida, and her faithful dog, Jake.

CHAPTER 14

As Marcella (her face black with grease), and Ral (his face white from road chalk), searched the truck for packets of wash and wipes, Maury trotted about, happily belching. He was investigating the other rear tire when Kevin Erlanger, sweating as he tried to make the hubcap fit the spare, called out, "Marcy!"

Marcella immediately picked up the jackhandle and waved it in a threatening manner. "Maury, you come anywhere near that tire and I'll brain you one!"

Maury immediately pouted and felt hurt. *Why did his mistress have to take that tone with him? Everyone took that tone with him, come to think of it. How unfair it was. How could they be so disloyal to him?*

"All right," Erlanger said, straightening up. "You're all set. But try to avoid going over any railroad tracks."

"I'm off like a herd of turtles," Ral responded.

"Wait!" Marcella caught Ral's arm. "Wait a minute."

"Why? What's wrong?"

"I've been thinking," Marcella said slowly. "Maybe it isn't a good idea to go back to the studio."

"What's the matter?"

"I'm just thinking of our masters," Marcella responded. "It occurs to me that they would cave in in a minute if the police called up to subpoena the tape. They wouldn't care if we hadn't finished editing the spot or not. They'd just as soon kill the story as offend any of the town fathers."

"So I'll get it duplicated at an outside film developing place," Ral countered.

Marcella gave Ral a look. "Think, junior. What's the only place like that open this time of night?"

"Quickie Flick," Ral said at once.

"And who owns Quickie Flick?"

Ral moaned, "Oh. The same people who own KCIN!"

Erlanger tried to scrub his forearms with an already dirty rag. "We better get back, Marcy. They'll have security seal off the building soon and we'll be doing some explaining as to where we were all this time."

"I know," Marcella said impatiently. "Listen, Ral. We need another place. Do you know anyone offhand who has an off-line machine?"

"Hey," Ral protested. "My roomies can barely afford VCRs."

"Damn." Marcella rubbed her eyes. "Who do I know who has an off-line machine? One person, Vic Kingston, and he's not likely to loan it to me. Where is he, do you think?"

Victor Kingston was above Marcella, at the window of a patient's room on the third floor, peering down at her through venetian blinds. So, he thought to himself. She got some film after all. Kingston recognized the young black kid as a cameraman Marcella used sometimes. *What*

had she caught? Anything incriminating? It didn't matter,
the veteran newsman thought to himself. His long-planned
murder of Linus Munch had been perfectly foolproof.

All of a sudden, Kingston heard noises in the hall. He
ducked down next to the bed of the terminal patient whose
room Kingston had chosen beforehand, precisely because
its only occupant was unlikely to raise a hue and cry.
Suddenly the man's eyes snapped open and the newsman
found himself pinned in the stare of the dying Dean B.
Crowder Westfall.

"What are you doing here?" the corpse-like man
croaked.

Kingston bit his lip to keep from crying out. "I'm . . .
avoiding the hospital security," he admitted.

Westfall nodded, the smallest of gestures, and raspishly
asked, "What did you do?"

"It's a long story," Kingston growled.

"I'm not going anywhere," the elderly academic pointed
out.

And so Victor Kingston told him everything.

CHAPTER 15

As she waited for Patricia Watson to return, Jackie sat next to Marcus Baghorn. "Say hey, kid. What do you know? What do you say?"

The old man nodded slowly. "Cagney. Very good. But can you do O. Z. Whitehead?"

Jackie smiled. "I don't think so."

"So where's the family?" Baghorn asked, carefully unwrapping a roll of Lifesavers.

"You saw them? They were only outside for a minute."

"You spend a lifetime in dark, smoky nightclubs trying to accidentally run into columnists, you develop good eyes."

"They're going to a phone to call me."

"I thought the phones went out in the hospital?"

"My phone works fine," Jackie said.

Marcus looked at the black leather case on Jackie's belt. "Shouldn't you use it to call for another herd of policemen?"

"Oh . . . I guess so. The truth is," Jackie admitted, "I'd rather not get too involved. Let the police handle this one. I just want to go home."

Marcus sighed and looked at his watch. "I guess I can understand that, *gevalt*. I wonder how Fred is doing?"

"We should go up and see him," Jackie proposed, without any real intention of doing so.

"Absolutely," Marcus confirmed. Of course he had no more intention of visiting Fred than Jackie did. The truth was the veteran cinematographer, normally a big, bluff backslapper with a booming voice that could be heard throughout the Longacre Communications Building, turned into a bit of a crybaby whenever he had one of his lumbago episodes.

"Fred really is a wonderful guy," Jackie tried again.

"Helluva guy," Baghorn confirmed. "Unless of course you've met a lot of people."

Jackie slapped Baghorn on the forearm. "Really, Marcus. The poor man is trussed up like Donald Sutherland in *Johnny Got His Gun*. The least we can do is say kind things about him."

"Who said different?" Baghorn demanded. "I think Fred Jackson should be stuffed with gold and patted on the back for being a whale of a male. But what do I know? I'm an old Jew who smokes cheap cigars. As the late Dr. Munch pointed out recently, I was stupid enough to think *Moose Murders* would run forever. God knows I'm not a Frankenstein genius."

"Einstein," Jackie corrected automatically.

Baghorn grabbed her wrist and gestured significantly. "Einstein! That's another story altogether. I assume you're talking about Harry Einstein. Called himself 'Parkyerkarkus.' Eddie Cantor's stooge."

"Parkyerkarkus? For real?"

"What's the matter? You don't show your students Eddie Cantor's fabulous musicals?"

"I remember *Roman Scandals,*" Jackie replied. "Was he in that one?"

"Eddie Cantor? Oh, sure. A Sam Goldwyn production. His real name was Goldfish, you know?"

"Eddie Cantor?"

"Sam Goldwyn. He stole his corporation name. Sam once had a company with Edgar Selwyn. They combined their names to make 'Goldwyn.' Now *that* man was a real nut."

"Sam Goldwyn?"

"Edgar Selwyn. Those powerful types always have a little screw loose. David Merrick, with his voodoo dolls. James Aubrey, 'The Smiling Cobra.' That man frightened sewer rats when he was angry. And Michael Todd—he would blow his stack and start hurling coffee. Remember, Jackie. When bigwigs go, they take people with them."

"Michael Todd threw scalding coffee on people he didn't like?" Jackie asked. She didn't know where this was going, but Marcus Baghorn had seen a lot in his day, and she always found listening to him an educational experience.

"Well, Todd wasn't organized enough to actually throw coffee *at* somebody. He'd just throw it up in the air. It'd land on me, it'd land on you, it'd land on Todd. Everywhere there were coffee stains. When he was married to Joan Blondell, it wasn't so bad. Very easygoing lady. Didn't mind a bit of coffee every now and again. Especially if she had a piece of strudel or a danish to go with it.

"Elizabeth Taylor, now that was a different kettle of herring. This woman, who marries and divorces every two years, is not a woman you take wacky chances around. She would wonder why her houseplants died. It was all those coffee showers. Yet she loved that crazy son of a gun."

Jackie smiled at the older man's vision of great romance. "And now that you've been married for almost a year, how are you and the former Ms. Pummer getting along?"

"I love her like Elizabeth Taylor loved Michael Todd."

"That's nice. Could I ask you one more question?"

"Anything, Lambchop. This body was built for talking."

"What did you see when you came down with Linus Munch? Really."

"I thought you weren't interested in this murder?" Baghorn pointed out.

"I'm not, I'm not," Jackie lied.

"Good, then we'll change the subject."

"Fine."

"How would you feel about Polly Merton coming back as Communications Studies secretary?"

"Oh, no. Really?"

"I'm afraid so," Baghorn said with a sigh. "It seems there's just no one else available to replace Ms. Zwieback. Now of course, thanks to your friend John Brooks, Ms. Merton is available again."

"Well, is it any wonder, Marcus?"

"I know. A pleasing personality she don't got. But the truth is, Mrs. Baghorn wants to come back to work. And of course, organized, she's not. So I figured if we used my little melancholy baby as the receptionist, and Miss Merton as the office coordinator behind the scenes, it might work."

"Will they get along?"

"Mrs. Baghorn and Ms. Merton are old friends."

"They are?"

"Sure, sure," Baghorn assured the amazed young film instructor. "Polly's a great gal outside of the office."

Jackie looked up and noticed John Brooks emerging from the corridor. He smiled at the sight of his friends. "Hello."

"Where have you been?" asked Jackie.

"With Officer Watson and the security fellow, looking at surveillance videotapes."

"Are they going to help?" Jackie asked.

"It would be a miracle," Brooks answered frankly. "Not only is their equipment cheap and poorly maintained, but they've been re-using the same tapes for the past six months. There's barely a schmear of emulsion left."

"What, they put cream cheese on videotape?" Baghorn joked.

"It may come to that," Brooks rejoined. "Anyway, I've offered my lab facilities, but if they're expecting *Rising Sun*–type miracles, they're crazy."

"All right!" Jackie said loudly. "I can't stand it anymore. Who saw what?"

"Well . . ." Brooks started.

Then, all of a sudden, Jackie's Fona-Dict started buzzing.

"Saved by the buzz!" Baghorn crowed.

As Jackie started to answer her call . . .

. . . Marcella, Erlanger, and Ral figured things out in the parking lot.

"I've got it!" Ral said suddenly. "I'll take it to the university and copy it there. They've got all the equipment we need. I could even call that editor guy . . ."

" . . . Dan Sotkin."

" . . . And have him meet me at the university. We can do a rough edit there."

"Perfect!" Marcella exclaimed. "Give me five."

Ral obliged, slapping his palm against her own.

"Give each other five," Marcella then instructed the two men.

The men obliged.

"Great! Now Kevin, give me a big kiss."

"What?" asked the amazed TV renter.

"Come on, don't be coy," Marcella rushed him. "I'm the busiest woman in Palmer and I don't have time to pussyfoot around. Pucker up."

Erlanger obliged and the two kissed almost as long as Valeria Golino bussed Paul Reubens in *Big Top Pee-Wee*.

"All right!" Ral applauded.

"Not bad at all," Marcella admitted, reluctantly pulling away.

"Wow," gasped Erlanger.

"One problem," Ral said.

"With kissing him?" Marcella asked, immediately worried.

"No, with me getting into the Longacre editing room," Ral explained. "I'll need a key from one of the co-chairmen."

"How about asking Jackie for her key?" Marcella suggested. "She was in the Emergency Room the last time I saw her. We can get it in two minutes."

"NG," said Ral reluctantly. "Ever since that guy got iced in the editing room . . ."

Ral referred to the demise of former Rodgers University Communications Studies chairman Philip Barger.

" . . . they changed all the locks. Jackie wouldn't have the key I need. Only Fred Jackson and Marcus Baghorn."

"Hm!" Marcella considered. "What about a security guard?"

"Ever since Mr. Hopfelt got killed, they've been more careful about handing out master keys."

"All right. Who should we approach?"

"Well," Ral mused. "I would say Mr. Baghorn would be the harder of the two."

"Really?" This surprised Marcella. "I've worked with Marcus Baghorn a few times. He's always struck me as a cuddly George Burns type."

"He's a nice guy," Ral confirmed. "Always talking. Always telling you stories. But he's tough too. You can't walk all over him. I'd have to tell him everything. And he may not go for it."

"You're right," Marcella confirmed. "Like it or not, he has to remember that he's an acting co-chairman now, and if this explodes in our faces, Rodgers U will get a whole heckuva lot of free publicity. What about Fred Jackson?"

"Call him Mr. Big, and he'll sign anything you put in front of him."

"My kind of guy. Where can we find 'Action' Jackson?"

"Right over there," Ral answered, pointing to the hospital. "He's in the traction ward with a bum back."

"Great," Marcella said happily. "If he doesn't cough up, we'll just tighten the ropes a little."

Ral and Erlanger exchanged looks at the newswoman's casual sadistic streak, but said nothing as Marcella called out, "Maury!"

The big dog, still a little dry, bounded back over.

"Hi, Maury," Marcella said in as cheerful a voice as she could manage.

Maury immediately nuzzled her hand, breaking two fingernails and bending a ring which had been in her family for generations.

"G . . . good dog," Marcella forced out. "Want to go back in the hospital and find a nice porcelain bowl to drink from?"

Maury wasn't quite sure what Marcella was proposing, but he was a good-natured lug, so he barked, "Sure!"

"Good dog. Let's romp, boy!"

When Officer Watson finally returned to the Emergency Room, she was perfectly willing to take Jackie first. However the film instructor was still on the phone. Watson therefore waved for Baghorn to accompany her into the research library, which the police officer was using as her interview area.

"Wait!" Jackie said too late. "What? No, Peter. I'm not talking to you. I was just going to talk to the policewoman. No, you don't have to hold. She just left with someone else. Just hope she takes your mother next. I don't want to sit here like a jade buddha all night. What? Oh come on, Peter. Since when did you become politically sensitive? Put on Merida, will you?"

As Jackie waited, John Brooks tapped Jackie on the knee.

"What?"

"I'm going down to the cafeteria to sit with Milly and the kids. Here's my beeper number." Brooks handed her his business card. "Call me when they want to talk to me."

"Hello?" an older, somewhat scratchy Thelma Ritter voice came on the phone.

"Just a minute, Merida," Jackie said quickly. "John!"

The science chairman turned back halfway.

"Would you do me a favor?"

He nodded yes.

"When you come back up, would you bring me a hot chocolate and a couple of blueberry muffin tops?"

"Sure," Brooks said (immediately deciding he would have a couple of those muffin tops too). *What a good idea,* he thought to himself, *dispensing with the bottom of the muffin. When,* he wondered, *will they come out with pizza tops?*

Then, having soothed her stomach with the promise of future succor, Jackie resumed her conversation. "Merida. Sorry."

"That's okay," she said. "I'm always comfortable in a bar. We're watching *I Confess* on my portable VCR. What a good little film and one of the few Hitchcocks that doesn't suffer on a postage stamp screen. Did you ever see it?"

"Many times," Jackie answered. "I used to sit up and beg for Montgomery Clift."

"Well, if you like that type."

"Tall, dark, and handsome?"

"Twisted, tortured, and homosexual."

"Well," Jackie shrugged. "As Joe E. Brown used to say, 'Nobody's perfect.' Let me speak to Jake, will you?"

"Of course."

The moment Jackie heard the friendly breathing of her beloved German shepherd, a sense of calm happiness broke over her like a warm wave.

"Hello, boy. How are you? Do you miss me?" Jackie smiled at Jake's guarded but still affectionate growls. She thought the fact that the dog found public displays of affection to be in slightly bad taste adorable.

Merida came back on the line. "Listen," Jackie said, "I need you and Jake. I'm in the Emergency Room. You know, the area where the ambulances drop people off. With the sliding doors. Remember? The problem is, the doors are locked and there's a big . . ."

Suddenly the air was split with an angry shout. "Siddown!" the security guard, Hidalgo Rojas, bellowed. "Siddown and shut up! You don't wait your turn, maybe someone will murder *you!*"

" . . . big and *mean*," Jackie amplified, "security guard. So you'll have to create some kind of disturbance. Get him to come out and then slip by him and meet me inside."

Merida repeated the plan, and Jake's snort and staccato bark in the background let Jackie know that it was a piece of cake.

"See you soon. Bye, Jake," she said, hanging up.

Just then, Bingo Allen, standing nearby, slid into Baghorn's vacated seat and said, "Say . . ."

Jackie laughed. She had told the lantern-jawed reporter long ago that he reminded her of Charles Lane. "What do you know? What do you say?"

"Was that your dog you were talking to?"

"Absolutely," Jackie smiled playfully. "And don't ask me how he does it, but Jake always knows what I want and does his darnedest to give it to me."

"Terrific. I wish I had a girlfriend like that."

"Dream on."

"So what have you found out so far?" Allen asked, taking out his notebook.

"I'm not here in my unofficial capacity as amateur sleuth," Jackie said haughtily. "I just happened to be here when the good doctor was killed. I'll do my duty as a public-spirited citizen, tell the police what I saw, and then go home."

"Yeah, right."

"I'm serious."

"Jackie, why did you solve all of those other crimes? Because you wanted to get a murderer off the streets of Palmer before he killed someone you knew, right?"

"I suppose so."

"Well, not all the facts are in yet. But it doesn't look like someone followed the doctor here from Colorado. So it looks like there is another murderer on the loose and if you don't solve it, we're down to the police—and nutcases like your neighbor Alice Blue."

Despite herself, Jackie laughed. She wouldn't necessarily dismiss Palmer's nosiest housewife as a nutcase, but it was true that Alice, despite her best efforts to steal the good words and publicity that Jackie had gotten by solving crimes before her, had been fairly ineffectual so far.

"I'm sure the police will solve the case without me, Bingo. One of the reasons I was somewhat helpful in solving the other cases was that I often knew the victims better than the police. I was able to follow up some sort of insight I had that the police weren't necessarily privy to. In this case, I didn't know Dr. Munch, and don't have any more idea of why he was killed or who did it than the next person."

"Are you sure this isn't just a matter that you didn't like Dr. Munch and so you don't want to go out of your way to solve his murder?"

"How did you know I didn't like Dr. Munch?" Jackie asked. Immediately the amateur sleuth extraordinaire felt like biting her lip. Of course he hadn't known and was just making a lucky stab, but now Jackie had given herself away.

"Thank you very much."

"Now listen, Charles Allen."

"With both ears and a hidden microphone, Ms. Walsh."

"I am not involved in this case, and I resent you mousetrapping me into making statements about a man I barely knew. Yes, I met him once, this afternoon, not under the greatest circumstances, and didn't particularly care for him. That's not news, and I'm telling you now that if you smear my name and picture all over the newspapers on something as silly as that, I will never cooperate with the press again on anything.

"In addition to not wanting my life disturbed with everyone calling or writing me to bawl me out or give me suggestions on how I should solve crimes, I'm tired of being a target for murderers. I've had my house broken into, my dog was stabbed, I was hit on the head, and my child was terrorized. The more you put me in the papers, the worse it gets. You're the one that's supposed to be the investigative journalist. Why don't you try to solve this one?"

"Okay, I will. How should I go about it?"

"None of that," Jackie said. "I don't have any ideas. I don't *want* to have any ideas. I just want to go home, take a nice long bath, have a bite to eat, and go to bed. Understand?"

"Sure," Allen said at once. "You're just lulling the murderer into a false sense of security."

As Jackie lunged for the reporter . . .

. . . Down in the parking lot, Marcella looked at a perspiring Ral Perrin and gave him one of her few remaining tissues. "You said a mouthful."

Kevin Erlanger, picking up the video camera he had carefully put to one side, wondered, "What the heck is so interesting about that toolshed, anyway?"

"I don't know," Marcella said wearily, running her fingers through her now utterly lifeless hair. "Jackie said something about him doing the same thing earlier. In fact, watch out for an open cesspool somewhere."

"Whoa!" Ral shouted. "I almost stepped into it."

"Don't do that!" Marcella cried out. "Okay, listen. We don't have to all stick together. Especially if things are heating up inside. Kevin, you work for the hospital, you can go in probably without too much trouble. So go to your cubicle and stash the camera somewhere. You said you have access to a VCR, right?"

"Right," Erlanger responded. "They use them for conferences. Also, I have a couple of 'play only' VCRs I've tucked away to rent to high rollers. I keep that kind of low-key, though, because we've had trouble with people stealing them."

"Good. Then I assume you have videotapes?"

"A few."

"Get a blank one, if you can. Put this sticker on it." Marcella reached into her bag and pulled out a peel-off KCIN logo sticker. "Play dumb if they ask you about it. Tell them I asked you to run the camera, and maybe you forgot to turn it on or accidentally erased it. Whatever. If they give you a hard time, blame it all on me. Say I must have switched the tapes when you weren't looking."

Erlanger made a face.

"What's the matter?"

"I don't want to get you in trouble, Marcy."

"Don't worry," Marcella instructed. "The network's got lawyers and they love to try First Amendment cases. It gives them the illusion of respectability."

"All right. The truth is," Erlanger explained sheepishly. "I don't want to get into trouble either."

"Of course you don't," Marcella agreed, understanding completely. "It would just be nice if the police didn't know what Ral and I were up to for an hour. I'm hoping they're so involved talking to other people that they don't even get to you in that time. But if they do, try to stall them by telling them only a little at a time. Tell them what happened in the ER, but try not to mention the part about us going out into the parking lot and talking to Ral. In fact, try to keep Ral out of it completely if you can. He's obviously not involved in the murder."

"We don't know that," Erlanger pointed out reasonably. "He could have killed Doc Munch, gone out another way, and drove up as if he didn't know anything about it."

"Kevin, thanks for playing devil's advocate, but could we save it for another time? My point is, I don't want them to run out to Rodgers U and scoop up Ral and my videotape before he can copy and edit it. At least not for a few hours. So if you have to answer questions about the videocamera, put it all on me. I stashed the videocamera without your knowledge. If they notice we switched the tape—I must have done it. If they ask you where I am— you have no idea. Okay? We have no previous connection. They won't suspect that you'll lie for me."

"How do you know I will lie for you?" Erlanger asked softly.

Marcella looked deeply into the young man's gold-flecked eyes. "You will, won't you?"

"Of course I will," Erlanger replied.

"Thank you." The couple considered kissing again, but a mighty belch from Maury interrupted them. Having broken his leash and eaten most of the two pieces, Maury was feeling dyspeptic.

"What are we going to do with him?" Ral asked.

"Have you got a rope in your car?" Marcella asked.

"I'll check," Ral promised.

"Anything you can use as a temporary leash. Hopefully it'll last longer than the last one."

As Ral rushed to do Marcella's bidding, the hoarse-voiced reporter turned back to Kevin Erlanger. "Remember, the only thing I'm asking you to hold back until the last possible second is anything about Ral. Tell them I'm still in the medical center if you have to, but don't mention Ral."

"Okay."

"Thanks, Kevin."

"You can thank me later."

"I will," Marcella promised. "Here."

"You're giving me a souvenir KCIN notebook?"

"Don't be a wise guy," Marcella ordered. "Write down your extension. Stay by the phone if you can."

"I'll write down the page operator, too. If you don't get me, call her. I'll have left a number where I can be reached, or she'll page me over the loudspeaker. I'll claim I have a pregnant sister or something."

"Good." Marcella leaned over and kissed Erlanger on the cheek. "Thank you again."

Erlanger nodded and shuddered to think he might be falling in love.

Ral returned.

"Did you find something?" Marcella asked.

"Just jumper cables," Ral announced.

The trio laughed and Marcella said, "They will have to do." In a moment she had attached the cables to Maury's collar and in two moments the playful mastiff had run around his three pals, tying their legs together and causing them all to fall on him in a heap.

"He's cute, isn't he?" Marcella forced out.

Ral and Erlanger took the Fifth on the matter.

CHAPTER 16

Inside the medical center, Officer Patricia Watson was still in charge of the investigation. Jackie, summoned by Sanji, stood in the doorway watching Marcus Baghorn wearing down the rapidly tiring Watson with one of his famous monologues.

"So you see, I'm more or less in charge of Communications Studies while Fred is recovering from his steady cam injury."

"I don't know what that is," Watson snapped.

"A large camera," Jackie explained. "With a gyroscope. It's for doing subjective shots. The 'Friday the Thirteenth'–type nonsense."

"Nothing new, of course," Baghorn said at once. "Mamoulian, another one of my clients, if I may drop a name, did it in the Fredric March *Dr. Jekyll and Mr. Hyde*."

"And Fritz Lang did it before him with *M*," Jackie added knowledgeably.

"I didn't represent Mr. Lang," Baghorn sniffed. "I didn't like the way his people handled their labor problems."

"So," Watson struggled to make sense of Baghorn's conversation. "This camera is heavy?"

"Heavy, awkward, fragile," Baghorn agreed. "And Fred Jackson likes to pretend he's Ernest Hemingway. I said to him, 'Fred, the beard you've got, not the back. Let one of the kids operate the steady cam.' I might as well have been talking in a deep-sea diving helmet under water."

"The steady cam is a tremendous rig that you have to support on your back and with your thighs, your shoulders, and forearms," Jackie explained.

"Picture a fireman holding a big firehose with a teenager on his back," Baghorn offered.

"Better yet, picture Mr. Freeze on *Batman,*" Jackie countered.

"This is all very interesting, but can we get back to the issue at hand?" Watson begged.

"Okay," Baghorn said. "You want to know who killed Dr. Linus, right?"

"Right!" Watson said decisively.

"I say you have two groups of suspects. One, is any person with AIDS, or perhaps someone who has lost someone to that terrible disease. I couldn't get him to admit it outright, but I think Dr. Linus knew his so-called vaccine was largely worthless. It was a cheap attempt to fool the public and the government into renewing his grants."

"He wasn't a very nice person, was he?" Watson commented.

"No, he wasn't," Jackie said in a strong voice.

"The other suspect is a newsperson."

"Why?" Jackie asked.

"Dr. Linus tried desperately to get along with them. He knew it was in his best interest to do so, but he couldn't

help it. He just hated them. Ever since they had given
the credit for all the discoveries he made along with his
brother to Marvin when he retired. As usual, it was Dr.
Linus's own fault. He didn't have time for interviews, he
said, so he just sent along a CV."

Watson looked blank.

"Curriculum vitae, dear lady, a kind of resumé."

As Baghorn talked, Jackie let her mind take the Latin
phrase and jump from it to the Dean of Faculty, B. Crowder Westfall, dying upstairs. She thought again that the least
she could do was stop in and visit him. After all, he had
hired her to work at Rodgers some years ago (principally
because she was her father's daughter—but still) and he
had never given her the slightest flak about missing dozens
of lectures and labs while investigating murders and other
acts of passion.

"What do you think, Jackie?" Watson asked.

Jackie stared at the patrol officer blankly. "I'm sorry. I
must have spaced out for a minute."

"I was telling the officer how Dr. Linus sent the press
his CV when they asked for a summary of his brother's career," Baghorn related. "They didn't understand, or
didn't choose to make the distinction, that the research was
done by both brothers. So, when Marvin retired, everyone,
including Linus's good friend Vic Kingston, made it seem
like Dr. Linus had just been standing around while his
brother did all the work."

Baghorn wet his whistle with a sip of soda and
then resumed. "He made a big show of researching
Alzheimer's the past few years, but my spies tell me he
really didn't accomplish much of anything. According to
informed sources, Dr. Linus spent his days in his office,
obsessively reading his old clippings and watching a tape
of his favorite TV appearances.

"The issue of who did what and who was the more important brother aside, when Marvin retired, Linus was finished too. There may not be any connection—Linus was no spring chicken—but his bolt was definitely shot. I think he picked this fight with the government so he could go out a last angry man.

"Dr. Linus was no stranger to playing the martyr or victim. You should have heard him when his brother retired. You'd think Marvin was insulting Linus by going off to a tropical island instead of checking into an institution to wait for eventual descent into complete senility."

Marcus Baghorn continued, "I think Dr. Linus came here in a very cynical mood. He was going to trash the government on TV—a spy of mine heard him practicing his off-the-cuff remarks before he came. Dr. Linus was going to stage this little AIDS extravaganza and shoot people full of vitamin C and bee pollen, which he got in some health food store, as a 'Cure for AIDS,' then he was going to blast and fume until someone slapped him down. At that point, Dr. Linus would sweep off the stage like Ethel Barrymore and announce that he was being 'driven' into retirement.

"No more hard days in the lab, just nice and easy retirement, reading the pages from his memoir some ghostwriter would concoct and making the rounds of universities, talk shows, and conventions, telling everyone how ill-used he was. You don't know how good that sounds to an old man. Sitting around schmoozing with people who think you're great, reliving your old triumphs, claiming you were prevented from making any new discoveries by various government officials.

"And this is more than just my theory. You can check it out for yourself. I was contacted by a friend in a Boulder, Colorado, publicity agency who had taken a lunch with the

Good Doctor. He wanted them to handle all this for him, for no money of course—not up front anyway—just the honor of being associated with such a great man. And of course promises of mystical millions down the line. You know what I think?"

Officer Watson smiled patiently and resisted the temptation to point out that she had been listening to him do just that for quite some time now.

"I think your prime suspect," Baghorn continued in a mysterious voice, "should be Victor Kingston."

"But they're friends," Jackie protested.

"You've never heard of friends falling out and killing each other?"

"I've heard of it," Watson stated emphatically. She was thinking of how she had almost shot Muhammed Sanji when he told her he was bailing out as her partner, just when she was assigned to patrol the dangerous part of town. The security chief, seeing her face, cast his eyes downward in remembered shame.

"Look at *Butch Cassidy and the Sundance Kid*," Baghorn suggested.

Jackie had heard something about the two men falling out in real life, but she protested, "They didn't become enemies in the movie. They died together the best of friends in a freeze frame."

"Think of a better example then, from the movies," Baghorn snapped. "I don't have to tell you. You teach the movies in your class."

"Well, I try to," Jackie responded, "but I so often find myself sidetracked in some dingy waiting room working with the police to make order out of some chaos."

Suddenly, the almost silent hospital was overwhelmed by the raucous sound of two dogs fighting. Jackie rushed out and was delighted to see Maury and Jake battling, the way Errol Flynn and John Huston used to enliven dull parties by beating the hell out of each other over some imagined insult.

In this particular case, Maury, always in the mood for a good wrestle, was taking the fight seriously while Jake, who seldom barked except for effect, was baiting the big dog by nipping him in the sensitive area behind his front legs and in front of his back legs.

"Ow! *Ow!*" Maury turned to stop Jake from tormenting him so, but the older dog kept getting behind the feckless mastiff, making the young elephant herder turn around and around until he finally collapsed dizzily to the ground.

Finally, Hidalgo Rojas ran outside to intervene. By carefully interposing himself between Rojas and a still-woozy Maury, Jake arranged it so that every time the guard lashed out, he hit Maury. Then, judging that the mastiff was now good and mad, Jake stepped aside.

"Oh oh," the big security guard said before being bowled over backward.

While Jackie's son Peter, Merida Green, and, finally, Jake slipped inside the Emergency Room . . .

. . . Marcella Jacobs and Ral Perrin took the passenger elevator to the fifth floor, where Fred Jackson was writhing in agony because his Jack Dolphin Talking Book was stuck on the phrase, "Murder had nothing to do with it."

Therefore, when Marcella and Ral burst into the room, the cinematography instructor and acting co-chairman sighed with relief. "Great peaks of Kilimanjaro, thank heaven you're here. Would you hit that player for me? There must be some dust making it skip and it's driving me bonkers."

"Oh sure, Professor Jackson," Ral said at once.

"Not so fast, Perrin," growled Marcella. "Jackson, listen. There's been an emergency."

"Murder had nothing to do with it," the taped voice continued insistently.

"What's that?" Jackson shouted above the talking book. "An emergency?"

"I'm afraid so," Marcella replied.

"Murder had nothing to do with it."

"That's terrible," Jackson replied finally.

"Worse for us, unfortunately," Marcella remarked.

"How so?"

"We need to edit some raw footage," Marcella explained, "and to do that Ral needs to borrow your keys. Okay?"

"Well . . . I don't know," Jackson considered.

"Murder had nothing to do with it."

"If Ral wanted to work on a teaching project," Jackson continued, "or if you were one of my students . . ."

"I will sign up for your class tomorrow," Marcella promised. "Want me to write you a check?"

"I don't know . . ." Jackson considered.

Marcella pulled down slightly on one of Jackson's leg stirrups. "Please, Fred."

"Murder had nothing to do with it."

"You'd really be helping us out."

"You bloody blackguards," Jackson said through gritted teeth. "I was tortured by the bloody Japanese in Burma. You think you can . . . ?"

Marcella turned to Ral. "Turn up the volume."

"Murder had nothing to do with it! Murder Had Nothing to Do with It!! MURDER HAD NOTHING TO DO WITH IT!"

"All right! All Right!! ALL RIGHT!!!" Jackson agreed finally.

Ral immediately turned the volume down.

"Murder had nothing to do with it," the talking book said more quietly.

"Take the keys, you bloody torturers," Jackson hissed. "They're in the top of that cabinet."

Marcella opened the drawer and flipped the keyring to Ral. "Catch!"

"Murder had nothing to do with it."

"Thank you, Fred," Marcella said sweetly. "Get well soon."

"Pray that I don't," Jackson said through clenched, oversized teeth.

"Mr. Jackson . . . I just want to say . . ." Ral considered the penalty for disloyalty, swallowed, and continued, " . . . I'm sorry about all this. It really wasn't my . . ."

"I understand," Jackson said manfully. "You're not to blame. The damn woman's turned you into a quisling."

"A what?"

"Doesn't matter," Marcella said quickly. She tapped the talking book player and the deep-voiced narrator resumed his tale. "We'll let you get back to your napping."

Jackson sighed, as if a giant rock had been lifted off his ribcage. "I don't suppose this thing you've taped and need to edit so desperately has anything to do with . . . ?"

Marcella, having gotten what she came for, tuned out what Fred was saying, and started to concentrate on the next task. "Ral, can you get out of this place okay by yourself? I couldn't help you anyway and I might hold you back if someone recognizes me."

"No, I'm cool," Ral said. "Thanks, Mr. Jackson."

"Yes. Godspeed," Jackson yelled after him.

"I'll just turn this up for you," Marcella offered, turning to the talking book machine.

"By the way," Jackson ineffectually called after her. "I saw your colleague, Vic Kingston, a few moments ago."

Marcella, unhearing or unheeding, switched off the lights, and left just as the hero was conked unconscious in the story. The rest was darkness.

CHAPTER 17

Jackie huddled with her son, her neighbor, and her partner in crime solving, well out of range of the infuriated security guard (who had been dragged into the open cesspool by the frisky Maury).

"All right," Jackie instructed them. "Remember, if anybody asks, you've been here all night."

"I feel like I've been here all night," Peter wailed. "I'm tired."

"There's a TV through there," Jackie said, pointing to the room where most of the witnesses, still waiting to testify, stared fixedly at a rerun of the original "Let's Make a Deal" with Monty Hall.

"Great." Peter took a couple of steps closer and laughed. "Look, Ma! That guy is dressed like a donut with chocolate sprinkles."

The security guard, automatically salivating, turned to look at the screen, his anger at Maury momentarily forgotten.

Jackie turned her attention to Merida. "How are you doing?"

"I'm fine, Jackie," the former Communications Studies chairman and Jackie's new friend, replied as she handed her neighbor a pair of tan denims, a large, comfortable, white fishnet sweater, and a change of socks. "I could do with a bite to eat, though."

"So could I, actually," Jackie said, remembering that John Brooks had never brought her back the hot chocolate and muffin tops. "Why don't you go down to the cafeteria in the basement?"

"I don't know." Merida made a face. "I don't like cafeteria food."

"No no," Jackie explained impatiently. "This isn't like the cafeteria at the university, Merida. This is one of those cafeterias where everyone eats together. Even the high mucky muck doctors, the executives, and the head of the hospital. So, the food is good. Really."

"I don't know," Merida hesitated.

"Well," Jackie said, "they also have a heckuva lot of vending machines."

"Sold. I'll just get a Snickers bar." As Merida left, Jackie turned to Jake.

"All right, Jake," she said quickly. "Let me show you what happened."

Jake trotted over.

"Through here." Jackie led the big German shepherd through the corridor of emergency care treatment rooms, through the unmarked (but not locked—by order of Officer Watson) door into a narrow corridor, tightened further by the protruding, heavy wooden frames on the painted portraits of former distinguished Marx-Wheeler administrators and heads of service.

At the end of the narrow corridor, they came to the back

entrance to the administrator's private elevator.

"The murdered man is a doctor."

Jake looked around at the different portraits.

"No. Nobody from Palmer. This fellow is from out of town."

"Rrrr . . . munkkk," Jake barked.

"That's right," Jackie said, pleased that her faithful pet had been watching the TV that her son never seemed to turn off. "Dr. Munch. The big shot doctor from Denver. He came here for evil purposes, Jake. And someone killed him."

The dog nodded wisely and then nosed around the elevator. "They came down from the administrator's office in this elevator," Jackie continued.

Jake nodded.

"Walked down the corridor, entered the Emergency Room and split up. That's what Marcus Baghorn says, anyway. And I believe him. I think if they had still been in a group, I would have noticed them. Marcus was . . . By the way, do you want to see him?"

Jake shook his head.

"I think you're right on that, Jake," Jackie quickly agreed. "Marcus is old, but he's observant and he doesn't really have an ax to grind on this one. He didn't really like Dr. Munch, but he wouldn't protect the murderer. Especially if it were one of the men he came down with on the elevator. Do you want to know about the other men now?"

Jake looked around distractedly.

"Not yet, apparently. All right, Jake. Talk to me. I'm only human. I can't read your mind."

Jake reached up and licked Jackie's hand, as if in consolation. Then he caught Jackie's eye and rolled over.

"Oh, you want to see the body? All right, sure." Jackie

led Jake out into the main corridor. As they passed the florist's shop, where Jackie had once bought flowers for Maggie Mulcahy, she felt a little stab of guilt, and decided to take a minute and call her mother.

Frances Costello, a little addled by the flu but still spry, answered on the first ring. " 'KROG plays the Old-Time Radio Re-creations I like,' " she answered.

"Congratulations," Jackie said at once, disguising her voice (it was terrible, she knew, but after all the grief Frances had given her over the years, she just couldn't resist opportunities like this to pull her mother's leg). "You have won dinner for two at a gala western fare restaurant in beautiful Wardville, Ohio! What do you say to that, Frances Cooley Costello?"

"Well . . . that's all right, I suppose," Frances answered dubiously. "But I was hoping for a Fibber McGee closet of party gifts."

"I'm sorry, Frances," Jackie said in her best not-very-sorry professional voice. "But in order to win the closet o'plenty, you have to own your own tam-o'-shanter."

"Wait! I have a tam-o'-shanter," Frances said excitedly. "I have to get it from the drawer in me daughter's room. Hold the phone a minute."

Jackie reached down and scratched her faithful companion behind the ears.

"I have it."

"Put it on your head," Jackie directed.

"All right."

"Now do a jig."

"A Scots jig or an Irish reel?"

"We want you to do a whirling reel."

"Ah me," Frances lamented. "That's the hard one, but if it's a matter of winning the grand prize."

"And while you're jigging, Frances . . ." Jackie switched

to her own voice in an attempt to clue in her mother that it was only a practical joke. " . . . cluck like a chicken."

"Buck, buck!"

"Mother."

"Chicka chick, bucka buck."

"Mother!"

"Ain't nobody here but us chickens." Frances had caught on, but decided to keep playing along and take her revenge. "Buck, buck. Cough, cough. Buck, cough, buck. Cough, cough."

Jackie winced as her mother went into a spasm of coughing.

"Oh dear, Mr. Monahan," Frances choked out as she gasped for life-giving air. "You'll have to excuse me. I've been in a sick bed these past few days and me wind's not what it should be. I asked my dear daughter Jaqueline Shannon to bring me some cough medicine, but you know how it is when your offspring go out on their own. Somehow they never have time for you any more and . . ."

"Mom! It's me, Jackie. Your daughter!"

"Jackie?" Frances said weakly. "Is that really you, dear girl?"

"Yes, Mother."

"What are you doing on the radio?"

"I'm not on the radio, Mother," Jackie explained. "I'm calling from Marx-Wheeler Medical Center."

"But I was just talking to . . . Oh, dear sweet tortoise in his shell. Don't tell me . . ."

"What is it, Mother?" Jackie asked, her mind racing.

Frances now sounded like she was near tears. "I thought it was the radio and that I'd won. Oh, dear. It was just a joke, wasn't it? It was just a terrible, mean-hearted . . ."

"No, no," Jackie assured the sick woman. "I'm sure if

you won a prize from the radio station, it's on its way to you, Mother."

"But I didn't give the man my address."

"Remember, they called you. They must already have it."

"They do?"

"Of course, Mother. Remember, the FBI routinely requisitions dental records to keep their security files on all United States citizens. If you've ever opened your mouth for another person, anyone who wants your address can get it."

"Well, all right then. If you're sure."

"Of course I'm sure," Jackie said very confidently. "How are you, Mother dearest?"

"Are ya daft, lass?" Frances roared, her old self again. "How d'ye think I am? I'm standing here in me living room, bare-legged and winded, coughing like a Canadian sea lion, and lookin' ridiculous wit me tam-o'-shanter on me head."

"Great," Jackie enthused, turning left at the security guard's desk and walking toward the elevator. As his mistress talked, Jake ran ahead and examined an old-fashioned mail chute opposite the elevator, which ran from the seventh floor to the mail room in the basement. "You're feeling better, then?"

"I'm at death's door and I hear the angel of darkness's footsteps," Frances claimed. "I'm just hoping the guardian on the other side will take me up and not down."

As if suiting her actions to her mother's words, Jackie pushed the up button on the elevator. "There's got to be some way to tell, Mother," Jackie joked. "What do the footsteps sound like? Do they sound like cloven hooves?"

"Ah, you laugh," Frances croaked out. "Go ahead, why don't you, and split a rib as your mother pants her life away in her final wrapping sheets."

"I'm sorry, dear Mother," Jackie promised, as the doors opened on the third floor (the pathology floor) of the medical center.

"And so you should be," Frances replied crabbily. "What the Hades are you doing in the hospital? Don't tell me you've got whatever is going around your ownself?"

"No, I'm glad to say," Jackie responded, turning left and walking down the corridor toward the Autopsy Room. "I'm here because Dr. Linus Munch, the big shot researcher, was murdered today."

"Oh sweet lamb of innocence," Frances groaned. "Don't tell me you're investigating another foul murder."

"I'm afraid so," Jackie admitted, stopping at the outside door to the autopsy suite. Unable to see inside the frosted glass porthole, Jackie pushed the metal strip in the center of the door (which protected the door from being scarred when dieners pushed stretchers through) and went inside.

"Are they paying you to find this awful fellow's killer?" Frances asked.

"No, I'm keeping my amateur status," Jackie answered, finding herself in the conference room (the place where the autopsy residents, visiting fellows, and Palmer Medical School students gathered with the prosector/intern who actually did the autopsy and a supervising attending pathologist to examine the gross organs removed from the autopsied patient for the purpose of determining the "path of death"—the diagnoses that would be listed on the final autopsy report). "Why do you say 'awful fellow'?"

"Well," Frances answered with alacrity, "haven't I been watching this news report here on the television which tells us how the fellow has been taking all this money in grants deducted from our hard-earned tax dollars to find a cure for the Alzheimer's disease, which is a terrible thing for us seniors to get because it . . . What was I saying?"

Jackie turned right, walked by the walls with see-through glass cabinets holding linen, autopsy forms, and reference books, a wide variety of souvenirs (including prosthetic implants and other foreign paraphernalia removed from the bodies of autopsied patients) and awful looking saws, scoops, and clamps for getting into every nook and cranny of the body, and approached the door to the Autopsy Room.

As she drew near, Jackie noticed a handwritten sign taped to the door saying, "Medical Examiner's Case in Progress"—then a larger, printed sign bolted onto the wall, telling her that under no circumstances could anyone enter the autopsy rooms without using full protective equipment.

"You were saying Alzheimer's disease makes people forget things, Mother."

"Indeed it does," Frances remembered. "And it would have been a lovely thing for someone—this doctor or anyone—to do something about something that concerns so many of us. But according to this Kinison fellow on the television . . ."

"Wait a minute, Mother." Having ducked into the changing room, put on her fresh clothes, gotten into baggy hospital greens, a baby-blue hair protector, elbow-length rubber gloves with ridged fingers and key grip reinforcers, and paper booties, Jackie was now trying to get Jake into his own footcoverings. She stopped short however when she heard her mother's last words. "You're watching the KCIN 11 P.M. news with Victor Kingston?"

"And the girl, your friend, whatever her name is."

"Marcella Jacobs."

"Yah, but she's not on tonight. They had a sports writer doing a lot of the program until the damn monkey bit him."

"Mother!" Jackie pleaded. "Listen! I'm trying to solve another murder down here at the hospital and it's just a matter of time before they take Jake away from me. So just answer one question. This report you're watching. It's on now?"

"It just ended," Frances answered. "There will be half a hundred commercials and then we'll get that mean chimp again. I don't see how they expect us to believe he knows what the weather is going to be like, when he can't even sit respectably at the news table and shuffle his papers like the rest of them."

"Never mind that," Jackie instructed. "Just take a look at the end of the program, and tell me you see Victor Kingston sitting at the desk when the weather is finished."

"I doubt we'll see any of them there," Frances warned her only daughter. "They're probably all frightened to death of the damn primate."

"Mother!"

"Aye, aye, Captain," Frances responded ill-naturedly. "I just hope my coughing and sneezing doesn't distract you from your good times."

"Please, Mother. I'm sorry you're sick, but this is important."

"Well, if it's important, what's a mother to do but drop everything, including any chance she might have for recovery, and . . . ? Ah, here it is. No, the set is empty. Except for what looks to be a young lad attacking the monkey with some sort of rolled-up newspaper. No. No. Victor Killian."

"Kingston, Mother. Victor Killian was the old flasher, on *Mary Hartman, Mary Hartman*."

"Ah, whatever. There are so many actors now, you have no hope at all of keeping track of them. They should wear numbers on their back like rugby players."

"And you're sure that Vic Kingston wasn't sitting at the desk at the end?"

"I just told you 'no,' didn't I? You think I wouldn't recognize such a nice fella as that if I saw him? You know he's got what none of these young people have, a nice, warm, fatherly way of telling you what's what that's very reassuring, when all the world is filled with rage and fear and starving people over there in wherever it is who need food from you one minute and another clip of bullets for the gun they're using to shoot you with the next . . ."

"Well, it's been nice talking to you, Mother," Jackie said, trying to escape.

"Wait a minute," Frances said, her voice growing fainter as she bent away from the phone and closer to the TV set. "We're getting the names of who wants all the credit at the end here and it says in letters much too wee to be seen by a normal person to read that 'Portions of the proceeding program were recorded earlier in the day.' "

"Great!" Jackie exulted, tearing a couple of earholes in Jake's bonnet. "Thanks, Mother."

"Wait half a mo, you daft child," Frances protested. "How did Maggie's funeral go?" It was too late, though; Jackie had broken the connection.

Remorselessly clicking her phone to dictation mode, Jackie left a reminder for herself. "Call Mother back later. First call Keith Monahan and tell him to send a Fibber McGee closet full of party gifts to my mother at my expense." The blue-paper-topped film instructor turned to her dog, now hatted and bootied and smocked in a plastic apron affair the dieners used to protect their clothing when hosing down the so-called gore tables. "Ready?"

Jackie barked something to the effect that he was whelped ready, and then proceeded into the adult Autopsy Room.

"Can I help you, Ma'am?" asked an older black man in bloody hospital whites who did not wear a head covering (for fear of messing up his Cab Calloway–style hair).

"I'm here to see . . ."

"Jackie Walsh!" a voice called out. "As I live and breathe—unlike this gentleman here. How are you?"

Jackie was happy to see that the autopsy surgeon, or "prosector" performing the autopsy, was Lee Humphries, the cheery acting chief medical examiner of Palmer, now wearing what seemed to be a spacesuit topped off with a clear bubble helmet.

"Hi, Lee!"

Dr. Humphries gave Jackie a rather ineffectual air kiss, then asked, "What brings you to our little house of horrors?"

"Well," Jackie said, a little uncomfortable to be looking into the open, empty abdomen of the late Dr. Munch, "believe it or not, I was upstairs when Dr. Munch here was killed."

"Oh, he *was* dead," Humphries joked, tapping the handkerchief covering the man's face. "I'm so relieved. Especially now that we've cut him up and hollowed him out and all."

Jackie forced a laugh. Dr. Humphries, like her predecessor Cosmo Gordon, tended to overindulge in black humor.

"Yes, he's dead," Jackie confirmed. "Did you find out what killed him?"

"I did, and since it's all on tape"—Humphries turned and pointed to the videocamera mounted in the corner—

"why don't you watch the playback while I wash up? Then we'll go down and you can buy me some pie and coffee and pump me with your questions."

"Fair enough," Jackie said.

"What about me?" Clutch Gillingham complained. "I'm about to sew him up now."

Jackie backed away from the needle and thread–bearing diener.

"Go ahead," Humphries said easily. "Jackie, you can go over there and watch." She pointed to a comfortable armchair. "You just rewind the tape that's in the machine and press 'play.' "

"Okay, fine," Jackie said, starting to move out of Gillingham's way.

"Just a minute," the diener protested again.

"Now what?" Lee asked.

"I don't know about bringing no dog in here," he justifiably complained.

"Don't worry about that either," Humphries assured the overworked diener. "I'll take full responsibility. Don't you recognize this dog? It's Palmer's premier canine sleuth, Fritz!"

"Jake, actually," Jackie reminded the pathologist, whose strong suit was not her ability to remember names.

"Oh, you changed it."

"Several times," Jackie admitted. "We didn't know what his real name was when we adopted him, then Peter tried calling him a few different names but none of them stuck— until Jake saw *Chinatown* and decided to adopt the name of the plucky sleuth played by Jack Nicholson."

"That is a good film," Humphries said. "For years I had a thing for John Huston that you wouldn't believe."

Jackie bit her lip, wanting to stay on the medical examiner's good side. "It's a fine film."

"Well, that's okay for you two!" yelled the aggrieved diener. "But I'm telling you now, if the inspector from the Board of Health comes in here and starts raising heck, you're paying him off. Not me."

As the diener went off to find a couple of empty Zenker's jars, Lee reassured Jackie, "Don't worry. It'll be fine. Sit back and enjoy the show. I'll take a quick shower, get dressed, and meet you back here in ten minutes."

Jackie looked around the white-tiled room, noting the four doors (one leading out to the gross conference room, another to a corridor, where the jars of removed organs were stored in a "cool" closet, a third to the changing room, and a fourth to an elevator down to the morgue); the two autopsy slabs (heavy metal sink tables almost seven feet long with teflon mesh tops, allowing for easy cleanup); the operating room–style lights above the tables; the drains in the floors; the built-in counters, where the doctors did their paperwork; the X-ray board and clipboards, where the prosectors could display the patient's hospital records; and the heavy trays of autopsy instruments, featuring everything from an electrical bone saw to an item that looked like an ice cream scoop. Then, a little queasy (she hadn't eaten since morning), she went over to view the autopsy footage.

Despite the fact that Jackie had investigated several murders, and despite the fact that she had written for a TV show with a police background, she wasn't really comfortable with autopsies yet.

Jackie had been in the City Morgue a few times (not a pretty picture) and had visited with the great English coroner Sir Keith Simpson (who had inspired a Canadian TV show about a grouchy coroner, played by John Vernon, and later still, an almost identical American series starring Jack Klugman).

Her other TV series, *Triumphant Spirit* (written with Celestine Barger), had also featured some autopsy room scenes. But in spite of these experiences, Jackie had never witnessed a real autopsy.

She witnessed one now.

The first thing the video depicted was the body of Dr. Linus Munch being hoisted onto the autopsy table by a very industrial-looking winch. The body was disrobed, weighed, and carefully sponged down. Lee Humphries started dictating.

"The body is that of a slightly obese, well-developed, elderly man measuring 163 cm. in total length, weighing approximately two hundred and seventy pounds, and appearing the stated age of seventy-four years old. Postmortem rigor is moderate and moderate lividity is present in the dependent portions."

Jackie watched with distaste as the body was opened by the diener (using a bonesaw), making a Y-shaped incision in the chest and abdomen and a U-shaped cut further down.

"The head is normocephalic and large with slight evidence of trauma. The scalp hair is white and sparse with a male frontal balding pattern. The pupils are round and equal and measure 6.5mm. in diameter. The irises are brown and the sclerae are white. The nasal septum is in the midline and the nares are patent. The ears are unremarkable and the external auditory canals are patent. The oral cavity cannot be examined because of rigor mortis."

As Jackie watched the autopsy surgeon go through her check list, she wondered if Lee Humphries had ever met Dr. Linus Munch in life. She wondered if the doctor could have this sort of dispassionate mechanic-working-on-a-car attitude toward someone she had liked, respected, or even loved.

Managing to keep a poker face while the on-tape surgeon took pictures, dissected and removed organs, and drained the body to better facilitate the examination of the skin, Jackie leaned forward as Lee started examining the skin. Finally she found it, a jagged tear large enough to put several fingers through. That was enough for Jackie. She immediately stood up and made a beeline for the elevator.

The doctor had been stabbed. Fine. Now she would think about something else. As Jackie took her mind off her queasiness by calling Keith Monahan, and by calling her mother back to apologize for being so abrupt . . .

. . . Marcella Jacobs tried to talk her way past Dannen Jeffreys, Dick Bellamy's personal security guard. "You don't understand, Dannen," she wheeled. "I was on the scene."

"Then you know what happened," the bodyguard pointed out. The fact of the matter was Dannen Jeffreys, who had asked for the evening off to go to the opera with a friend, now felt badly that he hadn't been around to keep his boss out of trouble, and was trying to make up for lost ground. "Why do you have to see Dr. Bellamy?"

"Because," Marcella all but flirted, "I want to get Administrator Bellamy's own private perspective."

Jeffreys was utterly unmoved by Marcella's charms. "If it's private, he's not going to give it to you to put all over the TV. That's what the word 'private' means."

Marcella, seeing that this tack wasn't working, immediately tried another. "Mr. Jeffreys, I think we both want the same thing."

"To see Bill Mazeroski elected to the Hall of Fame?"

"Well, that too of course," Marcella lied. "But I'm

talking about Richard Bellamy. You want to protect him. So do I."

"Protect him from what?" Jeffreys asked skeptically.

"Rumors, Dannen. Bad publicity. A whispering campaign. Why did Marx-Wheeler bring Linus Munch here? What was in that AIDS vaccine? Ice water? Honey and vitamin C? Or was it rat poison?"

"Come on," Jeffreys snapped. "What is this guff you're dishing? You're saying Doc Munch was going to poison people—in front of a hundred witnesses?"

"Maybe," Marcella chanced. "The vaccine disappeared. We don't know what was in it."

"I heard someone say it was interferon," Jeffries said in a superior tone. "What's wrong with that?"

"Nothing," Marcella conceded amiably. "Except that it doesn't work on AIDS. Everyone knows that."

"I don't know that," Jeffreys said stubbornly.

"And I don't know Bill Mazeroski belongs in the baseball Hall of Fame, but take my word for it, Dannen. It's common knowledge in the science world that interferon is not appropriate for a serum. Linus Munch would have known it and your boss would have known it too."

"So what?" Jeffreys demanded. "What does that prove?"

"Nothing," Marcella agreed. "That's the problem. Listen, Dannen. Like it or not, we have a story here. A man got killed. Not just any man, but a former Nobel Prize winner who claimed he had a vaccine for AIDS.

"Like it or not, a story will appear on the evening news, hosted by me. I will report the facts as I know them. If I say no one knows why Linus Munch was invited to practice medicine at Marx-Wheeler Medical Center, something he hadn't done in twenty-seven years, and Dr. Richard Bellamy, the administrator of the hospital refuses to tell us why, I won't have to say I think this is strange, suspicious, or a bad thing. All I have to do is report the facts and people will draw those kinds of conclusions automatically.

"If I report that moments after Linus Munch was killed in the Emergency Room of the Marx-Wheeler Medical Center the serum he was administering disappeared, people will wonder, and if I say that the administrator of the hospital is unwilling to comment on that, people will disapprove. And if I report that the only reason that anyone can think of why someone would kill Linus Munch is that maybe the administrator of Marx-Wheeler Medical Center finally figured out that his honored guest was playing him for a fool. And when he ordered him to cancel his appearance and the guest refused, he went a little berserk and killed him, and that the man whom this description seems to fit has locked himself away behind steel doors and bodyguards, refusing to cooperate with either the press or the police—people are going to feel, I'm sure, that Richard Bellamy has done something wrong.

"I know there are a lot of policemen—Captain Michael McGowan of the Palmer Central Division, for instance—who would not hesitate to come here and remove Dr. Richard Bellamy in handcuffs. I don't think his wife, Mayor Jane Bellamy, would like that. Do you? Do you want to drop a quarter and ask her? She is your boss, isn't she?"

"All right. All right," Jeffreys conceded. "I'll check with Dr. Bellamy and try to get him to see you. I won't make any guarantees, however."

"Of course not, Dannen." Having gotten her way, Marcella oozed niceness. "You do the best you can."

As Jeffreys went inside the office, Marcella checked her watch and whistled a little tune ("Nobody Does It Better," as popularized by Carly Simon on the soundtrack of the movie *The Spy Who Loved Me*).

The truth was, that while an interview with Dick Bellamy would not be a bad thing for her to get, Marcella wouldn't be too disappointed if the medical center administrator didn't see her. She could pick up that interview any time. After all, what was he going to say? That he committed the murder? That he saw who did? There wasn't much chance he was going to confess to something like that, especially with the bodyguard provided by his wife right there.

All Marcella really wanted at this point was her sur-veillance bug (which, unlike some listening devices, did not transmit voices to an outside tape, but recorded all that it could on a forty-five-minute tape).

Marcella was startled out of her reverie by the sound of a door opening. She turned, expecting the door behind her to have been opened. Then, when Marcella saw that it was still closed, she turned and saw Victor Kingston coming out of one of the patient's rooms.

The veteran newsman looked a wreck. His tie was gone; the collar of his blue-and-white striped shirt stood up on one side; his suit jacket looked rumpled and been rebut-toned the wrong way; his trousers were wrinkled, hiked up, and dirty at the knees and his shoes were scuffed and untied.

"Vic!" Marcella greeted him.

Kingston gave her a wild look, then dropped something into his left-hand coat pocket. "What are you doing here?" the telejournalist croaked out.

"I'm covering the story, Vic." As Marcella answered, she couldn't help but notice that her co-anchor was wear-ing the kind of rubber gloves used by surgeons.

"You're covering the story?" Kingston growled, putting his hands behind his back to pull off the gloves.

"I know," Marcella said quickly, trying to head off a

turf argument. "I came here to cover the strike and you came here with the doctor, but things developed the way they did and I think we can help each other. I have some great material, and I thought we could work together on this one. After all, you were with the doctor most of the afternoon and I could interview you."

"No, no. No interviews," Kingston muttered disconnectedly.

"Okay, whatever," Marcella said obligingly. "Tell you what. I'm just about to inter . . . talk to Dick Bellamy. Thing is, I've got another lead to follow up. What do you say, you take this one? After all, you're good friends. He'll tell you things he won't tell me."

"What . . . what's your other lead?" Kingston sputtered.

Marcella was debating what to say when Jeffreys opened the door behind her.

"All right," the bodyguard barked. "You have fifteen minutes."

Marcella turned again to Kingston. "What do you say, Vic? You ready?"

"No, no," the broadcast reporter said, backing down the hall as if he were Paul Muni at the end of *I Was a Fugitive from a Chain Gang*. "I'm not prepared. I don't have my tape recorder."

"*We* will be taping the interview," the bodyguard announced. "You may have a copy of our tape. If you wish."

"You see, Vic?" Marcella said, in as bright a voice as she could manage. "Piece of cake. Just get the basics, who, what, where, why, and try to get the doctor to mention the call letters of our station."

"No!" Kingston said loudly. "Can't you take 'no' for an answer, damn you!"

"But, Vic . . ."

"I said, 'no!' I can't do it. I can't . . . I can't . . . do anything right, anymore," Kingston rasped. "And for God's sake, don't insult me any further by acting as if you can't see that I'm drunk!"

As the veteran newsman rushed off, pushing through an exit door and stumbling down the stairs, Marcella turned to Jeffreys as if nothing unusual had occurred. "Well," she said. "Guess I'm doing the interview after all. Lead on, MacDuff."

CHAPTER 18

After eating her delicious muffin tops (always the best part, in the young film instructor's opinion) and hot chocolate, Jackie was able to summon up the energy to make a fuss over Milly Brooks's newly adopted daughters.

The two young girls were demure, blonde and blue-eyed and seemed totally innocent. They looked like a couple of Alices in Wonderland as drawn by Tenniel. Jackie, however, knew about their family history and wondered what was going on under the surface.

"Aren't they adorable, Jackie?" Milly asked for the hundredth time.

"I love their blue dresses," Jackie managed. "You know, when they were my neighbors, they never dressed alike."

"Please, Jackie," Milly said at once. "We're going to concentrate very hard to never mention Xenia and Matthew again. It just upsets the poor children."

As if on cue, Mia and Lea looked troubled and hurt.

"And besides," John Brooks added, neatly packing up the remains of his perfectly engineered snack. "We paid good money for these children and we intend to keep them."

"John, really," Milly said. "You would have never anticipated it, Jackie, but since my husband has become a father, he's become quite the kidder. Nothing's coming out very funny yet, but we're hoping that, with time, it will actually seem like John has a sense of humor."

Jackie smiled. She liked the petite curly red-haired English professor very much. They were the oldest of friends and Jackie had felt bad that because of the damage done by an IUD (since recalled) in their college days, Milly had not been able to have children of her own.

Milly and John had tried to adopt for many years, going through all sorts of contortions and disappointments. The opportunity to adopt Lea and Mia after their mother's tragic death had given the couple, who had given up their quest and were starting to have troubles in their marriage, a whole new lease on life. So, Jackie was careful not to let anything spoil her friends' happiness. "Well," she said. "I'm sure you guys will work things out."

"You can be sure we will," Milly asserted, putting her arms around her lovely new daughters. "Because we're a family now!"

"A family that is going home to their own place," John Brooks announced. "The police are through with me for the moment. Milly and the kids didn't arrive until after Dr. Linus was . . ."

Milly cut off her husband with a sharp elbow in the ribs.

"Indisposed."

Jackie caught the little girls, out of sight of their new parents, drawing their index fingers across their throats and giggling.

"So," John Brooks concluded. "We're off. Can we give anyone a lift?"

"I have my Jeep," Jackie said.

"Do you want us to give Peter and Merida a ride?" Milly asked.

"I don't know," Jackie replied. "Are they ready to go? Merida?"

Jackie got up from her seat and went to look for her neighbor. She went through the turnstile into the vending machine room and located Merida seated at a comfortable triangular table behind a stack of microwave popcorn wrappers.

"Have they been showing a movie in here?" Jackie kidded, placing her plastic-wrapped dirty clothes in Merida's shoulderbag.

"Actually, they have," Merida replied, pointing to a monitor in the corner of the room showing (silently) a film with subtitles. "But I'm on a popcorn diet to lose a few pounds."

"You just eat popcorn?"

"No, you have one of those milkshakes in a can with it," Merida explained. "The popcorn is just to give you something to do after you've bolted down your milkshake and your fat little tummy tries to make sense of what you're now consuming."

Jackie nodded, knowing that Merida, who had lost her boyfriend recently, was trying to lose some weight before throwing herself into the dating scene again. "How are you doing?"

"Eh," the Spanish-American film historian shrugged. "I'm a little tired, I guess."

"I suspected as much," Jackie said, sitting down and quickly consuming a few stray kernels of popcorn Merida had missed. "Want a ride home?"

"You ready to leave?" Merida asked.

"No. I thought I would hang around a little longer," Jackie said, frankly a little embarrassed by what she was saying. "You and Peter can get a ride home with Milly Brooks."

"Sounds good," Merida responded. "Is her husband going on this run?"

"Yes," Jackie answered.

"Then Peter will have to hold those adorable little *Omen* twins on his lap," Merida pointed out.

Jackie laughed guiltily. She knew her friend shared her uneasiness about the Dugan girls. "Well, he had Jake on his lap on the way over, right? I'm sure everyone involved will figure he's trading up."

"Not necessarily, Jackie," Merida teased. "Your little boy doesn't seem all that interested in girls."

"He just likes lady medical examiners better," Jackie cracked as she saw Lee Humphries approach. And it was true, Jackie's son had a powerful crush on the tall, deeply tanned, slightly horsey-looking medical examiner.

"Hola!" Lee greeted them, mindful of Merida's heritage and the fact that Jackie had been spending a lot of time in Los Angeles. "Qué pasa?"

"What it is," Merida replied.

Lee gave the woman, easily old enough to be her mother, a cynical look, then laughed aloud. "You two are too much."

"Why?" Jackie asked.

"I don't know," Lee answered, negligently throwing her thin, muscular legs up on the table. "So fire away if you have questions. What do you want to know?"

"What did the doctor die of?" Jackie asked, going to the soda machine for a can of carrot soda.

"He was killed," Lee informed the curious duo of film professors, "when a sharp object, jammed into his side, cut through his aorta. With the largest artery in his body torn in two, the doctor died painfully, bleeding to death, probably over a period of ten or fifteen minutes."

Jackie slowly put down her soda.

Seeing this, the medical examiner laughed loudly. "Wake up, Lee. I've got to stop doing that. 'Talkin' gore,' Roy calls it, when people are eating or drinking."

The "Roy" who Lee Humphries referred to was her boyfriend, Roy Thomas, another young pathologist and the new coroner of nearby Wardville.

"That's okay," Jackie said. "It's just that you remind me of how horrible it was to watch that poor man die."

"In a room full of doctors, a physician died without anyone lifting a finger to save him," Merida pointed out dryly.

"It wasn't quite that bad," Jackie said. "Everyone was standing up and Maury was making a commotion by attacking the pizza delivery boy. The minute people saw that Dr. Munch was hurt, several Emergency Room personnel rushed over to help him."

"It's very hard to do something constructive in a situation like that," Lee Humphries said, somewhat defensively (doctors hate to criticize other physicians, especially when they might someday need their testimony at a malpractice hearing of their own). "The problem is, unless you see the blood and understand immediately that the stab wound is a deep one, you assume that the patient has suffered a heart attack or stroke and you try to elevate the feet, or pump the chest with cardiopulmonary massage, or try to give mouth to mouth to force air into the lungs. Unfortunately, all these are disastrous choices in this case, since they force out the blood even faster. Dr. Munch was really beyond help the moment he hit the floor."

"So the cause of death was definitely the stab wound and not poison?" Jackie queried.

"It's interesting you should ask that," Lee responded. "You know, I've sent tissue samples from the area around the wound to a toxicologist in Canton. It looks like there might have been poison on the bottle the murderer used to stab him."

"Did you say bottle?" Jackie asked.

"I wouldn't swear to it," the young, acting medical examiner continued, "but from the fragments I've recovered, it looks like the type of bottle emergency rooms use to hold saline solutions."

"Saline solution," Merida exclaimed. "What would they use that for? To clean off your arm before sticking you?"

"No," Lee responded. "They usually use an alcohol-based scrub for that. The thing is, a serum, like the kind Dr. Munch was apparently planning to administer, is carried in a plastic bag in a concentrated gel-like form. In order to restore the gel into a form that can be injected into a person's veins, you need to add distilled water in a saline solution, which has been slightly warmed in an autoclave."

"Why?" Jackie asked.

"Well," the autopsy surgeon explained, "it's much harder to inject gel into a vein than a liquid. Ideally, to keep the contents of your syringe from flowing back out of the vein, you want to inject a solution that is thinner than human blood. So you add water. The saline part of the solution keeps the water and concentrated serum mixed, otherwise the serum would sink right to the bottom of the bottle."

"What sort of syringe was the doctor using?" Merida asked.

"He was actually using an inoculation gun," Humphries responded. "In my autopsy I found that he was fairly well crippled up with arthritis. He would have needed to use an automatic delivery system, such as a 'shot gun,' as they call it, in order to give the inoculations quickly and accurately. The gun would have been connected by a thin piece of tubing to the bottle of serum solution."

"Is it possible," Merida asked, "that someone could have accidentally upset the bottle? Perhaps even by trying to wrestle the shot gun out of the doctor's hand?"

"It's really not possible," Lee answered. She took a napkin and withdrew a black, fine-line marker from her bushy Afro. "See, the wound looks like this, with the shards of glass going in at an upward angle. If the bottle fell from the counter or dripstand, or whatever it was attached to, the glass would have entered the doctor's side at a downward angle. Plus, we would have found additional shards of glass around the wound. Instead, we see a wound caused by someone forcing a goodly hunk of glass with three or four sharp points through the doctor's clothing." Lee looked up at Jackie. "Jackie, you were there. When I saw the body it was nude. What was the doctor wearing when you saw him?"

Jackie thought back. "He was wearing his own clothes under a labcoat, I believe."

"All right," Lee nodded. "Then he had at least two layers of clothing, more if he was wearing a suit jacket beneath the labcoat or a T-shirt beneath his dress shirt, to go through. Plus, the area of the wound is significant. It may have been an accident of course. The murderer may have been trying to stick Munch in the chest or the middle of the back and just slipped. However, it is also possible that the murderer has some knowledge of medicine, or perhaps has killed someone in this fashion before."

Jackie looked up alertly.

Lee took a moment to get a burrito from a vending machine and put it in the microwave.

"Why do you say that?" Jackie asked.

"Because it is actually a lot harder to kill someone by stabbing them than it looks. A blade inserted through the chest must go between the ribs in order to pierce the heart, and in many cases, if it does manage to go through the peritoneal sac, the kind of rubbery bag below the surface of skin which holds the organs in place, the heart will immediately fold to cover the hole and minimize it.

"I would say the chances of someone jamming a broken bottle into a man's chest and killing him are four to one. The back is even harder to penetrate with a bottle since both the spine and the largest muscles in the body are in the way. That's why most of the assassins who stabbed Julius Caesar in what looked like vital spots didn't come anywhere near killing him. The proper way to kill someone with a broken bottle, dare I say it, is precisely the way the murderer killed Dr. Munch. You stab from the side backward, trying to catch the aorta. The lower you strike, the faster the blood will rush out of the body and the victim will die."

Jackie shuddered. Merida, however, was made of stronger stuff. "I don't get the part about the poison."

"Well, if the bottle was brought into the Emergency Room," Lee explained, "you would assume that the murderer himself . . ."

"Not a she?"

"It was a large piece of glass, shoved in very hard and very deep," Lee responded. "You would need a woman nearly six feet tall, with large hands and the muscles of a gorilla, to create this wound."

"Really?"

"Well," the medical examiner took a bite of burrito, then equivocated, "I suppose one of us could do it if we were insane with rage or hopped-up on some adrenaline-like drug, but I would be very surprised if the murderer didn't turn out to be male. I have studied hundreds of killings of this kind, and I don't recall a woman ever striking a man this way. We tend to strike overhand, with a sharp knife, trying to puncture the chest, throat, or face, or lower, using both hands to tear at the stomach or genitals. To create this kind of wound, a killer would have to stand to one side of and slightly behind his victim. He probably reached his left hand behind the doctor and pulled him closer in a one-handed hug, while stabbing up with a broken bottle, held in a cloth of some kind. Or perhaps he protected his own hand with a tough leather or rubber glove."

Jackie thought of the men she had seen in the Emergency Room. Which one could have been capable of such an act?

"I was saying," Lee continued, "that if the murderer brought the bottle in with him, he probably put the poison in the bottle himself. It is my impression however that the bottle was in the Emergency Room, which means that the murderer was familiar with the ER and had counted on there being a bottle handy when he got the opportunity to make his strike, or he came armed with another weapon and decided to switch to the bottle because it was a more effective weapon, or he thought it would be harder to trace back to him, or the act was unpremeditated. I tend to favor the third solution. I think the murderer, whether or not he had any strong feelings toward the doctor previously, only decided to kill him when he saw the doctor about to administer the shots.

"The noise and confusion created by your dog," Lee addressed Jackie, "gave him the opportunity to break the bottle and use the broken piece without being noticed. I wouldn't be surprised if a careful examination of the murderer's hand didn't reveal a laceration or bruise from the glass."

"But what about the poison?" Merida asked.

"I think, if there was poison, it was probably brought into the hospital by the victim rather than the murderer," Lee answered, coolly knocking back a swallow of her soda.

"Then you think that Linus Munch had come to Marx-Wheeler to administer poison to the people he was inoculating?" Jackie clarified.

"I think it's darn possible," the acting coroner responded. "What did he have to lose? He had a prostate carcinoma that had metastasized into the bone. It would have killed him, very painfully, within the next six months."

"How can you be sure he knew about it?" Merida asked.

Lee smiled wickedly. "A man might ignore an aneurysm, or a blocked carotid artery, or even an almost totally occluded heart, if he's really preoccupied or afraid of doctors, but he wouldn't have been able to ignore this.

"I'm sure the doctor knew he was dying. The question is, who decided to not only stop him, but kill him?" The autopsy surgeon finished her burrito with one last snapping bite. "You may want to consider, Jackie," she said, turning to the amateur sleuth, "whether you want to solve this one. Because if you do, chances are you will be less popular than the murderer. Even with a hard-boiled professional like me."

CHAPTER 19

Marcella asked Dannen Jeffreys for a drink of water, then coolly removed her bug, put in a new tape, then placed it into her shoulderbag.

Jeffreys returned from the administrator's private john with a white-and-green mug. She pretended to sip the drink, thanked the bodyguard, then followed him into the conference room where Richard Bellamy sat at the head of the table, stone drunk.

"Thank you for seeing me, Dr. Bellamy."

"What choice did I have?" Bellamy shrugged. "Tell me. How bad do you intend to hurt me?"

Marcella, amused, sat. She then put her cup on a cork coaster, thoughtfully placed on the highly polished walnut table in front of her, and crossed her legs.

"You personally?" she asked. "Or the Marx-Wheeler Medical Center?"

"They are the same," Bellamy pronounced.

"Are you sure?" Marcella asked.

"Quite sure," said a tall, curly-blond weightlifter in an English suit.

"Ms. Jacobs—my associate, Bronwyn Caruthers."

The Welsh-born deputy administrator leaned across the table and shook Marcella's hand with a grip that was meant to impress. Marcella was more impressed by the executive's platinum Rolex. "A pleasure, Ms. Jacobs. We have watched your rise with considerable interest."

"Really?" Marcella responded. "Who's we?"

"The hospital board," Caruthers said negligently. He carefully sat down and gestured to a burly bodyguard with a brown handlebar mustache and a football player's build to bring a brandy decanter over. "This is Mr. Ditko, of our security staff."

The big security guard nodded and set out crystal snifters for Bellamy and Caruthers. He started to put down a third snifter in front of Marcella, when the newscaster put up her hand, "No thanks, D. J."

"Oh," Caruthers smiled, showing perfect dimples on either side. "We have a sports fan among us. Did you ever watch Mr. Ditko play?"

"No," Marcella said coolly, uncrossing her legs. "I heard he'd fallen in with a bad lot. Tragic, isn't it, how the talents of our ex–football players are so often underutilized." Caruthers and Ditko exchanged "How much does she know?" looks, then composed themselves.

"For God's sake, pour the brandy," Bellamy demanded hoarsely, running his fingers through his sweaty, spiky hair.

Ditko did as instructed and paused. Caruthers tried again. "Are you sure you won't join us, Ms. Jacobs? Rumor has it that Jean Lafitte and Andrew Jackson bear-wrestled over a cask of this fine ambrosia during the battle of 1812."

"No thanks," Marcella said politely. "I'll stick with my water."

Bellamy made a face. Clearly he felt toward the substance the way W. C. Fields did.

"But you haven't touched your water," Caruthers pointed out reasonably.

"To be honest," Marcella said coolly. "With all this talk of poison in the air, I'm a little skeptical about drinking anything an employee of your hospital may hand me."

Now it was Caruthers and Bellamy's turn to exchange "How much does she know?" looks.

Ditko glared at the newswoman, then withdrew, placing the tray back in the concealed bar. Afterward, he sat at the end of the table opposite Dannen Jeffreys.

Caruthers decided to chance a remark. "Surely, Ms. Jacobs, you don't intend to maintain that Linus Munch was an employee of our institution?"

"So you concede Linus Munch was planning to inject volunteers for the AIDS serum with poison," Marcella said at once. It was a lucky stab, and Marcella had been lucky to grab ahold of the information. She had, by freak chance, been in the ladies' room on the traction floor, after visiting Fred Jackson, when she overheard an operating room scrub nurse named Candace (widely thought to be Dick Bellamy's mistress) confiding in a chubby little obstetrics nurse the rumor that Dr. Munch's serum pouch contained cyanide.

Bellamy finished his drink in a gulp and started coughing. Caruthers patted his superior on the back and reassured him. "Hold up there, Dick. You're okay. You're fine."

Marcella knew that Caruthers was trying to help Bellamy regain his composure before he made any damaging admissions and so switched her guns to him. "And just what is your role in all this, sir?"

"I'm Dr. Bellamy's assistant administrator," Caruthers answered easily.

"You're an M.D.?" Marcella asked.

"No, no. Not at all," Caruthers responded, sitting back in his chair, as a somewhat recovered Dick Bellamy wiped the drool from his own chin with a handkerchief. "I'm more of a facilitator. My background is in business."

"Isn't that unusual?" Marcella pressed.

"No, not at all," Caruthers said easily, sipping his brandy. "In this ever changing world, medical centers all over the country are dealing with the fact that a physician or a hospital administrator with a medical or scientific background is not necessarily the best person to handle the myriad problems confronting today's hospitals. I oversee Marx-Wheeler's Security and Publicity departments. I monitor and occasionally audit the Billing Department and coordinate the medical center's dealings with the vendors who run our cafeteria, rathskeller, gift and florist shops, and the snack carts and parking concessions. I'm also head of the team that negotiates union contracts. And let me say, off the record, that your organization of the pickets was most impressive. You drove us to the table a great deal sooner than we would have been otherwise motivated to do so."

"Spare me your compliments, Mr. Caruthers," Marcella snapped. "Where were you when Dr. Munch was stabbed earlier this evening?"

"I was at the Juniper Tavern," Caruthers said smoothly. "Partaking of the delicious dinner you and KCIN were kind enough to feed our employees."

"What?" Marcella sputtered.

"Please," Caruthers smiled. "I wasn't there under false pretenses; as a matter of fact, I was invited by your assistant, my girlfriend, Sandy Carlisle."

Marcella burned for a moment. No wonder Sandy had been so secretive about her new main squeeze. She knew Marcella would have never let her anywhere near the Marx-Wheeler story if Marcella knew her boyfriend represented management.

"I also," Caruthers continued silkily, "coordinate affairs with our legal representatives."

"And you're here in that capacity?" Marcella asked.

"He's here because I want him here," croaked Bellamy. "Listen, Jacobs. I could threaten you."

"You would have your hulking bodyguards beat me up?" Marcella pretended to be amused. "And how would you explain that?"

"We can make it look like an accident," Ditko assured her.

"And how do you know I don't know some tricky kung fu?" Marcella asked. "Like all those women on TV?"

Ditko laughed heartily and the others soon joined in. "As long as you don't know any more real fighting than they do, we'll be fine."

Marcella laughed too. "All right." She turned to Bronwyn Caruthers. "Is the threat part of our evening over now?"

"The physical threat part?" Caruthers elucidated. "Yes, absolutely. I am not interested in seeing you get hurt physically. Even if we could get away with it—which is certainly possible in this day and age—it doesn't stop the damage. The worst case scenario is it makes some sort of cultural icon out of you. A Karen Silkwood, if you will. At best, it inspires other reporters."

"But you have other ways to threaten me?" Marcella said alertly.

"The usual threats to get you fired," Caruthers said, almost carelessly. "Very hard to manage successfully though, as you know. We have some very powerful people on our board."

"Including my wife, the mayor," Bellamy said loudly, as he filled his glass again.

Neither of the bodyguards got up to help him this time. They both realized that if their boss was to be rescued, it would be his bright, young Welsh assistant who would save him.

"As the good doctor says," Caruthers continued smoothly. "You know, your parent company won't stomach a lot of heat right now. Especially for a story like this. Who in their right mind would run such a story? Who in their right mind would take the chance that the insane act of a dying man . . . ?"

"Dying? Before he was stabbed?"

"Cancer."

"A brain tumor, which pressed down on certain moral centers, making him act evilly against his will?" Marcella asked innocently.

"No," Caruthers said with a fine disgust. "This isn't TV. Dr. Munch was rotting away in the groin. An orchiectomy—you can imagine what is removed in that operation—was the next step, then gradual decline into disorientation and senility."

"Like his brother," Marcella commented.

"Far worse," Caruthers corrected in a mild voice. "Marvin Munch may live twenty years and with all of his reproductive equipment intact. That means a lot to a man, you know. Even if he's in no real position to use it."

"It means a lot to a woman too," Marcella said simply.

"There's one more thing."

"I'm really getting the full treatment tonight, aren't I?" Marcella asked.

"We're fighting for our life," Caruthers said simply. "Why hold back?"

"Then you may fire when ready, Gridley," Marcella responded coolly, quoting Lord Horatio Nelson at Trafalgar.

"We have a strong case that Vic Kingston killed Linus Munch."

"Come on. Like what?"

"The listening device you placed earlier . . ." Caruthers turned to Dannen Jeffreys. "Mr. Jeffreys, you kept your eye on Ms. Jacobs when she sent you out of the room . . ."

"Yes sir," Jeffreys said quickly. "Through the peek panel in Dr. Bellamy's bathroom door."

Marcella blushed hotly, even though she had never used the hospital administrator's bathroom, to think that she could have been the innocent victim of a peeping Dan!

"And did you see," Caruthers asked, "where Ms. Jacobs put the listening device she recovered from Dr. Bellamy's office?"

"Yes sir," the security guard answered at once. "She put it in her purse. After changing tapes first."

"Do you deny this, Ms. Jacobs?"

"You have no right . . ." Marcella started indignantly.

"Please." Caruthers made a disparaging face. "Spare us the manufactured outrage. Do you doubt that between the four of us, we could not wrestle your shoulderbag away from you?"

"You could try!" Marcella clutched her handbag until her knuckles were white. She had such a fierce look on her face that the four men laughed.

"I like this one," D. J. Ditko said. "I really do."

Caruthers smiled wickedly. "Well, Ms. Jacobs. You've made a new fan."

"Great."

"Don't be too quick to be dismissive," Caruthers commented wryly. "D. J. doesn't fall easily, believe me, and he's had a great many offers."

"Six hundred cheerleaders can't be wrong," Ditko asserted.

Marcella gave the men a "thanks, but no thanks" grimace.

"Quit jerking around, Caruthers," Bellamy rasped. "My wife will be here any minute. Let's clamp this down, shall we?"

"Sorry, Dr. Bellamy," Caruthers said at once, resuming his sober attitude. "Mr. Jeffreys, freshen the doctor's drink, will you?"

"Yes, sir."

Caruthers turned back to Marcella. "Are you sure we can't get you a drink?"

"Do you have something that's still sealed?"

"Like the saline solution bottle Dr. Munch put his poison vaccine in?"

"Ho, ho," Marcella responded. "I might as well stick with this." She picked up her cup of water and took a sip.

As Jeffreys circled around, pouring brandies, Caruthers resumed, "The fact of the matter is, Ms. Jacobs, we don't have to take your tape from you, legally or illegally. We took the liberty of making a copy of our own."

"You did?"

"Mr. Ditko?"

The burly security guard slid a tape recorder the length of the table.

"How do I know that what you're going to play is a copy of my tape?" Marcella asked suspiciously.

"Compare it to your own later," Caruthers said with an indifferent shrug.

"How do I know you haven't doctored the tape?"

"Have your experts check it," Caruthers snapped. He regained control and in a more convincing voice said, "Really, Ms. Jacobs. We haven't the facilities, and we certainly haven't had the time to do anything tricky. But I must tell you, either way, we intend to turn this tape over to your rival, KOPY. I don't think they will have any hesitation about using it to embarrass you."

"What's it say?" Marcella asked.

"Hear for yourself," Caruthers offered, turning on the tape recorder.

Marcella immediately recognized Vic Kingston's voice.

"I don't care who authorized it, damn it! You can't do this, Linus!"

She then heard the throaty tones of the late Nobel laureate. "What have you been talking about for the last four hours, Victor? Keep quiet a few moments longer and you'll have the story of your lifetime. You'll be able to write your own ticket. Hell, we'll do a series of interviews afterward and you can write a book or sell a videotape."

"No, goddamn it!" Vic Kingston was heard on the tape. "I'm not going to let you do this, Linus."

"Pah. You can't stop me."

"No? Hell's bells I can't stop you. I'll tell . . ."

"You'll tell whom, Victor?" Munch questioned angrily. "Your word against mine is it? Whom will they believe? The way you sound now, they won't even listen. Can't you hear yourself? No one will listen to you. No one will believe the words of a drunk!"

CHAPTER 20

As Bronwyn Caruthers turned off the recorder upstairs with a snap, Jackie returned to the lobby and was beckoned outside.

Jackie pushed through the still-unlocked wheelchair-access door and saw Bara Day waving to her. Wishing she had brought her raincoat with her, she said, "Hi, Bara!"

"Hi! Is that guard still there?"

"No," Jackie said. "He's catching a shower somewhere."

"Good! Cyril!"

Cyril Plum poked his head out around the corner of the toolshed (his yellowing white hair by now quite damp from the drizzle which had started again). "Okay?"

"Okay!" Bara said loudly.

And a moment later, Maury, cleaned up for the second time that evening, bounded into view. Maury smelled food on Jackie's hands, and he had a big red crumb remover ready to remedy that problem.

"Oh, dear."

Plum sneezed loudly and Bara Day grabbed the older man by his arm. "Darling, let's leave before you catch your death of a cold."

"Please, Bara. I told you. I was born in the north of England, where it was so cold they used to sharpen the legs of corpses so they could hammer them into the ground."

"Do you . . . should I ask the police officer if I can give you a ride?" Jackie offered.

"Not necessary," Cyril replied. "I have my old buggy."

"It's all right if you go?" Jackie asked.

"What could we tell them?" Bara demanded. "We didn't see anything at all."

"Well, dear lady," Cyril Plum protested. "We did see one remarkable thing."

As the elderly novelist told Jackie what they had seen . . .

. . . Marcella went out into the corridor and was surprised to see Kevin. He stood nervously at the exit door that Vic Kingston had disappeared through earlier in the evening.

"Hi, Marcella."

"What are you doing here?" Marcella asked, straightening a lock of her hair and pulling her jacket down in front.

"I was a little worried," Kevin said sheepishly.

Marcella noticed that the hot TV rental agent was still wearing his Catholic priest disguise. "I'm fine," she said, then shivered.

"Are you sure?" Erlanger asked. Then his urge to hug her, coupled with her urge to be hugged, brought the two together in the corridor.

"Hold me," she said.

Erlanger did.

"Did they ask about the videotape?"

"Not yet," Erlanger said, nuzzling the top of Marcella's head.

He was so strong, so loyal, so gentle and caring that Marcella figured, *What the heck—kiss him.*

"Mm."

"Am I a great kisser?" Marcella asked brightly.

"The best."

"So where are the police investigating Dr. Munch's murder?"

Erlanger took a moment to make the transition, then answered, "So far it's just Oficer Watson. I gave her my name and she's still working her way down to us. I suppose I should go back down pretty soon and check in."

Marcella shook her head in wonder. "What do you think is going on down there?"

Down in the Emergency Room conference room, Patricia Watson was answering the same question.

"I'm doing the best I can, sir," she tiredly told Palmer's richest citizen.

"That's not good enough!" Stuart Goodwillie raged, slapping his umbrella on the table. "I'll have your badge, you bumbling incompetent!"

"Back off!" Watson demanded, standing up. "Or I'll handcuff you to a lavatory stall and leave you there until the very end."

"Shoot her, Stillman," Goodwillie demanded. "Fill her guts with hot lead. No, check that. She's wearing a vest. Shoot her in the head."

Although Goodwillie's bodyguard made no effort to draw out his illegal concealed weapon, Patricia Watson was quickly on her feet and reaching for her own 9mm. Glock. "Muhammed!"

The startled security guard quickly pushed aside his half-consumed muffin top and sugar tea. "Yes, Patricia?"

"You'll back me up when I swear that Goodwillie was going for his gun when I blasted him?"

The security man, assuming that Officer Watson had a cheap .22 pistol in an ankle holster she could plant on the bullet-ridden industrialist, quickly averred, "You write it up, Patricia, I will sign it. Anything you like. Three times in triplicate."

"Please," Georgiana Bowman requested, as Goodwillie darted around his bodyguard. "Can't we all just get along?"

"I didn't start this," Watson responded through gritted teeth. She then pointed her pistol at the bodyguard and his employer. "But I'm sure willing to finish it!"

"Stuart!" Georgiana barked. "*Stu-art!*"

"Nobody here but us chickens," the cowardly bottled-water baron bleated.

"Apologize!"

"Sorry."

"Longer!"

"I'm most terribly sorry. What could I have been thinking of?"

"More sincere."

"My humblest apologies."

Georgiana turned to the police officer. "Is that acceptable?"

"I suppose so," Watson allowed, cocking her safeties back on.

"Now, young lady," Georgiana said in her best director's voice. "I know you are here alone . . ."

Muhammed huffed and the director quickly added, " . . . officially. Although Mr. Sanji is obviously doing a yeoman effort as a private citizen."

Satisfied that his leonine pride had not been dented, Muhammed Sanji sat back down and resumed snacking.

"Please, Officer," Georgiana pleaded with the younger patrolwoman. "This neck of mine has seen nine decades. Won't you sit down and let me hold it in a more comfortable position?"

Watson slowly holstered her pistol and sat down in her armchair.

"Stuart!" Georgiana raised her voice, but pleasantly. "Won't you rejoin us?"

"Is Dirty Mary still waving her weapon?" Goodwillie asked querulously. "Didn't half the nation recently riot over just such an example of police brutality?"

"Come on, Stuart," Georgiana offered. "Cut the cr . . ."

She was cut off by the entrance of a small boy and a noble dog. The latter of the two grr'ed loudly and all heads turned.

"Excuse me," Peter Walsh said, wiping a chocolate milk mustache from his upper lip (knowing that his mother, if she were here, would want him to look presentable). "You guys are investigating something, right?"

"Yes," Officer Watson said at once. "Do you know something that may help us?"

"Don't be daft," Goodwillie instructed. "What can a mere boy in short pants add to a murder investigation? Haven't we made it plain enough, Officer Torquemada? We'd like to go home!"

"It's not me," Peter said. "It's Jake."

The intelligent dog turned around and, although he was not a pointer, bent his left foreleg at the second joint, indicating that they should follow.

CHAPTER 21

Upstairs, Marcella and Kevin Erlanger had broken their embrace and were about to walk to the elevator when all of a sudden the co-anchor thought of something. "Wait, Kevin!"

"What?"

"This room . . ." Marcella pointed to the end room on the right side of the corridor, from which she had seen Vic Kingston emerge earlier. "Who are the patients here, do you know?"

Erlanger glanced over. "Well, this is the penthouse floor. It's a private room. I could go down and check my records. Get his name if he's rented a TV. But from the look of this . . ."

The TV rental agent put his hand on the red code cart outside the patient's door. "He's probably not watching anything."

"Let's go in," Marcella said.

"Why?" Erlanger asked. But he spoke only to the air.

This private patient's room was not a pleasant place. The only light came from a single overhead fluorescent bulb. The walls were beige with a single faded print of the moon, shining on a troubled sea. The blinds were drawn. The room's sole occupant lay on a single narrow bed surrounded by equipment. A Gomco pump on the bedstand pulled fluids and mucus from the patient's throat. An oxygen stand held two small blue tanks, hooked by tubes to the patient's nose. An intravenous drip stand held two thick plastic bags of glucose and other fluids, delivered through a thin plastic tube to the patient's arm. A urinary catheter, lower down, took waste fluids out of the patient and emptied them into a container under the bed.

Marcella picked up the patient's medical chart and noted the name. "B. Crowder Westfall," she said aloud. "Do you know him?"

Erlanger shook his head.

"Hm. He works at the university," Marcella mused. "I guess I could ask Jackie about him. Is she still here?"

Jackie was indeed still on the premises. Having thanked Bara Day and Cyril Plum for their help, she had seen them to their car, and then returned to the hospital with Maury in tow.

As she entered the waiting room, Chubb Greenway shrunk back in terror. "Don't let him near me!" the young pizza boy begged piteously. "I don't have any more pizza. Honest!"

Maury affably licked gum off the floor and Jackie took a quick look around. "Where's Officer Watson?"

"She took off down the hall over there, with some kid and an Alsatian dog," Chubb answered.

"Jake's a German shepherd," Jackie said automatically.

Suddenly, the elevator opened and Merida Green and the extended Brooks family spilled out into the Emergency Room.

"Well, we're off!" John Brooks announced.

"Say goodbye to Ms. Walsh, girls," Milly requested.

"Goodnight, Ms. Walsh," the girls said sweetly.

"Where's Peter?" Merida asked.

The two girls giggled. They both had tremendous crushes on the sexy young hockey player.

"Apparently he and Jake have launched their own investigation," Jackie answered. "Don't worry, John. He can ride home with me."

"Okey dodlee doo," Brooks chortled. "Come on, troops!"

Merida stood, confused for a moment and wondering whether or not to follow. "Do you want me to stay?"

"No," Jackie said. "I'll be fine. Go ahead home. Keep an eye on the place."

Merida nodded, knowing that the Walsh duplex had been plagued with a wealth of burglars and break-in artists. "Good luck, Jackie," she said, giving her friend a kiss on the cheek. "Call me, if you have any problems."

"Thank you, Merida," Jackie said warmly. "Goodnight, everyone!"

As the Brooks and Merida Green contingent exited the hospital . . .

. . . Patricia Watson, Muhammed Sanji, Stuart Goodwillie, Georgiana Bowman, and Evan Stillman had caught up to Pete Walsh and the intrepid Jake.

"Look!" Peter said.

"What is it?" demanded Goodwillie.

Patricia Watson looked carefully at the mail slot where Jake was pointing and pulled out a towel-wrapped package consisting of the traveling serum pack that Dr. Munch had transferred to the saline bottle before starting the inoculations, and a pair of bloody surgeon's gloves (one of them cut and lacerated by little shards of glass). "Exhibit One!"

"Pah!" Goodwillie scoffed. "Say those are the gloves of the person who did the knifing? What of it? Anyone could pick up a pair of gloves like that. They're lying all around the hospital. They could have even bought them at a pharmacy and brought them in from the outside."

"That's quite true," Watson willingly conceded. "But do you notice something?" She held the gloves up to the light.

"No!" Goodwillie said loudly, obviously speaking for the rest of them. "We are not mind readers. I suppose we could contact those foolish illusionists."

"He's referring to Bill and Lil Reigert, twin magicians," Georgiana contributed.

"But it would be easier, I suppose," Goodwillie crabbed, "if you just told us."

"I'd be happy to, Mr. Goodwillie," Patricia Watson said quickly, happy to be doing some real detecting at last. "What do you see here? No, better yet, what don't you see here?"

Goodwillie started the ball rolling. "Well, I don't see the principality of Monaco. Is that relevant?"

"What you don't see," Watson answered her own question, "is talcum powder. Many glove companies pre-fill their gloves with talcum powder in order to help medical personnel slide their gloves off and on more easily." Watson spoke from experience. Her mother, Gail, the rehabilitation nurse with the knee brace, had taught her well. "When you don't have these pre-treated gloves, you shake a little talcum powder on your hands before putting on the glove. That is, if you do it all the time. Someone not experienced with putting on and taking off rubber gloves is likely to tug them on, without the powder, as this person did. Therefore, I conclude, the murderer was not a member of the medical center."

"Capital surmise, Patricia," Muhammed Sanji exclaimed.

"In no sense of the word," Goodwillie crabbed. "It could mean that. It could also mean that some bloodthirsty white coat intentionally eschewed the use of talcum powder, thinking that the fat-headed constabulary would come to precisely that conclusion.

"You seem to forget, Madam, that people are aware of police techniques. There are, are there not, four or five thousand real-life police shows polluting the airwaves—plus, dozens of mystery programs. I myself occasionally tolerate the shows aired on that *Mystery* program on PBS. In addition, we have a hundred years of murder mysteries filling the shelves of our bookstores to overflowing, and perhaps they have not only entertained the poor deluded few who still buy books, but also educated a few murderers on how to commit a more perfect crime. I say your surmise, therefore, is spinach, and to heck with it."

"Thank you for your warm words of encouragement, Mr. Goodwillie," Watson replied, as cheerful as before. "But whether I'm right or not, I know one thing. I've got whoever did this crime cold."

"How so?" Goodwillie sneered.

"If you'll notice, Mr. Goodwillie," Watson answered. "The person who wore these gloves had to turn them inside out to remove them. And because they didn't use talcum powder, they left fingerprints, and if I'm not mistaken, I have ten clear prints."

CHAPTER 22

As Jackie watched Maury knock over a paper-only refuse bin, inspect its contents, and swat it across the room, the elevator again opened up behind her. Sensing a special aura, Jackie turned and saw the rumpled newsman staring at her.

"Mr. Kingston!"

"What?" The anchorman's hand immediately dropped into his pocket. "What do you want?"

"Are you looking for Officer Watson?" Jackie asked. "I know she was looking for you earlier."

"No, no. I . . ." Kingston did not wait to find out that Watson had left the area and that he could waltz right out the Emergency Room exit. Instead he feverishly stabbed at the "door close" button. "Tell her . . . I have to use the men's . . . I'll be right back."

Not really very concerned, Jackie turned back to little Horace Greenway. "What do you say, Chubb? They haven't talked to you yet?"

"No, but it's not the policewoman's fault. She started to ask me questions before and I got a nosebleed."

Jackie shook her head at the pathetic pizza delivery boy. "Did you call home and tell your parents where you were so they wouldn't worry?"

"I tried to," Chubb said. "But the phone's not working. Mr. Allen said he'd call them when he got to his office."

"When did Mr. Allen leave?" Jackie asked.

"Right after that man got killed," Chubb blubbered. "He got killed and I got fired."

"Now, now," Jackie said. "Maybe Mr. Allen's story will save your job."

"He's going to be too busy to write about pizza now," young Greenway accurately predicted. "Besides, it's too late. They sent a tow truck to pick up my putt-putt. I watched them through the glass here."

"Well, I'm sure you can do better than that awful pizza delivery job," Jackie said soothingly.

"I already have," the boy responded. "Mr. Goodwillie offered me a job."

"There you go."

"But how am I going to get home?" Chubb sniffled.

"I'll give you a lift," Jackie offered. "If . . ."

"Thanks a lot, Ms. Walsh," Chubb effused.

" . . . *If* you help me mind Maury."

"Oh, no."

Maury turned to Chubb with glee, and licked a dried piece of cheese off the lad's leg. It was like having his clothes dry-cleaned while he was still wearing them.

"Come on," Jackie said. "You can do it."

"No, I can't," Chubb responded miserably.

"Horace Greenway the sixth . . ."

"The seventh," Chubb corrected. "Dad's name is Horace

too—he gave himself the name 'Max' when he played football."

"Listen to me!" Jackie demanded. "You are an adult now."

Chubb snuffled again and sorted through his pockets full of comic books, penny candies, and trading cards for a napkin to blow his nose.

Jackie reached into her fanny pack and handed him a tissue.

"Thank you."

"You're welcome. Now you have to get a grip on yourself. You can't live at home forever."

"Yes, I can," Chubb pointed out as he tried vainly to clear his sinuses (he was of course allergic to dog fur). "According to the latest census, one out of seven kids my age lives at home."

"Chubb!"

"Yes, Ma'am?"

"I'm trying to have a constructive dialogue with you. Shut the hell up!"

"Yes, Ma'am."

"Whether or not you *can* live at home, you shouldn't live at home."

"Why not?"

"Because you are a responsible human being."

"I am?"

"You should be. And you better get used to pulling your own weight. The people of this country are tired of working long days and nights to support deadbeats. There's a will in this country," Jackie informed the indigent ex-pizza deliverer, "not only to reform welfare programs but to do away with them completely. And people, especially young people like you, are going to have to pull their own weight for a change."

"I'll never have to pull my own weight," Chubb replied without triumph. "I have rich parents."

"Chubb!" Jackie roared. "Do you ever want *anyone* to respect you?"

"Yes," the young Greenway heir answered in a quiet voice. "I wish you'd respect me enough to stop calling me 'Chubb.' Do you think that's a nickname I picked for myself?"

"What would you like to be called?" Jackie asked at once.

"How about 'Hoss'? That's short for Horace, and it's kind of friendly. It reminds people of the guy on *Bonanza*."

"Okay, Chu . . . Hoss," Jackie enthused. "Maury, you listen to Hoss now. You understand?"

Maury ate the penny candy young Hoss Greenway offered him, then turned back to his former mistress to see if she had some as well.

"Does he really understand what you're saying to him?" Hoss asked.

"Maury," Jackie said, struggling to keep a straight face, "has a mind like a steel trap."

As Jackie and company made their way toward his room, B. Crowder Westfall opened his eyes and stared blearily at his unexpected guests. "Who are you?"

"Marcella Jacobs," the co-anchor introduced herself. "KCIN news. Care to make a statement?"

"And what would I make a statement about?" Westfall choked out. "Dying? Very well, it's very painful. I would recommend against it. And you may quote me."

"Thank you," Marcella said, reaching into her bag and turning her taping device on. "I will. Did you know Linus Munch?"

"The Nobel laureate?"

"Yes."

"No, but I know who he was. I knew what he was."

"What's that?" Marcella asked negligently.

"I heard talk . . ." Westfall's voice cracked and he gasped for breath.

Erlanger handed him a drink bottle.

Westfall managed to move his breathing tube to one side, and take the built-in plastic drinking straw into the corner of his mouth. He sucked weakly, then reapplied the breathing tube. "Thank you."

"Don't mention it."

"You were telling us what you heard, er . . . Professor."

"Yes." Westfall adjusted his mouthpiece so he could speak more comfortably. "I heard them talking in the administrator's office."

"Really?" Marcella asked, sitting at the foot of the bed. "How?"

"Through some freak in the ventilating system," Westfall replied weakly. "I can hear every word. See for yourself."

Erlanger gave Marcella a questioning look. She nodded and he went to the overhead vent in the room. Pushing down a lever, the cantilevered slides opened and the voices of Dannen Jeffreys and Richard Bellamy could be clearly heard.

"What are you doing?"

"I'm pouring you another cup of coffee, *Doctor*."

"I've already had two cups."

"I know, sir, but your wife is on the way. Won't you just drink this and then take a shower?"

"Damn it, Jeffreys. I am tired of you acting as my nursemaid. You want to know what I think about my dear wife the mayor? I don't give a good gosh."

"Kevin!" Marcella then called out.

Erlanger shut the vent, cutting off the sound.

"So you could hear everything," Marcella marveled.

"More than enough," Westfall agreed weakly. "I heard you."

"You did?"

"Just a few moments ago, yes."

"And you heard them playing me the tape incriminating Vic Kingston?"

"I heard that, yes."

"And Vic was in here earlier."

"Yes, he was," Westfall confirmed. "Hiding. He knew the hospital staff was preparing to set him up."

"Did he confess to you?"

"No, just the opposite," Westfall replied, his voice growing stronger now.

"Come again?" Marcella asked, baffled.

"I said, I confessed to him," Westfall wheezed. "And now, sir . . ." The elderly Latin scholar turned to Erlanger. "I would like to confess to you."

Kevin was taken aback. "What?"

"You are a priest, aren't you?"

Erlanger turned to Marcella. She nodded vociferously. "Yes," he responded. "Yes, I am."

"Well, I would like to confess to you." Westfall reached way down for additional resources, then said, "Bless me father for I have sinned. It has been many years since my last confession."

"Forget the eating meat on Friday crap," Marcella instructed. "What's this about you killing someone?"

"I didn't say I would confess to you, Madam," Westfall wheezed. He then raised his heavily lined face crowned with its fringe of rust-colored hair off his pillow and glared at Marcella. "Now be quiet or you'll stand outside in the corridor while I die."

Marcella shut up at once. Westfall then slowly let his head sink back onto the pillow. He then started mumbling in Latin, "The method you have pursued, my dear Pliny . . . if indeed the crime be proved . . . it must be punished . . . as it introduces a very dangerous precedent . . ."

"I'm sorry," Erlanger responded patiently. "I don't understand."

"No, of course. You're Vatican II. Probably don't know a bit of Latin."

"Not much," Erlanger confessed.

"It's just as well," Westfall sighed. "The word 'scholar' has been profaned in our time. It made me almost fit to bust to hear that self-aggrandizing phony called a 'scholar' when all he was was a failed physician, living on the glory of his brother's discoveries."

Marcella said nothing, hoping the Latin professor would give her a better insight into the reason he had for killing Linus Munch.

"I became a Latin scholar, you know, because I was encouraged by a brilliant man of your church."

Erlanger nodded.

"Today I would be lucky, I am sure, to find a father who could confer with me in English. I killed Linus Munch."

"Why?" Kevin Erlanger asked simply.

"Such a large question for such a small matter," Westfall sighed. While the elderly teacher's mind drifted back to the words of Pliny the Younger, Kevin brought the drinking straw to the man's lips. Westfall noticed it, nodded gratefully, and drank as if taking his last drink.

Marcella quietly turned her tape over.

At last Westfall resumed speaking. "I heard them talking. I realized what Munch was going to do. I heard the newsman arguing with him, threatening him, even after the doctor disclosed that he was a dying man. Such foolishness . . . to argue with a dying man. What hold do you have over him?"

Erlanger and Marcella shared a guilty stolen look as Westfall paused for more words.

Words. There had been so many in his lifetime and now, as he lay here, slipping away, he realized how few he still needed. "After the last episode—cardiac fibrillation, whatever it was—they injected me with adrenaline, epinephrine, whatever free samples they had been recently sent by pharmaceutical companies. Normally, they inject you again with Demerol, or some sort of opiate to help you sleep.

"Not this time. Perhaps they simply forgot. Perhaps they resented the number of times I've come so close to dying and they've had to leave their pornographic comic books to come up and save me. Anyway, with the electricity running through my skin and the invigorating drugs running through my veins, I felt . . . well, normal, for the first time in a long time. Not just merely alive.

"So I got up and considered going to the nurses' station and showing them how well I was, but then I realized they wouldn't care. They would probably be angry with me, as if I'd been faking before.

"So I went the other way, to the administrator's elevator. It was on this floor and open. Not working correctly, I suppose. I went in and pressed the button for the ground floor. A mad desire seized me to die in the open air, on a piece of grass—to expire with the earth on my back and the stars in my eyes. When I touched down on the Emergency Room floor, however, and saw him there, with poison he intended to inject in innocent young men's veins . . ."

Westfall faded out for a while, then slowly came back. "You don't know how many times I considered taking poison. Particularly when I heard a young man who I was . . . involved with . . . had died of AIDS."

Marcella and Erlanger exchanged looks. If what this dying man was saying was true, the weakest, frailest, gayest of them all had brought down the mighty Munch before he could harm a single one of them.

"But to murder that way . . . because he had nothing to lose? Because he was bitter that his career was going to end at seventy-three? Bitter? Can you believe it? After forty years of comfort, fame, and glory?

"I am sixty-five. My career is ending along with my life. After years of bitter effort, putting myself through college and graduate school, I finally obtained my doctorate and worked as a librarian for three years at Rodgers University, waiting for the most junior position to become available. I taught for thirty-four years for a salary the government now tells us is below the poverty line. I became chairman of the Latin Studies division the year the department was cut to one full-time instructor. Myself.

"I wrote sixty-seven scholarly treatises and sent them to the two Latin academic magazines in the English-speaking world. They accepted one and published it, much edited, with my name spelled incorrectly.

"I never had a love affair that lasted longer than the rental of the room. I went on two vacations in my life. Came back with dysentery and venereal disease, both times.

"After a lifetime in education, I was elected to the post of dean of faculty and immediately was confronted by the ludicrous specter of political correctness coupled with an incurable case of congestive heart failure.

"And so I had no hesitation in giving my life for his."

Erlanger and Marcella received the news in silence.

"Mr. Kingston was here earlier. He felt very guilty. Guiltier than I felt . . . or feel now, for killing someone. He felt guilty that he hadn't been the one to destroy that madman. I tried to calm him, but he would not believe that I was telling the truth."

"Are you telling the truth?" Erlanger asked, knowing Marcella would want him to.

"As God is my witness," B. Crowder Westfall gasped, his breath coming with shuddering sobs, "and as I soon will be his. I took a bottle from the cart. Broke it and plunged it into that evil man. And I regret only . . . that I could not live to stand trial, so I could tell . . . all of the world that I am glad I did what I did, and would do it again a thousand times."

As Kevin Erlanger administered the last rites to the now-deceased dean, Marcella turned and opened the door, where she was surprised to see none other than Vic Kingston.

Kingston wheeled, wide-eyed, and pulled the hand grenade he had brought with him from his office out of his pocket. "Hold it right there!"

"Vic," Marcella called to him, stepping forward. "Don't! You don't have to do . . . anything."

Kingston pulled the pin out of the grenade and for a long moment it seemed as if it would go off. Then Marcella clamped her hand on her co-anchor's hand, holding the trigger clip in place.

"Don't let go, Vic!" she demanded.

"I have the right!"

"No! You don't," Marcella said. "Especially not in this way. Not when you will hurt or kill so many others besides yourself."

Kingston raved and waved his free hand. "I killed Linus Munch. He deserved it and I was glad to give him what he deserved."

"No, Vic," Marcella said patiently. "We just talked to Dean Westfall."

Vic looked past Marcella's shoulder and tried to go back inside. "He's dead?"

Marcella nodded and established eye contact. "Just a few moments ago."

"That's too bad," Kingston said sincerely.

"Yes it is," Marcella agreed quietly. "But he was resigned to his illness. You have a chance to cure yours."

"I intend to," Kingston said through clenched teeth.

"Not with a hand grenade," Marcella said.

"Why not?"

"Because it is pointless," Marcella said. "People will know you weren't the killer and your suicide will just make people think you were just some kind of nut."

"No. I left a note on the administrator's door. They'll gladly distribute it, and give me full credit—full blame, they'll consider it—for the death of Linus Munch."

"No, Victor. They won't. People will be told that Mr. Westfall killed the doctor. Not you."

"Who will tell them?" Kingston roared. His tight, red face was now only inches away from hers. "You said you just heard it from the Latin professor. Then you didn't have time to broadcast it on the air. He'll be dead. He won't confess to anyone else. I'll be dead. I won't confirm it. You'll be dead."

"He won't be dead," Marcella said, referring to Kevin Erlanger. "My body will take the impact of the blast."

"He's a priest. He can't testify to what was told him in confession."

"I'm not a priest," Kevin Erlanger shouted, coming to the doorway. "I was a priest, but . . . I gave it up to rent TVs."

"And I know about it too, Mr. Kingston," another voice said.

Kingston turned to his left to see Jackie, Hoss, and Maury (who had come up the stairway).

The film instructor went on to explain, "Two people, Bara Day and Cyril Plum, saw Dean Westfall stagger past them in a blood-stained hospital gown, mumbling, 'The king is dead. A tyrant has been slain.' "

"Melodramatic balderdash!" Kingston roared. "If you put that line in the docudrama, they'll laugh it off the screen."

"There's more proof than that!" Officer Watson (leading her contingent from the administrator's elevator, which she had commandeered). "We have a video of the ER that clearly shows you more than an arm's length away when the doctor went down. And," Watson held up the rubber gloves. "We have the fingerprints of the killer. It won't take the lab twenty minutes to confirm that these prints belong to Westfall."

"So you see, Vic," Marcella said quietly. "You won't die a hero."

"Maybe not," Kingston growled. "But what makes you think I want to live an ineffectual old fart?" With that, whether or not he intended to do it, the grenade squirted out of Kingston's hand and skittered across the floor.

Erlanger threw his body over Marcella's.

Peter dragged his mother out of range.

Stuart Goodwillie yelled for his bodyguard to shield Georgiana Bowman.

Jake grabbed Vic Kingston by his sleeve and pulled him down, just as Patricia Watson yelled, "Hit the deck!"

And Maury, not knowing any better, swatted the grenade toward the window.

It went through the cheap, substandard glass and fell down, down, down, until it landed on the toolshed, blowing it into a thousand pieces. This in turn resulted in the complete and utter barbecue of the tiny field mouse who had, just as Maury suspected, been hiding underneath.

Later, after the mess had been cleaned up, statements had been taken, blame and congratulations had been shared, and the witnesses had been released, Maury ate that little mouse. And it was delicious.

EPILOGUE

The funeral for B. Crowder Westfall was better attended than the rites for the late Maggie Mulcahy.

A great many people from the university and from the town, wearing red ribbons in solidarity, said their silent goodbyes.

The personnel of the medical center were not implicated in any way, for their attempt to cover up what happened was largely suppressed. The networks happily played along with this cover-up. It was the sort of story, they realized, which would not sell cars.

Charles "Bingo" Allen did a long piece, which was eventually considered the definitive story of what happened to Linus Munch, the Nobel laureate, when he came to Palmer with the stated intention of administering a serum that inoculated people at risk against the possibility of contracting AIDS.

The *Daily Chronicle* edited the already much-censored article and buried it in the science section of the newsstand-only version, and published it on Thanksgiving. Thanksgiving is traditionally not a time when a great many newspapers are sold on newsstands. The article, as unseen as it was, was nominated for several journalism awards. Bingo Allen was not a member of any of the "in" journalistic circles so he didn't win a thing.

Marcella Jacobs was elevated to the sole anchor position on the evening news.

Victor Kingston announced his retirement and checked into a substance abuse clinic.

Drew Feigl was designated lead roving reporter and would fill in for Marcella as anchorman on her days off.

Sandy Carlisle, much to her surprise, because of her contacts (Bronwyn Caruthers, et al.) and her pretty figure and face, became KCIN's youngest cub reporter.

Ruben Baskette, a young man in an older person's job, was made the fall guy for Vic Kingston's spectacular collapse. Baskette was fired (and quickly hired in the same position by KOPY) and replaced at KCIN by Stan Gray who was happy to come to Palmer with a TV job instead of one in boring old academia.

A grateful Jackie, after resting up from her ordeal, had gladly volunteered to go to Florida at Christmas to try to persuade Ivor Quest to come back to Palmer and resume his old duties.

Jake, perfectly happy not to have been shot, stabbed, clubbed, kicked, or rib-punched in bringing this particular murderer to bay (as he had in his previous exploits), happily spent the next week letting young Petey Walsh teach him to retrieve hockey pucks that missed the practice net by such a wide margin that they flew out into the street or neighboring alley.

Maury Jacobs, formerly Walsh, pig-happy in his new quarters (with his new pals Kevin and Marcy), handled his new status as hero dog with aplomb. He was only a puppy, after all. He thought everyone acted that way all the time.